Spanktown Papers

Jane Hulse

Published by Open Books

Copyright © 2026 by Jane Hulse

All rights reserved. No part of this book may be reproduced, scanned, or distributed in any printed or electronic form without permission except in the case of brief quotations embodied in critical articles and reviews.

Interior design by Siva Ram Maganti

Cover image © OpenArt.ai openart.ai/ and Shutterstock AI Generator shutterstock.com/g/ai-image-generator

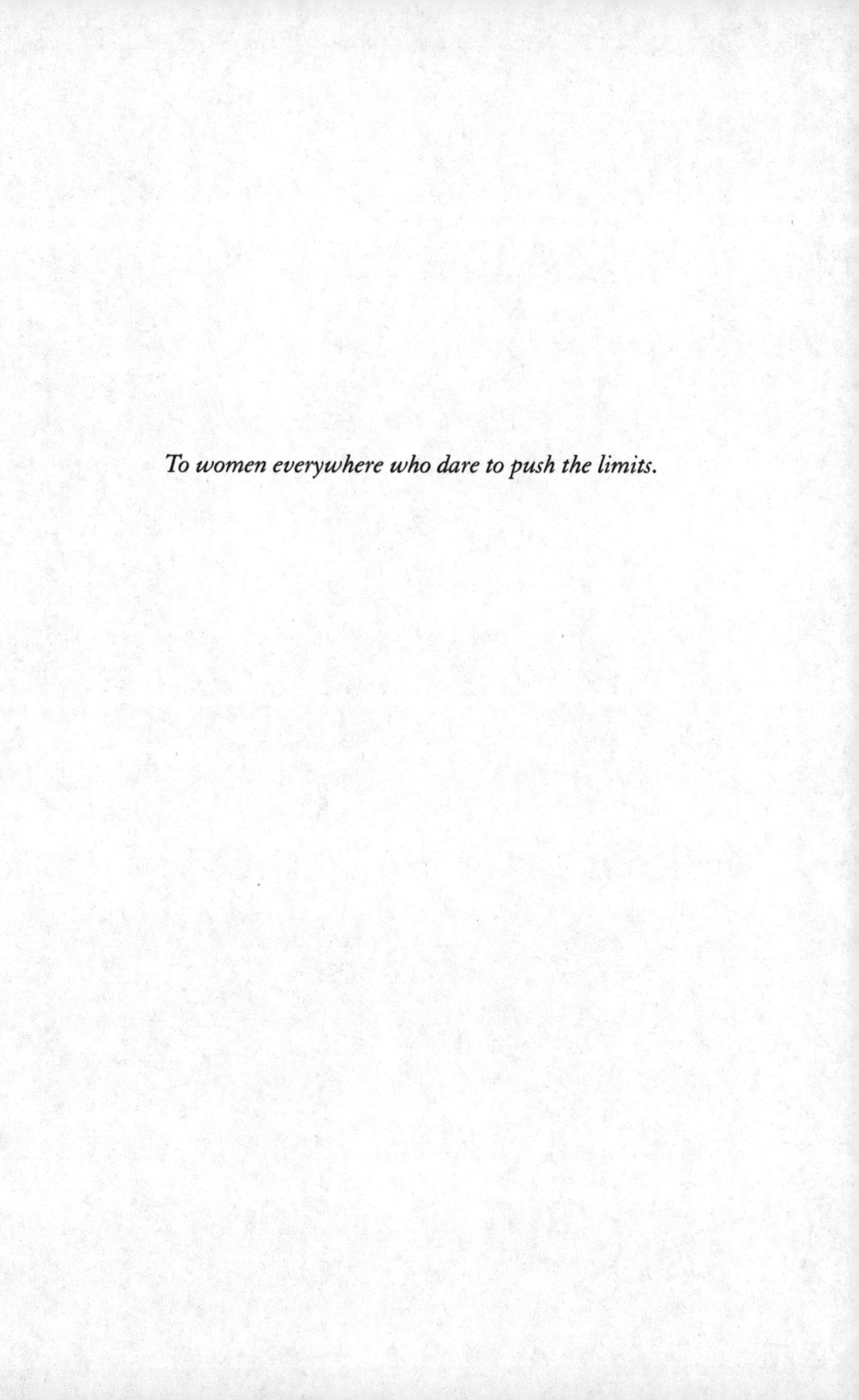

To women everywhere who dare to push the limits.

CHAPTER 1

It's sweltering, not a hint of a breeze, when I slip into Lloyd's Coffeehouse. I brace myself for the usual scowls and whispers.

The place is bustling with Philadelphia's most prosperous merchants, lawyers and tradesmen—bewigged citizens who still go pale at the presence of a woman in their sacred space. I put up with it because Lloyd's is the best place to pick up the latest chatter about the war—essential to my employment at the *Philadelphia Weekly Sentinel*.

"Good morn to you, Sarah," chirps Rip Ripley, the dashing blond proprietor who enjoys the daily outrage my presence elicits. "Coffee?"

"Yes, strong as you have it, and your biggest slice of gingerbread."

"Overslept again?"

I sigh. "I know, it's sinful, and a certain hell awaits."

"Doubt that," he laughs, his bright blue eyes lingering on my face.

"What do you hear about the fighting, Rip?"

"Our men spotted British troops less than 40 miles away. Could be here any day."

"And Washington's men?"

"They're in dire straits," he says. "Some don't even have shoes. Clothes are rags. They're sickly and low on food."

I think of Tom and my stomach lurches. Still no letter. It's been over a month since our hurried goodbyes in New York when he set off to join George Washington's troops. I fear the worst, and knowing Tom's appetite for danger, it's not a frivolous worry.

"They need a miracle," I say.

By the time I arrive at the *Sentinel*, a three-story red brick mansion with white shutters, Amos Tinkleton, esteemed editor and publisher, is in a silent stew.

"Would it trouble you to be on time?" he says with cool detachment. I never know if he's deadly serious or joking.

"Won't happen again, Amos."

"MISTER Tinkleton."

Deadly serious. I remove my bonnet, and my cascade of red curls goes amok, drawing an exasperated look from my eternally composed lord and commander. But these days, everyone is on edge. The British are closing in on the city.

I try to jolly him with a tasty morsel of news. "I was at Lloyd's and I heard—"

"Never mind that. I need you to write an article for tomorrow's edition—that is, if you can spare the time."

"Of course, Mr. Tinkleton," I blush. If he weren't a handsome gentleman of 35, and the most respected newspaper publisher in Philadelphia, I'd put up a fuss. But I've learned to hold my tongue, except for the most extreme situations.

His desk is a tribute to orderliness. Papers stacked with precision. Quill pens lined up like soldiers. Ink bottle gleaming. His person is the same. His dark hair tied neatly at his nape, he's tall as a barn door and lean as a racehorse. He's so fastidious that the slightest stain sends him off midday for a fresh shirt or breeches.

He's a far cry from my previous employer, who bellowed orders to his terrified workers and wasn't happy without a meat pie dripping down his front. But that was the *New York Gazette*, where I started out sweeping the floors but ended up exposing the hellish British prison ships in the city's harbor. That and a few other scrapes sent me packing to Amos's door in Philadelphia.

Amos lights his long-stem silver pipe and strikes a thoughtful pose. "It's high time we call out these Quakers for what they are—wolves in sheep's clothing."

"What do you mean?" I've learned never to assume I know what he's talking about. Amos doesn't suffer fools.

"They hide behind their religion, claiming they can't possibly support the war—too violent," he says. "But they're aiding the British in their confoundedly pious ways."

"Aiding how?" I ask, risking a lecture. "They won't fight for the British either."

"How can you be so naïve?" he asks, not expecting an answer. "They've bedeviled us for the past year. They won't pay taxes if even a penny goes to the fighting. They won't accept the new Continental paper money—the only way we can pay for this bloody war. Last month Simon Plummer turned away my good money for a shipment of paper. Had to go clear to Boston."

"Old news," I say. "You've written about all that."

The patriots, desperate for ammunition, asked everyone to dig the lead out of their clocks and windows for the cause. Last month, the Quakers refused, and Amos blasted them in print.

"Why are you riled up now?"

"Blankets. Washington put out a call for blankets and woolen socks for his men. The good people of Philadelphia offered up their best—but not the Quakers. Violates their religious beliefs to help in the least way, or so they say."

With a starched handkerchief, he wipes imperceptible sweat from his aristocratic upper lip.

"It's the last straw, the final insult," he seethes.

It is galling when I imagine Tom, his feet bloodied for lack of shoes, no warm clothes for the coming winter, and his gritty determination to fight the British to the end, whenever that is.

"That's what I want to write," he says. "We've been patient too long. It's time we inflict consequences for their obstinance—jail, fines, loss of property."

What he really means is he wants me to write it. I look at the grandfather clock in the corner and curse my tardiness.

"Of course, Mr. Tinkleton. Anything else?"

"Dress it up with your usual thoughtful and convincing verbiage."

Empty praise, though I thought my—rather, *his*—last article damning the British for some ridiculous tax was clever, even witty.

He starts to walk away, then stops. "And my library needs a

good dusting. Make sure Tess does a decent job this time. I know someone has been in there poking around. If I find out who it is—"

"Wasn't me," I say, with mock innocence. But he's already gone.

His library, which takes up the entire second story, is his precious baby. He claims it rivals Benjamin Franklin's collection of 4,000 volumes. I only go in there when I know he's out of town, and I can safely sneak out a volume and return it by morning.

I find Tess, a petite former slave with a serious but pretty face, cleaning the privy with lye soap and a bucket—an unpleasant chore she faces daily, per Amos's orders. He won't tolerate a hint of filth.

"Tess, Mr. Tinkleton would like you to dust the library." She looks up at me, sweat coating her face. I don't have the heart to tell her to do a 'decent' job of it this time. She already pours everything into keeping the print shop immaculate, along with his quarters on the third floor.

"Yes ma'am."

"Thank you, Tess. Please call me Sarah."

"Yes ma'am."

Amos can be demanding and insulting at times, but he bought Tess's freedom last year, so I can forgive just about anything he does to annoy me. He's never spoken to me about it. As for Tess, she's said no more than ten words to me since my arrival at the *Sentinel* last month.

At my desk, I open a bottle of ink, dip my quill pen, and begin to write what I hope will satisfy Amos yet also be somewhat married to the truth.

He hangs over my shoulder, eager to criticize. It irks me but not as much as my other duties: combing through old newspapers from here and abroad for news Amos deems fit to reprint in the *Sentinel*. Today's find is a warning to ladies venturing out in stormy weather: Steer clear of metal hair pins to avoid death by lightning.

At noon the owner of Nelson Mercantile, Andrew Nelson, strides through the front door with heavy purpose. Being a Quaker, he doesn't remove his broad-brimmed felt hat—no doubt irritating Amos. They disappear behind closed doors for two hours. By the time they emerge, both men look worn to a nub and unhappy.

I know the Quakers have not had an easy time of it lately. For decades, they held sway over the government of Pennsylvania. Rich and powerful, some ride in grand carriages and retire to summer homes when the rest of the city swelters. But now the patriots control the government, and business for the Quakers has dried up.

I hear the press creak to life and see Amos's apprentice, Jacob, begin to print the latest pamphlet that the Continental Congress is disseminating about the war. When Amos isn't printing the *Sentinel* every week, he prints anything and everything, from books to almanacs to new laws to sermons.

All afternoon I struggle with the words that usually come fast and furious. I'm conflicted about the Quakers. The truth is, I live with a Quaker family—Charles and Rachel Porter, and their five children. Amos knows this, though it doesn't stop him from ranting about the Quakers.

The Porters rented me a bedroom in their spacious home overlooking the Delaware River when no one else would. Apparently, it's scandalous for an unmarried woman such as myself—Miss Sarah Barrett—to seek lodging in the city of Philadelphia.

So when I knocked on the Porters' front door, I'd concocted a little white lie to smooth the way. I introduced myself as Sarah Jordan, whose husband Tom Jordan is away fighting with General Washington's troops. At least part of it is true.

Finally, I finish writing and present it to Amos. "A fair effort," he says. "I'll just make some changes."

Just once, I'd like to hear him say, "That's perfect, Sarah. I wouldn't change a word." Nor will I get any credit for writing it. It's his name that graces the newspaper's masthead. But I stifle my resentment. I know how lucky I am to have this job. I'm the only newspaper *woman* in the entire city, maybe the entire colony.

I glance at the clock. It's a bit past 5.

"Tomorrow be prompt. Even better, be early," he says as I head for the door.

"Why?"

"I have it on good authority the city will be in an uproar. We must be the eyes and ears of our readers when it happens."

"Is it the British?"

"No. I've already said too much. God willing, no one will be hurt."

CHAPTER 2

As usual, supper at the Porter home is a raucous affair. Three of the five children are under 6 years old. Rachel Porter comforts a squalling baby while corralling 5-year-old twin boys intent on bathing the cat.

When the entire family finally sits down at the long walnut dining table, Charles Porter bows his head in silent prayer. I bow mine as well, not in thanks for the food we're about to eat, but in vainglorious hope for Amos Tinkleton's elusive approval. Of course, I hope that tomorrow does not bring the end of the world, as Amos suggested. And one final hope: that my little white lie is safe.

After a few minutes of anxious waiting, the Porters' maid, Molly, finally appears with a platter of bacon dumplings and cornmeal pudding. With Molly, it's never certain when food will arrive at the table, or if it will be edible. Even after a year with the Porters, meals are sometimes haphazard, owing to her casual attitude toward cuisine and her employment in general.

If I were in charge, I'd have dismissed her by now, but the Porters seem to have infinite patience for those less fortunate.

Tonight, Charles Porter is irritable and anxious, not in his usual good cheer. He makes no comment on the near perfect dumplings Molly has somehow managed to produce, nor does he ask Rachel about her day.

"Charles, was there more trouble from the patriots today?" she asks, while dishing up plates for the younger children.

"Trouble? It was outrageous! Shameful!"

Charles is barely 40, nearly bald and almost never uses strong language. "What happened?" I blurt out.

"A committee from the Council stormed into my store, disrupting everything and demanding a look at my books," he says. "All right in front of customers who were lined up to buy kettles and skillets."

"What were they looking for this time?" Rachel asks.

Charles pushes his plate away in disgust. "They can't wait to find me shoveling money to the British. I suppose they think I'm a loyalist who's just disguised himself as a Quaker."

"Why can't they leave us alone?" Rachel says. "We want no part of this."

Rachel is slightly younger than her husband and has a long, serious face, framed with honey-colored hair that offsets her customary drab gray dress.

"Sarah, I almost forgot!" she says, practically jumping up. "There's a letter for you on the mantle."

A letter from Tom? I almost choke on a dumpling. I fight to control the flush creeping over my face as she hands me the letter.

Sadly, I recognize the handwriting immediately. "From my mother."

"Open it, Sarah," says the Porters' oldest child, Abigail. "Read it to us."

"Give Sarah some privacy," her mother scolds.

"It's all right," I say, anxious to hear Mother's news from Nova Scotia. I've told the Porters all about her adventures as a fearless midwife, braving the wilds of Canada to birth babies and tend the sick.

I glance at the neat writing, comforted by her words. "She says she is well but had a close call with a bear," I tell them. The room is silent. "I'll read it to you:"

> *I was paddling a canoe across a swift-moving river to go tend a birth. The river was high after mighty rains, and it was all I could do to maneuver to the other side. When I pulled up on shore, I was suddenly confronted by this immense creature standing tall on his hind legs.*

"What happened?" wide-eyed Abigail asks.

I continue reading.

I don't know what possessed me, but I started swatting him with the paddle and yelling. Mr. Yardley came to my rescue, firing his gun. He missed, but the bear ran off. Not an hour later, I delivered Mrs. Yardley of a fine son.

Abigail claps, and even her father releases a "Glory be!"

I don't read aloud the next part, where she says she misses me terribly and pleads for me to join her in Canada. I know she wants me to be her apprentice again. But I'm 19 now, and I've made it clear a thousand times over that I'd sooner eat worms than catch another newborn.

"We could certainly use another midwife in Philadelphia," Rachel says.

"No chance of that," I say. "Mother is an ardent loyalist. That's why she fled to Canada. She supports the British and wants to be with others of like mind."

Molly surprises everyone when she sets down a frosted cake on the dining room table. Even Charles is buoyed. "Carrot cake! My favorite."

"No, Mr. Porter," she says with a sly look. "Carrots are hard to come by, what with all the troubles. I used parsnips instead."

Charles is crestfallen. I feel my stomach churn at the memory of Mother's loathsome parsnip soup. With some hesitation everyone tries it. But it's Rachel who pronounces it a success. "Well done, Molly."

Molly is clearing the table when a rap on the door startles everyone. It's already dark and no one calls at this hour. "What now?" Rachel says.

I remember Amos's dire words and worry the uproar—whatever it might be—is already starting.

Charles opens the door to Andrew Nelson and the Tilden brothers, John and Ebenezer: all prominent merchants and all Quakers.

"Apologies for the intrusion but we must talk with you," Nelson, the mercantile owner, says. "We can't abide this treatment from the

Council and their patriot gangs."

Charles leads them into his study and closes the door. I linger in the dining room, sweeping up crumbs from the table in hopes I'll hear more than muffled voices.

"Sarah, no need to clean up," Rachel says. "Abigail will lend a hand."

"I don't mind—"

"No, no, you must be tired." She takes my arm and leads me to the stairs, either out of genuine concern or to keep me from eavesdropping. "Forgive me, my dear, I never asked about your day. I hope it was productive."

I wish I could tell her about my day and warn her about whatever hell will break loose tomorrow. But she assumes I have little to do with gathering or writing the news at the *Sentinel*. And, in any event, I'm totally in the dark.

"It was nothing out of the ordinary," I say. "Just keeping things orderly."

"And how is Amos Tinkleton?" she asks with the slightest smile that gives her long face a warm glow.

"He's fine."

"Sarah, you know his family is one of the wealthiest in Pennsylvania. And he's not taken a wife, yet. He'd make an excellent husband for some lucky woman. Not you, of course," she laughs. "Have you any word from your husband?"

I bristle at the words but force a smile. "No. Any day now, I presume."

Climbing the stairs to my room, I strain for a word or two from the study, but I hear nothing. Perhaps they're in silent prayer.

In my room, I look at Mother's letter again and wish it was from Tom. I can't fight the wave of sadness that comes over me. Why hasn't he written? He knows I'm in Philadelphia at the newspaper.

I think about those final days we had together in New York. As I undress for bed, I try to remember his touch on my body, caressing places even I had never explored before. And the final rush of pleasure we both felt at the end.

With just my shift on, I trace the outline of my breasts and hips and feel my nipples harden. But then I stop, embarrassed. What would Rachel think? What would anyone think? Does it matter?

I open the window and feel a rush of hot, humid air. No chance of easy sleep tonight. I light the candle, take out my quill pen and open my diary on the little table that serves as my desk.

September 1, 1777

"I fear Tom has forgotten about me already. Was I naïve to think it was more than a lark?..."

Tom and I were hardly strangers. His sister Emma was my best friend. I still marvel how two families in a small New Hampshire town could have been so different. My parents were loyalists to the core, and the Jordans were ardent rebels—like most other folks in Essex.

As a gentle breeze finally blows through the room, I remember how sick and desolate Tom was after Bunker Hill. He'd nearly lost his leg, and I helped him recover. At the same time, my father's newspaper was wrecked, and he was run out of town for his stinging editorials against the "treasonous rebels." He survived, only to die of smallpox.

Things have a strange way of working out. If I hadn't fled to New York…if Tom hadn't been stuck on that horrid prison ship...if I hadn't helped him escape…It's a long story, full of grisly, stomach-churning details. It would shock Rachel Porter's gentle Quaker sensibility, and sometimes it even shocks me. Another reason to hide my identity.

I lay down my pen and open the window wider. That's when three dark figures creep up to the house and heave rocks through the windows of Charles' study.

The crash shatters the quiet of this palatial neighborhood.

Charles and his two friends dash out seconds later, but the vandals have fled. I can make out Charles, with blood streaming from the glass shards that nicked his face.

He's practically shouting: "Gentlemen, I fear it's begun."

CHAPTER 3

It's barely dawn when I wake to someone pounding on the front door. What now? Through the fog, I can make out a crowd of two dozen men, armed with muskets.

"Charles Porter!" one of them yells. "Come out peacefully. Don't make us use force."

I dress quickly and race downstairs to find Rachel, her long hair undone, clutching her husband's arm.

"Don't go out! Nothing good will come of it."

A wise woman, Rachel. The men look like they're out for blood.

Charles gently frees himself from his wife's grip. "I'll go out and reason with them," he says. "Surely, it's a misunderstanding."

Rachel and I follow him outside, trailed by Abigail and her younger brother Jack.

"What's happening?" Abigail asks. Her face is white.

"Be calm. I'm sure I can straighten this out," Charles tells them, his voice shaky. Turning to the crowd, he yells, "What is it you men want? Whatever it is certainly doesn't call for the entire militia to come out armed and ready for battle."

"Don't get smart with us, Porter," says a bearded beefy man in his thirties who appears to be in charge. "We're here to take you into custody."

"Whatever for, Sam Parsons? I've done nothing to warrant this!"

Rachel steps forward. "Leave him be," she shouts. "You've got no right." I'm pleasantly stunned by her boldness.

But Parsons brushes her off like a mosquito. "We've got every right," he growls.

"Men, search the house for weapons. Tear apart his desk—look for any papers that prove his Tory sympathies."

"For shame!" Charles yells. He plants his feet wider and folds his arms across his chest. "I'm not going anywhere until you tell me what you're charging me with."

"How about this?" Parsons says. "Aiding and abetting the enemy. That's treason."

"Not true," Charles says. "I want nothing to do with either side in this unholy war."

"He's a damned Tory," someone in the crowd yells. "We don't need more evidence. Let's take him."

Rachel cries out, "No! We've taken no side in this conflict. We don't want trouble."

With the children clinging to his shirt sleeves, Charles says, "Our religion forbids us from joining in your war. I'll not go against my God, and neither you nor anyone else in Pennsylvania can force me to do so."

"This isn't about religion—it's about politics," Parsons says. "We have the backing of the Pennsylvania Supreme Executive Council and the Continental Congress. Now come with us."

It's clear that Charles is no match for the mob. "Rachel, I have no choice," he says. "I'll not have my children witness violence."

They lead him to a waiting wagon, toss him in like a sack of potatoes, and within a few minutes they're all gone.

Rachel consoles a furious Abigail and young Jack, who's in tears. "Come inside and we'll figure out what to do." I stand there useless, unable to help, but finally understanding what Amos meant when he spoke yesterday of big things to come.

Inside, Rachel paces. "I must get word to the others. Find out where they're taking him. Oh, my poor Charles!"

I finally gather my wits. "I have to go to work, Rachel. I know I'll have some useful information for you when I return."

"Yes, Sarah. Mr. Tinkleton will know what's happening."

"No doubt," I say.

But I fear it won't be good news for the Porters, or any others in their tight Quaker circle.

At the *Sentinel*, Amos is issuing orders to his lead apprentice Jacob Stafford.

"Prepare enough ink for a special edition. We did it for the Declaration of Independence, and we can do it now!"

Jacob is oiling the press and appears none too happy. Amos has enlisted Tess to clean the metal type, letter by letter, with rags and horse piss, a solvent I know all too well from my father's print shop. In her ink-stained dress, she sits on the floor surrounded by drawers of type and a cloud of stink.

"All this for one arrest?" I say to Amos. I'm anxious to tell him about the militia hauling off poor Charles.

"One?" He looks at me as if I'm daft. "There are at least 20 – nearly all of them leaders in the Quaker community—being rounded up as we speak. It's about time they suffered the consequences of their so-called faith."

I can barely speak. "Twenty-two men arrested for refusing to fight?" I ask incredulously.

"You know it's more than just refusing to fight," Amos says, settling at his desk and uncorking his ink bottle. "It's being against our whole civic enterprise. It's being anti-American!"

"Surely you don't mean that," I say, but he ignores me.

"I can't wait to set this good news to paper," he says with uncharacteristic enthusiasm. "Sarah, go to Nelson's Mercantile. Rip told me Andrew Nelson is putting up quite a fuss."

Passing the coffeehouse, I duck in for a quick word with Rip. He's brewing another vat of coffee for today's bigger-than-usual crowd. Even his brother Ethan is helping out, roasting coffee beans in a skillet over a fire. The aroma is intoxicating. Rip breaks free when he sees me.

"Big day," he says, his face grim. "I wager Amos is happy as a pig in clover."

"And you're not?"

"I'm conflicted. Of course, I support the patriots, but this doesn't feel right. Too extreme. I hear old Nelson is holed up inside his office and won't come out."

Nearly forgetting to thank him, I dash out. Two blocks away, I see a crowd outside the mercantile.

"Come out peacefully, Andrew Nelson," the militia's Parsons yells. "Don't make us take you by force. No one wants that."

Someone yells "Tory traitor! Tory traitor!" and the crowd picks it up as a chant. The noise is deafening. One of the militiamen smashes the mercantile's front window with the butt of his musket.

I feel a tug on my sleeve and see Agatha Nelson's frantic face beneath her black bonnet.

"Sarah, they'll kill him," she cries, though I can barely hear her over the din. "His heart can't take it. He's 60 and ailing from the gout."

Before I can open my mouth, Parsons and the crowd kick in the front door. Moments later, four large men drag out the struggling merchant, sitting atop his massive office chair.

The diminutive Nelson is loaded into a waiting wagon, chair and all, as if the mob somehow reckons that destroying furniture goes a step too far.

Agatha nearly collapses, and I tighten my grip on her arm. A few other Quakers show up to protest.

"You have no right!" Nelson yells. "I've broken no laws. Our attorneys will destroy you. You'll pay for this!"

I rush to the wagon and manage to learn that there's no room left at the jail. One of the militiamen, leering at me, says Nelson and the others are being hauled to the Freemasons Lodge, "where they can ponder their disloyalty for a bit."

Back at the *Sentinel*, I write up the chaotic scene and hand it to Amos, who seems as pleased as I am shaken.

"What will happen to them?" I ask. I imagine a fine, or maybe the kind of penalty that's handed out to debtors, like forfeiting property.

Patiently, Amos sets down his pen. "The Council intends to keep them locked up so they can't cause more trouble for Washington and his men."

He says it casually, as if being locked away were some minor inconvenience.

"But they have families and businesses," I say. "Rachel Porter has five children. They'll struggle without Charles."

Amos raises his manicured eyebrows. "And don't you have family—a husband I believe, bravely fighting with Washington's men, Mrs. Jordan?"

I can only nod. What would he think if he knew the truth about my "husband"?

Hours later, the special edition comes off the press, one sheet at a time. Silently, Tess hangs each to dry on a line strung around the cavernous room. Soon a stack of papers is ready to go. The first stop is Lloyd's Coffeehouse, and I can't wait to hear the reaction.

When I finally arrive, the place is crammed and noisy. They're all reading Amos' denunciation of the Quakers.

"It's about time someone did something about the pious fools," one of them says. "It's hard enough for our boys to beat the bloody redcoats. They shouldn't have to fight the Quakers too."

Another one pipes up: "The least they can do is donate blankets and food. They're a lot richer than we are. They can afford it!"

Cheers echo through the room. I look for Rip but don't see him.

Finally, someone notices me. "It's the woman from the *Sentinel* skulking around for news," he hoots, raising his bowl of coffee. "Tell your employer, he's done a great service for the patriots."

The only response I can come up with on the spot is a lame one. "Tell him yourself," I say, inviting more laughter before I slip out the door.

At the Porter house, Rachel has taken charge. Molly puts out a supper of hash and biscuits, and all the children are assembled at the table. Rachel has spent the day, calming them and most of her friends, who streamed in to learn about the "trouble." They didn't leave without a cup of tea and one of Molly's rock-hard biscuits.

"When is Father coming home?" Jack demands as soon as I sit down at the table.

"I don't know."

"But you work at the *Sentinel*," he says, as if I should know things even before they happen.

"I can tell you there were at least 20 men, all good businessmen like your father, rounded up today and they're being held at Freemasons Lodge. I wish I knew more."

"I must go there tonight," Rachel says. She hasn't touched her food. "My Charles will need a clean shirt, and his spectacles, pen and paper, and something for that cough. Poor, poor man."

When I offer to go with her, she perks up for a second.

"That would be a great comfort," she says.

Comfort isn't exactly what I had in mind. I'm anxious to know more about the arrested Quakers. I don't know whether it's to impress Amos with my diligence or to satisfy my own dark curiosity.

"We'll go as soon as I gather a few things," Rachel says. "Abigail, I'll need you to watch the twins and tend the baby."

"But I want to go too," she pouts. "I want to see Father as much as you do."

"I know, but I need you to do as I ask. This is not the time to be selfish."

In a half hour, Rachel and I are out the door, walking three blocks to the Freemasons Lodge. She starts at every noise and eyes the few people who are out and about with suspicion.

"Surely the men won't be held more than a fortnight," I say. "Won't the Quaker community rally to their aid?"

"The lawyers are already hard at work appealing this unlawful imprisonment," she says. "My Charles has never broken a law. His faith in God guides him in all his deeds."

I believe her, but I have a feeling others won't see it that way. Especially Amos. And honestly, I see their point. So many others, like my Tom, are giving everything they've got to win independence from Britain.

I want to ask her why it would be so immoral to hand a blanket to a shivering soldier. But I don't want to offend this kind soul who opened her home to me.

Nor am I ready to tell her the whole truth about Tom. I don't know whether it's my shame for lying to her, or the more shameful possibility that he's forgotten me by now and taken up with one of the camp followers whose services go well beyond cooking and washing.

We hear the commotion before we even see the Freemasons Lodge, a two-story plain brick house that gives no clue to its purpose. Several women in their plain Quaker dress are having a row with the militia guards stationed outside.

"We only want to go inside and see our husbands," one of the women yells.

"We have orders. No one is allowed inside," a guard yells back. "Now hush up! Or I'll find room inside for you ladies as well."

I hate being told to hush up, especially by a fool playing soldier. I feel my anger rising. But Rachel is calm and reasoned.

"We just want to see that they're well and give them things they need," she says in a voice that would soothe a rabid dog. "Mine is sick with a cough and suffers from rheumatism. Surely you can understand that."

"You'll see them when we take them away," the guard says with a smirk.

"Take them away?" I confront the guard. "Where are they going?"

Now he's enjoying himself. "Far, far away," he laughs.

"You mean banished, exiled?"

He nods and breaks into a toothy grin.

"No!" Rachel says. "I need my husband. I can't manage alone with five children. He has a business."

Just when I think this scene could not take a more bizarre turn, Rip storms out of the Freemasons Lodge.

"Rip, what are you doing here?" I ask.

"I might ask you the same, but I suspect you're here in the pursuit of news. If that's what this is."

He's clearly perturbed, but I don't see why he's being short with me. "I'm only trying to comfort these poor women and give them what scant information I have."

He looks at the desperate women surrounding me, and his face softens.

"I see," he says. "You can tell them this: If my information is correct, their men have the law on their side. The papers accusing them are a fraud, and—"

The door of the lodge bursts open, and Parsons, the head militia man, storms out. "Ripley, I told you to get out of here. Now what's going on here?"

"Nothing you need concern yourself with," Rip says, turning to leave.

"We've got no use for your wild talk," Parsons yells. "You spread more of it, and you'll find yourself at the end of a rope."

CHAPTER 4

I WAKE JUST BEFORE DAWN TO the awful sound of vomiting. The gagging and choking echo through the house. Sleep is impossible, so I head downstairs to see who is so violently ill.

In the hall I encounter Rachel carrying a fouled basin to the privy. Her hair undone, she is still dressed in yesterday's clothes. Her eyes are bloodshot and puffy.

"Little Henry is doing poorly," she says. "He's had a dreadful night. I couldn't leave his side."

Henry, one of the 5-year-old twins, has been sickly the entire time I've stayed with the Porters. Not nearly as hefty as his brother Harry, he's lately seemed frailer and paler than usual.

"You look so weary. Let me empty that for you," I offer, reaching for the basin.

"No, I'll do it," she says yanking it back.

That's when I make the mistake of looking inside the basin. Worms, some still writhing! I cry out and jump back as if I've seen a rattlesnake. I know Mother has treated such digestive disorders, but I can't hide my revulsion.

Rachel ignores it.

"Poor child is worse than I realized," she says, near tears. "I gave him a tea to purge the sickness from his little body. He's still feverish. Nothing seems to help," She can't hold back the tears now.

"How can I help you?" I ask, hoping she doesn't pass the

basin back to me. My stomach has always been sensitive. The slightest unsavory sight can set me to puking my innards out—even further proof that I'm unsuited to midwifery.

"I must see my Charles and bring him whatever supplies they'll allow," she says. "But I can't leave my boy's side. He doesn't have the strength to walk across the room."

"I'll gladly go in your place," I say, especially if it spares me from making up yet another excuse for skipping church on Sunday. The fact that I'm uncertain about the very existence of God is something I keep to myself.

"Charles and the others are writing so many appeals for their freedom that they need more paper, ink and pens," Rachel says. "Poor soul could use horehound tea for that cough."

"I'd be happy to bring all that," I say.

It also might be a chance to find out more about the jailed Quakers and why Rip was there last night, and just what his row with the militia is about.

He's a patriot through and through. When his brother went off to fight with Washington's troops, Rip wanted to go too. But he promised his father he'd stay put until Ethan returned to help run the family's coffeehouse.

Rachel and Molly put together a bundle for Charles, and I offer some of the paper from my small stash. An hour after sunrise, I'm out the door in my good blue dress and matching bonnet.

Now that I'm 19, I take more pains to look pleasing. My curly hair has been brushed into submission. My breasts are "sufficiently ample," at least that's what Tom told me when we last held each other in New York.

There's a feeling of fall in the air as I walk to the Freemasons Lodge, past maple trees just beginning to show their autumn colors. I pass stately brick mansions like the Porters' and a stretch of rowhouses with shops on the first floor. Few people are on the street, except for a boisterous family loading their belongings into a wagon.

"Good morn to you," I say, recognizing the rebel sympathizer Peter Abrams, the owner of Abrams Hats for Gentlemen.

"'Tis a sad morning," he says, wrestling a grandfather clock into the wagon with the aid of his two sons.

"Why is that?" I ask.

"Moving to Reading. I fear the British will be here any day, and I want to be long gone when it happens."

"Sorry to see you go," I say. "Others are fearful too."

"With good reason," he says. "The patriot leaders—John Adams and the like—are all here, right under the Brits' noses, plotting the overthrow of the government. I fear this won't end well."

"Safe travels," I say, moving on. His fears make me wonder what Amos Tinkleton and his family will do if the British move in. Amos has made no bones about his hatred of the redcoats, ripping them apart regularly in the *Sentinel's* pages.

More importantly, what does it mean for me? I've been careful not to tell Amos or the Porters too much about my past. In truth, I've upset people on both sides of this bewildering war—all with good reason, of course.

When I arrive at the Freemasons Lodge, a guard greets me with good cheer, so unlike the scene last night. I'm immediately suspicious.

"I have supplies for Charles Porter," I announce in my most official voice. "If you would kindly see that he receives them."

"You may go inside and see him yourself," he says. "They're in the parlor." He even opens the door for me.

I had expected to see bloodied faces, rancid, bug-infested scraps, men tethered to beams—all fodder for Amos's newspaper columns. But inside I find a cozy scene: Charles with a half-dozen other men sitting around a table laden with law books, paper, quill pens, ink bottles, and here and there, a cup of tea. Charles jumps up to greet me.

"Is Rachel unwell?"

"No, little Henry is ailing, so she's at his bedside. Rachel fears he may have eaten watermelon too close to the rind." A lie to spare Charles an additional worry.

"Oh, my poor boy," he says. He looks weary, his fringe of hair loose and stringy. I give him the bundle.

"More paper. Excellent!" he says. "Thank you kindly, Sarah."

We settle into corner chairs by the two doors that lead into a big meeting room. "Seems they're not guarding you as strictly as last night," I say.

"They're now calling this a 'gentle imprisonment.'" he explains. "They haven't charged us with any crimes, perhaps because they know we're not criminals. One of our good men is a lawyer, and we're petitioning the Supreme Executive Council of Pennsylvania and the Continental Congress to free us. After all, how can they hold us without charges?"

"Have they mistreated you or the others?" I ask, hoping to present Amos with at least a bloody gash or a good face-pounding.

"No, and they haven't deprived us of food or visits from our families." Charles shakes his head sadly. "Still, this is particularly hard on our wives and children. They're the ones suffering."

"Rachel sends her kind wishes," I tell him. "She'd be here if she could. She's asked her sister to come help with the house and children while you're gone."

"Good. I expect my brother Benjamin will be tending to my business affairs with Rachel's help," he says.

"How much longer can they keep you here?" I ask. "Surely there's a limit."

"In fact, they've offered to set us free. That is, if we sign an oath of loyalty to the patriots and their cause."

I mull that for a moment. "Is that such a hardship? It's not fighting or contributing to the war or helping in any way."

I look at the men around the table reading and sipping tea and wonder what their imprisonment would be like if they weren't prosperous men of good standing.

"Will you and the others sign the oath?"

"Our captors expect that we will, that we'll cave in to spare our families and businesses. Then they can call an end to this embarrassing miscarriage of justice."

Makes sense to me. Just sign the bloody oath, and all this unpleasantness will be over.

He knows what I'm thinking and gives me a patient, patronizing smile. "I wouldn't expect you to understand this. We Quakers do not sign oaths of any kind, if we follow our religion to the letter."

I want to ask him if being letter-perfect is worth putting his family through terrible hardship? Does being a Quaker mean following blindly, leaving all common sense behind? I don't even have to ask the questions for him to immediately answer.

"No, I will not sign. Nor will the others," he says without hesitation. "I know Rachel supports me in this, even if it means tougher days ahead."

I wonder if there isn't just a little piece of Rachel that would be relieved if he simply took the easier—and, to my mind more sensible—way out.

"What will they do to you if you don't sign the oath?"

He pauses to wipe his brow. "I don't know, but I'm sure our imprisonment will not stay this comfortable. Wherever they put us, they'll make us suffer. I can only hope it's not for too long."

CHAPTER 5

It's chaotic when I arrive at the breakfast table. Henry is no better, and Rachel has sent for the doctor.

"He's too weak to stand," she says while futilely trying to soothe fussy baby Mary. "And this little one is cutting a tooth."

Molly is nowhere in sight. Rachel is clearly at her wits' end. I want to help, but I'm ill-suited to the whole mess of babies and childcare.

I offer a pittance: "My mother says chamomile is helpful for teething babies. Would you like me to brew up a pot?"

"That would be most appreciated, Sarah," she says, near tears. Between the fussy baby and ailing Henry, she's been up for two nights running.

"I miss Charles's wise counsel," she says, barely audibly.

I know better than to say what seems so obvious: If Charles would just sign the loyalty oath, he could be at her side straightaway.

But she makes clear where she stands. "Of course, I agree completely with his decision to walk the Quaker path. I wouldn't want it any other way."

I would. Why be the martyr if it only makes everyone else miserable? Does that make me selfish? Or is it the martyr who's the selfish one? I don't know anymore. I only know Rachel doesn't have a selfish bone in her body. Not one that's obvious to me, anyway.

I stop at Lloyd's Coffeehouse on my way to the *Sentinel*, hoping to see Rip and glean some news. He's deep in conversation with Ethan, who, not surprisingly for a brother, has the same sandy-blond hair. Rip sees me and trudges over.

"Good morning, Sarah. You're a much-needed spot of sunshine today."

He hands me a large mug of coffee without my even asking. Lowering his voice, he gestures toward his brother.

"Ethan's a bit changed," he says.

"I know he just returned from the fighting. Now you're free to join Washington's forces."

"Not that easy," he says, taking a seat beside me and drawing some stares from customers. "Ethan saw some unthinkable carnage and was wounded in New York."

"He seems to have recovered just fine."

"He's not fine," Rip says. "His hands shake. He gets headaches. Sometimes he lashes out at me or a customer for no reason. Yesterday he was grinding coffee beans and was so startled when the door slammed that he spilt the lot of them on the floor."

I've read about soldiers like Ethan who return from the fighting as different people, unable to pick up where they left off. Some of them are plagued by nightmares. I remember the horrors Tom endured at Bunker Hill.

"I'm so sorry," I say, wishing I had some more meaningful words of comfort. "Poor Ethan."

"What about me?" he laughs. "I'm the one who can't go off to fight the damn redcoats. Ethan isn't fit to manage the coffeehouse in my absence. At least, not at the moment."

I feel sorry for both, but I'm happy Rip isn't leaving. He's not only my best source for news but also my only real friend in Philadelphia.

"By the way," I say. "What brought you to the Freemasons Lodge the other night? And what fraudulent papers were you talking about?"

Rip clams up. "Can't say more. It's not my place."

At the *Sentinel*, Amos is in a quiet frenzy: His cravat is loosened ever so slightly.

"It's fortunate you're on time today," he says with icy precision. "We have a problem."

"The British?"

"No. Something far more sinister. Another book has gone missing from my library."

"What is it this time?"

"*Gulliver's Travels* by Jonathan Swift. It's a rare copy—signed by Swift himself," he says.

"Perhaps you mislaid it. Remember, that's what happened with your first edition of *The New England Primer.*"

After an hour-long, exhaustive search by everyone at the *Sentinel*, the book—which was used as a children's reading primer for nearly a hundred years—finally turned up under a pile of papers on his desk.

"Don't make light of this," he scolds. "This is deliberate. I'm sure of it. The thief knows full well the book's value and just wants to make some easy money."

I nod, trying to look sincere. "I'll ask everyone to be on the lookout."

He shrugs, knowing it will be a fruitless effort. "I'll be at the London Book Shop, asking them to let me know if anyone tries to peddle my precious volume."

While he's gone, I make a half-hearted effort to locate Gulliver and the odd companions he encounters on his travels. I find Tess washing the windows for the second time this week.

"Tess, Mr. Tinkleton says another book is missing from the library. This time it's *Gulliver's*—oh, never mind." The book's title is of no use to a woman who's illiterate. "Please keep an eye out for a stray book on the floor or wherever. I'm sure it's around here somewhere."

"Yes ma'am," she whispers, clearly flustered by the interruption.

"I'm sorry. I didn't mean to startle you," I say.

She turns back to the window. "No trouble."

Tess is a conundrum, a complete mystery. I wish I knew her better, but it doesn't seem as if she'd welcome that.

When Amos returns an hour later, he bursts in with a handful of papers. "Sarah, do you know what I have here?"

"Of course not, I—"

"It's all the proof we need to show that these Quakers are traitors," he says, his face flushed with excitement. "It's clear evidence they're aiding the loyalists."

"Well, what is it?" I ask, half-expecting a tongue-lashing for my ignorance.

"The Spanktown Papers," he says gleefully. He holds them up as if he's struck gold.

"The what?"

"Spanktown Papers—I finally got my hands on them, and we're going to print them in tomorrow's edition. I need your help, so don't expect to leave early."

Then he sits me down and lectures me as if I'm a dimwitted child. It seems the Spanktown Papers are so called because of Spanktown, New Jersey, where a group of Quakers held their annual meeting in August. According to Amos, a report from the meeting proves the Quakers gave British forces crucial information about American troop movements and weaknesses within the ranks.

"How do the Americans know all that?" I dare to ask.

"I'm getting to that. The information comes from Major General John Sullivan, a highly respected patriot from New Hampshire—one of your people."

Amos explains how Sullivan said he found the incriminating papers among the belongings of an American soldier, who he accused of being a turncoat.

"It's all there," Amos says, spreading out a slew of pages. "More than enough evidence to arrest those lying Quakers and convict them of treason. The Continental Congress and the Pennsylvania Council just got their hands on this. So the Quakers—Andrew Nelson and the whole bunch—don't have a leg to stand on."

I've never seen Amos so exhilarated, and my head has never ached so, with all this new information.

"What do the Quaker leaders say?" I ask.

"They say it's not true—of course that's what they would say," he blusters. "And because they're so damn 'pious,' people believe them. That's why they're so dangerous."

"Charles Porter dangerous? Ridiculous!"

"Harden your heart, Sarah. Maybe you're not cut out for this work," he says.

I have no response. None that I can utter that wouldn't sound childish. He infuriates me so.

Amos stands suddenly, indicating the lecture is over and the real work is starting.

We labor together for three hours, transcribing the Spanktown Papers and explaining their importance to readers.

Amos's enthusiasm is infectious, no matter how hard I fight it. I imagine how pleased the patriots must be to have this new evidence. Perhaps it will save Tom, and who knows how many soldiers, from slaughter by the redcoats. I can't wait to press Charles Porter for an explanation—that is, if he's ever released and back home with his family.

By the time we finish, it's past 3 o'clock, and the apprentices have yet to print the paper and get it on to the streets. I see Tess silently cleaning type and wonder if she's had a moment all day to catch her breath. When she's not scrubbing this and that, she lives in a room in the basement.

The parlor, printing press and Amos's office take up the first floor. The library occupies the second. He lives in spacious quarters on the third floor—that is when he isn't lounging at his parents' lavish country estate. Tess cleans it all and still finds time to cook for her notoriously fussy boss.

I'm putting on my bonnet to leave when Tess approaches, a worried look creasing her forehead.

"Ma'am," she whispers, eyes darting to see if anyone is listening. "The missing book. I found it." She hands me *Gulliver's Travels* as if it's a delicate ornament of the finest crystal.

"Oh, that's wonderful news, Tess. He'll be so relieved. Where did you find it?"

"In the library, ma'am."

"The library, of all places," I laugh.

"Yes, ma'am. It was in the wrong place."

"Mr. Tinkleton is gone for the day, but I'll make sure he knows you found it, Tess."

"Yes, ma'am."

"Please call me Sarah."

"Yes…Sarah."

I'm so happy about the book, I practically skip all the way to the Porters' house. But when I arrive at the front door, a strange thought overtakes me. How did Tess find a misplaced book? I didn't think slaves could read or write.

CHAPTER 6

Gertrude has seized command. Tall and stern, Rachel's spinster sister took one look at the disorder in the Porter home and knew exactly what to do. Tonight's supper—corn and potato chowder, with crusty brown bread—is served on the good china, with napkins. The children are scrubbed and well-behaved, and Molly, under Gertrude's tutelage, outdoes herself with an apple pie.

I'm amazed to discover just how far Gertrude's passion for order extends. When I open the door to my room, I find it tidied far beyond my admittedly casual standards. The bed made. Books piled neatly. Papers put away. Clothes folded and stored in the chest.

I feel violated, my nakedness on display. My room is *my* room. Gertrude has touched my things. My half-finished letter to Mother is in full view. I'm furious, but I rein in my anger as I rush downstairs.

"Gertrude, thank you, but there's no need to straighten my room," I say with excruciating politeness. "I'm sure you already have your hands full."

"Hmm." She views me with disdain, as if I'm an ungrateful child.

The knocking on the front door distracts her. Despite the hour, three of Rachel's friends are eager to chat. Their husbands are also being held at the Freemasons Lodge.

"How is little Henry today?" Agatha Nelson asks Gertrude as she steps inside.

"Not as poorly. I advised the doctor to do a bleed, and that helped."

How she knows anything about medicinal procedures or child-rearing is a mystery to me, as she's never birthed children or even wed.

"How are the captives faring?" I ask.

"Poor souls are preparing for the worst," grim-faced Agatha says.

"Terrible, terrible," the others chime in.

"We're here to talk with Rachel about the latest injustice," Agatha says, removing her bonnet and shawl.

"You must mean the Spanktown Papers," I say. "What have you heard?"

I'm anxious to know how the Quakers can defend the Spanktown revelations, if the evidence is as damning as Amos says.

"Rest assured our lawyers are frantic to get the word out: It's not true—not one word of it. That's what we're here to tell Rachel, so she won't fret. Our men have demanded a hearing, and God willing, the militia will listen."

Gertrude, itching to say something, draws the three women closer. "I brought Charles a fresh shirt and handkerchiefs today, and he told me the militia has no intention of hearing their side or letting them go free. Banish them, that's what this government wants: Send them far, far, from here until the rebels win and the war is over."

An hour later, I go to sleep wondering just how far the militia will go to squeeze some patriotism out of old men dead set against war. How far would I go, I ask myself, if Tom's life were in the balance?

In the morning, I hurry to the *Sentinel*, eager to ask Tess if she can read. Along the way I see two more families headed out of town with their belongings piled high in wagons. I wonder when the British will swoop into the city with their troops and horses and cannons.

At the *Sentinel*, Tess is nowhere to be found. She's always there cleaning, straightening, putting something in its rightful place. I check the library and even venture to the sacred third floor, where Amos's bed is still unmade. Surely, something is amiss.

Finally, I open the door to the basement and teeter down the dark stairs with a lantern. It's musty but cooler. I stop when I hear something skitter. I pray it's not a mouse—I hate mice.

"Tess?"

At the bottom of the stairs, I see a slight figure motionless on a narrow straw mattress on the dirt floor. It's Tess, with a damp rag covering her eyes and forehead, and a basin at her side.

"Tess? Are you ill?" I say too loud, fearing at first, she's unconscious. Then she removes the cloth from her red, swollen eyes.

"Ma'am, you shouldn't be here," she whispers.

"Why not? What's wrong?" The only furniture is a single chair, and I pull it closer.

"My head hurts so bad. The light makes it worse. Go, before I puke again," she moans.

"I'll go, but I'll return. I think I can help you, Tess."

It's a few blocks to Marshall Apothecary where I breathlessly ask for what I need. A young but intensely serious druggist pulls aside several glass bottles and slowly mixes a concoction of ground-up leaves and oils. His precision tests my patience. Finally, he hands me a salve in a tiny glass jar, and I shove coins at him before dashing back to Tess.

"This should help," I say as I kneel next to her. "My mother is a midwife, and she uses a salve of feverfew leaves and willow bark to treat head pain."

She looks terrified.

"Trust me," I say, realizing immediately how empty my words must sound. She has no reason to trust me. I'm a stranger who has invaded her privacy.

"Tess, I've never poisoned anyone."

She looks at me startled, then breaks into a slight smile. "Don't expect you have."

I open the jar, and I'm about to smear the ointment on her forehead when she grabs my arm.

"Just in case, I'll do it myself."

As she dabs on the salve, I notice the book on a crude shelf above her bed.

"You have a copy of *Robinson Crusoe*, Tess?"

She doesn't answer.

"You *can* read." Still nothing.

I feel triumphant, having solved one mystery about this strange woman. But she looks frightened.

"Is the book from Mr. Tinkleton's library? I won't tell. Your secret is safe."

"Thank you."

I notice a delicate china cup and saucer on the shelf next to the book.

"Beautiful!" I say, admiring the blue flowers painted on the tea setting.

"A gift," she offers.

"Someone special," I say, hoping to elicit more.

"Indeed. Taught me to read."

"And write too?" I ask, noticing the paper, pen, and ink bottle on a small chest that apparently serves as a desk.

"Yes, ma'am."

I want to find out more, but I hold back. I've been told I'm sometimes too forthright and nosey. She seems revived, and in a hurry to return to her chores.

"Mr. Tinkleton will be plenty riled up," she says. "Haven't tidied his quarters."

"You rest," I tell her. "I'll deal with Amos. Did I tell you that *Robinson Crusoe* is my favorite book?"

"Mine too."

"What was your favorite part?" I ask.

"When he finds the footprints in the sand and realizes he's not alone on the island." She seems to come alive as we talk more.

"What did you think of the cannibals," I ask.

"Disgusting!"

I can't help myself. "Tess, about *Gulliver's Travels*? Was it really misplaced?"

She doesn't answer, but the corners of her mouth rise slightly.

As I climb the stairs, I wonder how many books Tess has read.

Amos is in a quiet frenzy, pacing, but it's not Tess he's upset about.

"Where have you been?" he demands. "Soldiers on patrol just found a body behind the Freemasons Lodge."

I gasp. "One of the Quakers?"

"Don't know."

I'm out the door before he can say more. I fear it's a prisoner, caught trying to escape. I futilely scan the crowd outside the Lodge for Rachel or one of the other wives. Militia men are trying to keep everyone away from a crumpled body on the ground, covered with a blood-soaked linen sheet.

I feel sick. "Who is it?" I demand of a militia man.

"Young Ripley from the coffeehouse. Now step back."

"Rip?" I try to push past the guard. I don't believe it. "Let me see him," I scream.

"No, Miss. Next person who sees him will be the gravedigger," he says, pushing me back.

It's then I notice Rip's brother Ethan, sobbing. I want to comfort this young man I barely know.

"I'm so sorry, Ethan. Rip was my friend. Do you know what happened?"

He seems to recognize me. "He was on his way to Father's house with the day's receipts," he says haltingly.

"Somebody slit his throat ear to ear," Sam Parsons, the despicable militia leader, says. "He then relieved our Rip of the money."

I can't stop looking at Rip's covered body sprawled on the cobblestones. *He can't be dead. Someone should call the doctor. It's not too late.*

Suddenly, I'm back in Essex. I see my brother Seth with a gaping wound in his chest. He's dying in the dirt just outside our house. A patriot shot him—a supremely ironic gesture, as Seth was preparing to join the patriots the very next day.

"Who did this?" I ask Parsons.

"Don't know. But we'll find him—and the money."

I want to cradle and comfort Rip, just as I did my dying brother. As I try to move closer, Parsons steps in my way.

"It's a grisly sight. Trust me, you don't want to look any closer."

CHAPTER 7

Back at the *Sentinel* I'm in no condition to face Amos.

The horrible memory of Seth's murder makes me realize I still haven't recovered from it, though it's been a full two years.

Tom called it a terrible accident, but it was much more than that. Seth wanted to join the militia, against the wishes of our rabid-loyalist father. When they came to the house to enlist him, a fistfight led to gunfire, and Seth lay dying from a rebel's musket-ball.

Now Rip is dead too. My only friend in Philadelphia. I'm cursed—the men in my life keep dying. First Seth. Then Father, dead of smallpox. Now Rip.

Amos is in no mood to comfort me. "Well, what happened? Who was it?"

"Rip from Lloyd's Coffeehouse," I say, barely able to form the words. "Militia thinks someone killed him for the cash he was carrying."

Feeling dizzy and nauseous, I reach for Amos's arm before I crash to the floor in a dead faint. Everything is black. When I come to, he helps me to a chair.

"You sit a spell, and I'll fetch you a cool drink," he says with unusual warmth. My head has stopped spinning by the time he returns with a cup of cider.

"Are you feeling better?" he asks.

"Yes," I answer, my voice quavering. "Never happened before."

"You look pale, white as a ghost," he says. "You're not going to become ill, are you?"

"Don't think so." Is he worried I'll foul the premises?

"Maybe you should go home and rest. I can handle everything here, with Jacob's help."

I nod. Why not enjoy this rare show of kindness?

By the time I reach the Porters, I'm feeling better and wondering how Rip's brother Ethan is faring. Still tormented by the war, he now faces the viciousness of Rip's attack. The coffeehouse was closed when I walked by, a black ribbon draped across the front door.

The Porter house is blessedly quiet. Rachel is off visiting Charles with the two older children, and Gertrude has commanded the younger three to take naps. It's a perfect time to reflect on how different—maybe safer—my life would be if I'd given in to Mother's nagging, embraced midwifery, fled to Nova Scotia, and become her apprentice.

But first I spot a letter on the mantle for me. My heart leaps, thinking it's Tom, finally. But I recognize the handwriting of my best friend Emma from New Hampshire. Almost as good.

Emma, Tom's sister, has stood by me through all my troubles and adventures, and I sorely miss her. She's the only one who knows I've taken the Jordan name: *Mrs. Thomas Jordan*. I rip the envelope open.

Dearest Sarah,

I wish I had better news for you. We have heard nothing from Tom, and Mother and Father are worried sick he may not have survived the fighting in New York. But we both know what a fighter he is. If anyone can cheat death, it's my brother.

I'm bored to tears, teaching school to the young ruffians of Essex. I swear children are a miserable curse, something I wager you never thought I'd say. You're right to forsake them.

Father has decided the butcher, Isaac Ward, is my last chance for a respectable husband. Even if I could tolerate the stink of blood and guts, his clumsy and unceasing advances have made me swear off marriage too, as well as progeny.

Your urging that I take up residence in Philadelphia is tempting. Honestly, I'm still troubled by all the heartache of my time with you in New York. You are my dearest friend, but you wear me to a nub convincing me to do things that are clearly foolhardy.

Affectionately,
Emma

PS: Ezekiel is the best mouser in Essex. Mother still keeps score.

I reread the first part again. Tom missing? Feared dead? I don't believe it for a second. The Tom I know survived a near-fatal wound at Bunker Hill, only to plunge back into the fighting after he recovered. He nearly died of starvation and other tortures on that foul British prison ship in New York Harbor. No one survives all that to simply die in some battle. I won't let him.

At the mention of Ezekiel, the huge, murderous, ever-famished feline, I'm homesick for New Hampshire. I had to leave him and so much else that I loved when I fled to New York two years ago. Maybe that was somehow divine retribution—if there is such a thing—for blowing up the patriots' cache of ammunition with a flaming arrow. It's not as crazy as it sounds, though Emma would argue differently. I wanted to stop a bloodbath between the two sides. And I did—at least on that particular night in the little town of Essex—but it nearly cost me her friendship.

Then, I convinced her to move to New York and help me rescue Tom with an insanely dangerous plan that nearly drowned us all. She has every right to be wary of me.

I'm rereading the letter for the third time when Rachel bursts into the house. I'd never seen her anything but composed and cheerful, and now she's close to hysterical.

"They're sending our men away tomorrow, banishing them to western Virginia," she cries. "Who knows how long they'll be gone?

I can't manage without Charles! I don't know if he can even survive such an ordeal."

So far, the "ordeal" hasn't been such a trying time for the tea-sipping, well-fed merchants—a fact I don't have the heart to tell Rachel.

"They can't just banish them," I assure her. "They haven't had a hearing yet. They haven't even been charged with a crime. They have rights."

"Doesn't matter to these fools," she says, in unusually strong language. "They're determined to do it anyway. Those papers, those Spanktown Papers—that horrible collection of lies—they were the final straw."

Then she looks at me oddly. "Why are you home in the middle of the day?"

"I fainted at the *Sentinel*, and Mr. Tinkleton took pity on me," I say. I give her the sickening news about Rip.

"Dreadful!" she says. "All for a few coins. The streets aren't safe—not for Rip, not for our poor husbands, and now, certainly not for me and the other wives."

Abigail, her oldest, is predictably angry about her father's exile. "Mother, can't we do something—write to the Council, the Congress?"

Rachel pats her shoulder tenderly. "Your father and the others have done nothing but draft letters about the injustice since they were taken from us. And all our people support them. It's done no good."

"We can't just abandon him," whimpers brother Jack.

I offer what I think is the sensible path to freedom: "It's not too late for them to sign the loyalty oath." But they react as if I'd suggested they dance naked outside the Statehouse.

"He'd sooner give up his life," Rachel scoffs. "I know my husband, and he would not forsake his religion, never forsake God."

Abigail eyes me suspiciously. "Don't you believe in God, Sarah?"

"Of course I do," I say far too quickly. "My husband Tom would also give up his life for what he believes in—independence." I'm not ready to share more about the only man I've ever loved. Just thinking of him makes my body quiver and yearn, but I fear—if he's alive—that he remembers me only as a bit of attractive fluff on his glorious path to war.

Rachel is too distraught to think about supper, so Molly and Gertrude wrestle over how best to season the lamb stew. The pungent smell of garlic and rosemary reaches my tender stomach and sends me racing to the privy.

My retching doesn't go unnoticed by Rachel. "Poor child, you've had a terrible fright today. No wonder your stomach is unsettled. You rest while we make you a cup of tea."

I don't argue. If only she knew the whole truth. Emma's letter is sinking in: Tom could be dead. Then what would become of my little white lie about my "marriage"?

I sip tea in silent panic while Rachel pulls together a list of things for Charles: his greatcoat, breeches, shirts, Bible, razor, soap, tobacco, wine, biscuits, a teapot, and assorted herbs for his cough, his touchy stomach, and his heart tremors.

Because little Henry is still feverish, Rachel asks Jack to bring the parcel to the Freemasons Lodge. Off he goes, barely able to carry it.

"It will do him good to have a grown-up chore," Rachel says. I marvel at how well she understands her children.

"How will you get by with Charles gone?" I ask, wondering how she stays so calm under the most trying circumstances.

"If Henry takes a turn for the worse, I don't know what I'll do," she says. "I can handle nearly anything but the death of a dear, sweet child."

At dusk, we hear a commotion of horses and raised voices.

"Could it be the British?" Abigail asks.

"No," I assure her. "They aren't that close to the city."

"Then who is it?"

I peek out the front curtain and see a crowd of some 50 people carrying torches. They start jeering, louder and louder.

"Good riddance to you, pious Quakers! Wolves in sheep's clothing! Wolves in sheep's clothing!"

"Here's a little taste of real patriotism," one of them yells, before heaving the contents of a bucket all over the front steps.

I watch in disbelief from my window.

"Blood and guts!" He motions for the others to take up the chant. "Blood and guts!" The gloppy mess is all over the steps, and spatters streak the front door.

I hope to God it's animal and not human.

He yells his parting shot. "We'll see that your men have a bloody good sendoff tomorrow!"

CHAPTER 8

At first light I'm out on the front steps with a bucket of water, cake of lye soap and a brush. I don't know what possessed me to clean up the most foul-smelling mess I've ever encountered. Maybe it was the thought of poor Rachel out here on her hands and knees. Maybe it was just a way to avoid thinking about Rip or Tom.

I nearly slip and fall on the sticky, stinking goo coating the steps. Struggling to hold onto the contents of my stomach, I tackle the gore. If my day weren't already bleak enough, Gertrude emerges to survey the damage.

"Looks like someone was murdered and dismembered right here on our front steps," she says, holding a lavender-scented handkerchief to her nose.

"My guess is chicken guts," I say, "and whatever entrails the butcher had lying around."

"Best we get it cleaned up before the day heats up and makes the stink any worse," she says. "I'll get some rags."

Gertrude is as tough as an old boot.

When we finally finish, I go inside and find the household in unsurprising turmoil. After all, we were barraged with animal innards last night, and today, Charles and the others will likely be dragged off to some godforsaken spot for who knows how long.

Rachel is rushing to mend a pair of breeches in hopes of taking them to Charles before the men leave. Abigail is swatting at Jack for sampling the biscuits she's packing for their father. I'm in no mood for the clatter. I change my clothes and prepare for work, hoping my odor isn't too foul.

"Are you feeling better, Sarah?" Rachel asks as I head for my escape. "You had quite a day yesterday."

I'd like to give her an earful about the grief that's been so unfairly piled on me. But I can't.

"Yes, better," I lie. "Though I must hurry to the *Sentinel*. They'll want an article about Charles and the others."

"Good!" she says. "Everyone should know about their suffering and this terrible injustice."

Something in me bursts.

"Suffering? Injustice?" I say, incredulous. "Patriots like my Tom are dying on the battlefield so that you can go off to your meeting house and pray in peace for the divine light, or whatever it is that you call God. No warm biscuits for the soldiers! I know injustice! Oh, I know all about it!"

I expect Rachel to lash out at my rudeness; any sane person would. She looks at me long and hard.

"We'll sort this out later." She calmly goes back to her sewing.

As soon as I leave, I regret what I said. I didn't mean to hurt Rachel, though her righteousness wears thin. As I trudge to the *Sentinel*, I realize she has every right to make me find another place to live. A dreadful prospect.

To make matters worse, I walk in and find Amos ecstatic.

"Did you hear? They're banishing those traitorous Quakers today. Riding them out of town in full humiliation. I want to publish every detail of their inglorious exodus."

I decide to risk my own humiliation by asking a logical question.

"How can the Council and the Congress exile them when they haven't been charged with a crime or given a hearing? Don't they have rights?"

"Not important," he declares, brushing me off. "I need you to scour the city for every detail of their departure. Every tomato heaved at them. Every rock thrown."

Gone is the compassionate Amos of yesterday. I swallow

my irritation before asking whether he's heard any more news about Rip's murder.

"Just another robbery gone bad." The man is infuriating.

I find Tess in the back, scrubbing a coffee stain out of Amos's cravat. "Feeling better today?" I ask. She looks up, and for the first time I see a big, beautiful smile that perks me up.

"Yes. Thank you," she says. "But I'm afraid I can't repay you for the salve."

"No need." Then I give her a sly look. "Any books missing from the library today?"

Tess lowers her eyes and her voice. "Only *Moll Flanders*."

"Ah, the thief must be enamored with Daniel Defoe," I say.

She nods. "I wager it will be back in its rightful place tomorrow."

"Fast reader, this thief," I say.

At the Freemasons Lodge, a crowd waits for the prisoners to emerge after nine days of captivity. Groups of Quakers in their plain dress pray silently for the men's release. Some of the women weep.

A very different group are jeering the piety all around them and cheering on the militia who will soon be carting away the Quakers' venerable leaders. They mock the Quakers praying for peace rather than praying for more soldiers to beat the British.

"I say we seize more of their belongings to help pay for the war if they won't pay taxes like the rest of us," one of them yells.

At the moment, I'm not as concerned with the rights and wrongs of the debate as I am with the mess I've made of my immediate future. The Porters and their Quakers friends have been nothing but kind to me, and now I fear I've burned that bridge. Will supper and a comfortable bed await me tonight?

As for the 20 prisoners, they'll be traveling in high style. The caravan includes two ornately tasseled carriages, followed by six big wagons piled high with luggage. Some will even be riding their own horses. Andrew Nelson's servant Moses will accompany them, should the men need to have their toast buttered or some similar service.

Rachel has come to see Charles off with a basket of food and a parcel containing his neatly folded, mended breeches.

"Here to add your voice to the chorus of protesters?" she asks me in a painfully polite voice.

"No. I'm here to report on the day's events for the newspaper," I answer, just as politely.

"Then perhaps you can make it known to readers that those so-called patriots are treating our men as unjustly as they say the British are treating them. If that isn't the pot calling the kettle black!"

"Good point." Suddenly the lodge door opens, and guards haul out short, stout Andrew Nelson, arms and legs flailing. Digging his heels into the dirt, he screams: "I protest this unlawful act!"

As guards shove him into the carriage, his broad-brimmed felt hat falls to the ground and a horse stomps it into the dirt. The patriots, laughing at him, take up a mocking chant:

"I protest! I protest!"

Appalled, the Quakers add their voices to the din. "You'll be sorry!" one of them yells at the guards.

I'm stunned to hear such fighting words—however tame—come from the mouth of a Quaker, but the crowd seems to perceive them as comedic.

"I'm quaking in my boots," someone yells. More laughter.

Then armed guards shove and drag the rest of the men toward the waiting carriages. Some resist more than others. Charles emerges calmly, clutching his Bible and a satchel stuffed with papers. Rachel thrusts the food and breeches toward him.

"Back away from the prisoner," a guard shouts.

Someone in the crowd flings garbage at the all-but-imprisoned Quakers still dressed in their finery. A glob of rancid bacon fat hits Charles in the face as he's shoved into the carriage. Someone else hurls a rock at him and, instead, hits the back of Rachel's head, knocking her to the ground.

Blood gushes from the wound as I rush over to help.

"Clear the way," I shout, forcing a path through the crowd.

Agatha Nelson, the merchant's wife, comforts Rachel as blood streams down her cheek. Away from the crowd, we lower her to the ground under a sprawling elm. I gently untie Rachel's bonnet and grab Agatha's lace handkerchief to stanch the scarlet flow from a gash the size of a napkin ring.

She moans softly as the crowd hurls insults at the departing caravan. A half-dozen Quaker women gather around Rachel, forming a kind of human bandage.

"Heathen!" Agatha wails.

"I want to go home," Rachel says shakily.

"No, you mustn't get up," I say.

"I insist," she says.

There's no use debating it. As we help Rachel up and gently walk her away from the crowd, I link arms with Agatha.

"Our people will have a lot to say about this sorry treatment," she murmurs.

As tactfully as I can, I ask her why the entire Quaker community isn't here in protest.

"We've written countless letters and printed a slew of handbills," she says, clearly irked by my question. "Some of us are crying foul with our silence. Many others are at the meetinghouse praying for our men."

Rachel gives me a cautious look, as she wipes blood from her face with a torn sleeve. But I forge ahead.

"Why did Mr. Nelson put up a fight, when he was so clearly outnumbered?" I ask, trying to understand this confounded religion.

"That reflects our beliefs," Agatha explains, enunciating her words so carefully that even a witless soul such as myself might comprehend. "He feels strongly that we must not help the war effort in any way, even by stepping peaceably into a carriage."

"That makes no sense to me," I say.

Agatha shrugs. "You're not a Quaker."

Rachel stops to lean against a tree, and I tell her she needs to see a doctor immediately.

"No," Rachel insists. "I'll be fine once I'm gone from here."

"I'll see you home to bed," Agatha says.

The caravan of exiles is slowly rolling away, led by members of the militia and the armed guards—a ridiculous sight. Do they think these prisoners, these generously upholstered old men, would try to break free?

"Banish them! Good riddance!" The crowd is breaking up but their shouts persist.

It will take several days for them to reach their destination: Winchester, Virginia, some 200 miles away. I fear they'll suffer worse than mere taunts all along the way. Who knows how long they'll be held captive in the backcountry?

As I hurry back to the *Sentinel*, I hear the distant boom of cannon and see people gathering in the street. They know the British are coming, and many—including myself—are wondering what new hell awaits.

Amos already knows what's going on. It's maddening how news seems to travel directly to his delicate ear.

"The rebels are getting crushed at Brandywine Creek," he says. "There's no doubt now that the King's men will sweep in and take Philadelphia. The only question is whether they'll get any kind of fight from the patriots. I doubt it."

Amos has already moved on to the next big story—how soon the redcoats will take command.

I try to bring him back to the Quakers. "Amos, I have all the details you wanted. Some of the men had to be dragged from the lodge. And there's an important issue: Were their rights violated? No arrests; no charges. It seems unlawful—"

He just chuckles. "Nobody cares about some rich, pompous Bible beaters who won't fire a musket for liberty."

"But—"

"Let them stew in their own juices in some far-flung outpost where they can't do us more harm!"

Then he turns to Jacob. "Get that press going! We've got real news out there. In just hours, the Brits will march in and take over!"

Amos is so excited he's actually sweating. Probably hasn't happened since a hard summer's day of lawn bowling out on his parents' estate.

Turning to me, he says, "Go out there and find out if patriots—those that are left—are planning to flee the city."

I can't believe what I'm hearing. My world has gone topsy-turvy. "What about us? What about the *Sentinel*? Are we packing up? Everyone knows you're no friend of the British."

Amos gives me his best smug look, the one that says I'm an imbecile for even opening my mouth.

"We're not going anywhere."

CHAPTER 9

By the time I arrive home, I find Rachel tending Henry, whose fever has returned. Even though he's five years old, she cradles him in her arms, gently rocking him to and fro like a baby. Compared to his twin brother, he looks so frail.

Gertrude takes me aside. "I tried to coax Rachel to bed but she wouldn't have any of it. I don't know why she won't let me tend the child."

Gertrude has a good heart but all the tenderness of a charging bull.

"How is her head wound?" I ask.

"I cleaned it up. Put a bandage on it."

Upstairs, Rachel lays a shivering Henry on the bed, tenderly covering him with a wool blanket despite the day's heat.

"I'm worried sick," she says to me. "I didn't let on to Charles this morning. He would be frantic."

Back in New Hampshire, when my mother dragged me on her midwifery rounds, I saw too many little children who were sick and dying. I don't tell Rachel, of course, but I can't help thinking that Henry's time is near.

"How are you feeling?" I ask. "That was a nasty gash."

She pats the back of her head. "It's nothing, a trifle," she insists a little too forcefully. She motions to me to sit. "I would like a word."

I brace myself for the full force of Rachel's displeasure. After all, it was just this morning that I so rudely insulted her convictions.

"I wanted to thank you for helping me to safety today," she says, hands folded in her lap. "I don't know what would have happened if you hadn't stepped in."

Relief floods me. "Anyone else would do the same. I'm sorry I spoke so harshly this morning. If you would like me to find other living accommodations—"

"No, my dear!" she laughs. "The Lord would never forgive me if I cast you out."

Then she leans toward me with a serious face. "But I believe I'm entitled to an explanation for such strong words."

Her kindness overwhelms me, and in a rush of tears I tell her the whole story of Tom—his brush with death at Bunker Hill and again as a prisoner. I leave out the part about us not being married.

"Tom's belief in the patriots' cause is unshakeable," I say.

"I see." Rachel sounds horrified, and I don't know how much detail I should share with her.

"Maybe sometime I'll tell you how my friend Emma and I managed to rescue Tom from a British prison ship in a creaky rowboat that could have splintered in a rough wave!"

She looks at me as if my life has been ripped from the pages of a Daniel Defoe novel.

"And then you married this young man. Where is he, your husband, now?"

"I don't know," I admit. "I don't know if he's still with Washington's troops. His family hasn't heard from him. Nor have I."

Rachel's face turns sad and I know what she's thinking.

"He can't possibly be dead," I insist. I can't bring myself to tell her that the marriage is a sham. A convenience. Even though, ultimately, it's what I want, and I'm sure he does too—or at least did.

"You obviously care deeply for him," she says.

"More than anything."

"Then I understand why your loyalties lie with the patriots in this abominable war," she says.

I race to correct her.

"I've seen evil on both sides," I say. "The people of Essex hated my parents for supporting the British. They so despised my father that they destroyed his press and threw him in jail when he wouldn't sign the loyalty oath."

"How difficult for you—to be caught in the middle," Rachel says. "Though it seems now you must favor the patriots, given your husband's loyalty to the cause."

I'm about to tell Rachel that I can make up my own mind about the war, when the blast of cannon fire makes us both jump.

"The British are closing in," I say. "I hope your men are safely out of harm's way."

"I guess we both must live with uncertainty," Rachel says. "I will pray for you, Sarah."

I nod politely. I should respond with the same offer, but prayer has never worked for me. Until I see evidence, I'll pin my hopes elsewhere.

Days later I attend Rip's funeral at Christ Church. Save for a smattering of family members and a few friends, the cavernous church with its ornate columns and huge arched window is nearly empty. Not surprising, I guess, as patriot sympathizers are leaving town in droves.

With its towering steeple, Christ Church is the tallest building in all the colonies. All the city's bigwigs have attended services here—Washington, Benjamin Franklin, members of the Continental Congress. Now, with the British set to invade at any hour, it's eerily empty. They've all fled, many of them to other parts of Pennsylvania.

It's so sad—Rip knew everyone. I take a seat just behind Ethan and his father in a straight-back pew. On the other side of the aisle, I see Sam Parsons, head of the militia, and a few of his chums. Sam scowls at me, and I wonder why he's even here.

Ethan has the same thick, wavy hair as Rip, tied at the back of his neck. He's sweating, though it's not hot. He taps his foot nervously until his father comforts him with a hand on his shoulder. Rip told me that their mother died of yellow fever when he was ten and Ethan was 12.

The minister arrives late and hastily climbs the stairs up to the pulpit without apology. Is he itching to leave town too?

"Robert Ripley was a good, kind man," he says without much spirit. "He had many friends. It's unfortunate that more of them couldn't be here with us today. Rip, as his friends called him, had plans to join the patriots and fight for victory over the British. Just as his brother Ethan did, and just as their father did in the French and Indian War."

Ethan is weeping. I hear his father tell him to get ahold of himself. "Won't be long," the old man says.

The minister is speeding things along. "Rip was taken from us in a most cruel way. Simply for the money he was carrying home from the coffeehouse. Please join me in silent prayer for the soul of our dearly departed."

All too quickly it's over, and the minister is calling for Rip's simple pine coffin to be carried to the church burial grounds. After nearly 300 patriot deaths at Brandywine Creek, they were lucky to secure a coffin. Ethan and his father are among the pallbearers, along with Sam Parsons.

After Rip is lowered into the ground, I approach Ethan.

He flinches, and I realize his nerves are still raw. "I just wanted to say how sorry I am about Rip."

He looks bewildered, and I rush to explain.

"I'm Sarah Jordan, and I knew him from the coffeehouse. He was always kind to me."

He nods and gives me a blank look.

"I hope they find his killer soon," I say.

"I do as well," he says in a shaky voice. "I feel responsible."

"It wasn't your fault, Ethan," I say. "They'll find whoever did this."

His eyes are full of pain, and his hands are shaking. His father steps in, as if on the lookout for anything that might upset his son.

"Come along," he says, taking him gently by the arm.

At that moment, the odious Sam Parsons sidles up to me.

"On the prowl for news, I see."

With his shaggy reddish hair and tall frame, he might be considered handsome by some. But his lip rises to a sneer whenever he speaks, giving him an evil countenance.

"No, I'm here to grieve," I say dispassionately. "Rip was my friend. Why are you here? Not to grieve, I presume."

"You're a smug one," he says. "Rip was a good patriot. I aim to find his killer."

"Any hunches?"

"Maybe." he says. "Wouldn't tell you if I did."

"Forget about me. I hope you do tell the authorities because the town's not safe with a murderer on the loose. Could happen to anyone lucky enough to have a few coins on them."

"I'll find him," he boasts. "If anyone can. You do know the old man put up a reward for the killer's arrest, don't you?"

"No, I didn't know."

"Fool's errand, if you ask me," he snorts. "Killer could be right here under our noses."

CHAPTER 10

Rachel pulls an envelope from her tattered Bible. "A letter from Charles," she says, practically giddy with excitement. "I know you'll want to hear about it."

He's been gone nearly two weeks, and I'm astonished that he managed to get a letter through. Philadelphia is in chaos. British troops are massing outside the city, and any day now they'll make their grand entrance.

"A messenger brought it," she says.

"How—"

"Our people have ways."

I'm in awe of Quaker ingenuity and solidarity.

Scanning the letter, she says, "Seems the caravan is taking a circuitous route to Virginia to avoid the fighting. Listen to this."

We stayed in the homes of some generous souls in Potts Grove and Reading. Our latest appeal of this unlawful banishment has fallen on deaf ears."

"No surprise," she remarks.

"We were stoned and shoved by rebel ruffians on our journey. Some of us were badly bruised and shaken. One night we were quartered in a tavern surrounded by guards who barely

managed to fend off an angry mob."

"Awful," Rachel says.

"Is he all right?" I ask, picturing him bloodied, his spirit wounded. Such a kind, gentle man.

"He insists he's fine," she says. "I'm not so sure."

"Don't trouble yourself with worries about me. You are burdened with quite enough."

Rachel tears up. "He has a few encouraging words for each of the children."

"That must ease your mind," I say. I know she barely sleeps at night, and her dark-circled eyes tell a tale I can't even imagine.

As usual, she prefers not to talk about herself. "I see you're leaving without breakfast again, my dear. Molly has some porridge left on the hearth."

I politely demur. For some reason, I nearly gag at the mention of porridge though I've been on good terms with the horrid mush for as long as I can remember. Maybe my childhood tastes are finally changing.

"At least let me fix some bread and cheese. A bird eats more than you do."

As I walk toward the *Sentinel*, the streets are eerily quiet, especially compared to the ruckus of the last few nights. I was kept awake by the thundering exodus of carriages and wagons laden with household possessions. From everywhere and nowhere in particular, there was sporadic gunfire.

Usually Market Street is raucous with peddlers hawking fish, meat, live chickens and produce. But not today. Gone is the baker tempting me with sweet tarts and buns piled high on his cart.

Even Lloyd's is uncrowded this morning. Ethan is helping a customer when I walk in for my usual brew. Taller and slimmer than Rip, he's a far cry from his chatty brother, but today he seems calm and in control. I see his father in the back roasting coffee beans. The aroma is heavenly.

"Good morning, Sarah," he says with a shy smile.

"Good morn to you, Ethan. You're looking well."

"I am?" he laughs. "Inside I'm jumpy as a cat."

"You're as calm as can be, especially with all the turmoil in the air."

He leans in toward me. "I heard the most preposterous story," he says, and I feel like I'm talking to Rip again.

"I'm all ears."

"The patriots knew the British would try to seize Philadelphia," he says, clearly relishing the tale. "So, a few days ago, under cover of darkness, a band of them removed all 11 of the city's great church bells—even the 2,000-pound behemoth in the Statehouse."

"Let me guess," I say excitedly. "They stole the bells so the British wouldn't melt them down for bullets and cannonballs?"

"Exactly! A bunch of farmers were in on it. They loaded the bells in Conestoga wagons and covered them in manure and hay."

"Where did they go?"

"Allentown. They hid them in a church basement."

We both laugh and Ethan breaks into a rare smile. "Guess we showed 'em!" he says.

It feels good to see him happy and relaxed.

"Any more information on Rip's murder?" I ask.

"No. But Sam Parsons has been here a lot asking questions."

He hands me the coffee, and I see the tremor in his hands.

"Any gingerbread for you today?"

"No thank you, Ethan. Not the least bit hungry." Even gingerbread, which normally makes me swoon, sounds loathsome.

"Please come again, Sarah." He smiles, the same playful grin that endeared me to Rip.

At the *Sentinel*, the apprentice Joshua is regaling Amos with the latest rumor.

"The Brits will be marking patriot houses with chalk," he says, almost laughing.

"Why?" I ask.

Joshua's jaw drops at what he takes for my profound ignorance. "Well," he drawls slowly, "it might have something to do with who the Brits will evict so they can sit themselves in front of a nice roaring fire."

"They won't get a warm welcome at my quarters," Amos laughs. "I'll not take kindly to sharing my accommodations with anyone, no matter who they are."

Then he's all business. "This invasion is big news. Maybe Howe and his men will be stopped by Washington's troops at the last minute. Could be a major battle right here in Philadelphia. The whole city is on tenterhooks."

"What's left of the city," I remind him. So many have left, and if he had any sense, he'd be among them.

Joshua, the know-it-all apprentice, pipes up with his thorough analysis of military logistics.

"Washington's men were trounced at Brandywine—they're no threat to anyone. All that talk about them burning down the city to spite the British? Hogwash! They'll want to come back here someday."

"Enough of this chatter," Amos says impatiently. "I need you both to go out there and find out what's happening. I want to know every detail of their arrival, every *Huzzah!* shouted, and by whom."

As I head for the door, I pass Tess, who is frantically straightening a stack of newspapers.

She gives me a terrified look.

"Be careful out there, Sarah," she whispers.

On the street, word of the British advance has been out for hours. The cabinetmaker, and the silversmith, the provisioners—all the shopkeepers—are boarding up their windows.

"Just in case there's trouble," the wig maker Daniel Ballard tells me. "We don't know what kind of reception the King's men will get."

If Washington's men intend to defend the city, there's no sign of them. I head in the very direction from which the redcoats will be arriving, ignoring Tess's warning and all common sense. Walking past homes, I see an occasional face at the window. The waterfront, normally bustling, is still.

Now I see a smattering of people gathering on the side of the road. Still no sign of Washington's men.

Drums roll, but no gunfire. I see people waving the British flag, likely loyalists relieved that the reign of the patriots is virtually over.

Soon I see the redcoats, thousands of them, led by fife and drummers. Now the crowd around me is abuzz. As the units approach—some on horseback, their swords clattering, others on foot—I'm struck by the sea of crisp, bright red and white uniforms. The crowd cheers. Clearly, people are relieved that it's a parade instead of a massacre.

Somewhere out front is Lord Cornwallis, the general—or, if you listen to Amos, the pompous twit—who led the redcoats to victory at Brandywine. Beside him is lawyer and politician Joseph Galloway, Philadelphia's most famous loyalist.

As the men stride past, a military band plays "God Save the King." Still, the crowd is sparse.

I hear one of the happy onlookers orate to his friends about a return to civility. "Good riddance to those stinkin' rebels!" he says.

Later, celebratory fireworks rock the city, and I wonder how Ethan is faring.

At the *Sentinel*, Amos is gleeful. He rubs his hands together like a child anticipating a bowl of strawberry ice cream. He's hardly the starched, proper Amos I thought I'd gotten to know over the last month.

"Let's mark this day and celebrate!" he exults. "Let's ever recall September 26, 1777, as the day the British took over the city with a mere 3,000 soldiers, leaving the other 9,000 troops at Germantown. And let's remember that they did it without a peep from Washington and his men. Too bad they didn't get the huge, boisterous reception they were expecting."

"Hardly anyone left but a few loyalists," Joshua offers.

Amos is smiling, and I don't know why. I finally blurt it out: "You've bashed the British at every turn, and now they've taken over! Doesn't that give you pause?"

Amos's rollicking guffaw makes me wish I'd kept my thoughts to myself.

"You think I've gone mad!" he says.

I'm not sure whether he's gone mad or I've gone sane. I just know he's a puzzling, frustrating, impossible man.

"The other newspapers with patriot sympathies, the *Journal* and the *Packet*, fled the city as soon as trouble appeared," he says. "Just like John Adams and the Continental Congress—all of them fleet on their feet. Meanwhile, we'll take profitable advantage of their loss. It's business!"

"What about your hatred of the British? They're likely not fond of you either," I remind him.

"No matter," he says. "I can adjust my thinking. Lawyers do it all the time."

Then he shoos us away. "Back to work. We have much to do. We must give this story the pomp and circumstance befitting our beneficent new rulers."

I walk away wondering how Amos can change his political views as easily as changing his silk stockings. He's not the least bit troubled. Maybe I should be equally magnanimous toward the victors, whoever they might be, tomorrow or in years to come.

By the end of the day, I've managed to write something that seems to satisfy him, and I even helped Joshua set type. Yet somehow, my biggest achievement was choking down Rachel's bread and cheese. I knew I needed to eat but it was the absolute last thing I wanted to do.

Just before I leave for the day, I see Tess helping Amos off with his vest, just as a loving wife would do. There's a tenderness in his eyes I've not seen before. Both are conundrums in their own way.

Before heading home, I stop at Lloyd's. They're closing early, and I meet Ethan's father at the door. I can tell immediately something is wrong.

"Ethan? Is he—"

"He's not well," Mr. Ripley says. "Today was too much for him, with the noise, all the soldiers and the fireworks."

"May I see him?"

"I don't think—well, maybe a quick visit would calm him."

I already have the door open, and I can see Ethan is rocking back and forth on the edge of a stool, his arms wrapped tightly around himself.

I walk up slowly. "Ethan, may I sit with you?"

He keeps rocking, but I take a seat opposite him and say nothing. He's hunched over, head down, breathing fast.

"Sorry you . . . have to see me . . . like this," he finally says, still rocking.

"No need to apologize," I say, not sure what else to do. We sit for another minute as the rocking slowly subsides and he raises his eyes to meet mine.

"I was all right until the fireworks," he says. "All of a sudden, I was—well, somewhere else, the battlefield."

"That must have been terrifying," I say. "The important thing is that you made it out."

His hands are trembling. "I wish I hadn't."

Walking home, I agonize over what I should have said or done. I feel so lacking when it comes to helping others—something Mother is so well equipped to deal with.

I wonder how she'd deal with poor Ethan.

And I wonder about Tom. I wonder what horrors he's waded through on the battlefield. I wonder how he copes with them. And I wonder, most of all, if he's still alive.

CHAPTER 11

"You're late, again," Amos says slowly and with precise diction. "In case you're interested, British troops have attacked Fort Mifflin on Mud Island."

"Mud Island?" I'm here not 10 seconds, and Amos is literally spitting words at me. I can't make sense of it. My mind is on my roiling stomach.

"Mud Island in the middle of the Delaware River," he says, enunciating every syllable as if I were deaf. "We need to write an account of it, a glowing account that will make the British and General Howe so pleased they'll look to the *Sentinel* for their printing and advertising needs. Could be nicely profitable for us."

"Of course, Amos I'll—"

There's a volcano of porridge rising in my throat, and I can't stop it.

"I'll get—"

"What ails you, Sarah?" he barks.

I can't answer. The volcano is cresting. I cover my mouth and run to the privy outside, arriving just in time.

I'm still there a half hour later, relieving myself of whatever else I managed to choke down this morning. I can't deny it any longer—something is terribly wrong with me. At first, I thought I was just greatly upset by Rip's murder. But I can't think of a single food that doesn't make me gag. And I'm tired all the time.

The one thing that makes total sense is such an unlikely prospect that I force it from my mind. Tom and I were lovers, but only once. What are the chances? No, it's not that. It can't be that.

Tess finds me sprawled on the floor, hair undone, drool down the front of my dress.

"Mr. Tinkleton asked me to check on you," she says. "How are you feeling?"

"Not so good," I whisper, embarrassed. "I think it's dysentery. I might be dying."

"Let me help you up," Tess says, not the least bit put off by the sight of me. She puts her arm around my waist and lifts me up. Somehow this tiny woman raises me to my feet.

"You come down to my quarters where you can rest, and I can tend you," she says, taking my arm. I'm still wobbly and nearly fall before she rights me again.

"What about Amos?"

"I'll take care of him."

I let her guide me down the stairs in the dim light.

"I can't lie on your bed. I'm a mess."

"You think I've never seen sickness?"

She lowers me onto a quilt with stars and flowers embroidered on it.

"It's beautiful," I say. "I don't want to foul it."

"My mother made it," she says, ignoring my protests and covering me with a threadbare blanket. "I don't have the patience or the fortitude for such precise labors."

I'm surprised by her vocabulary. I've never heard a slave—former slave—talk that way. Of course, I've known very few, no less one who could read. Around Amos and the others, I've only heard her whisper, "Yes sir, and no sir," with eyes lowered.

"You look much improved," Tess says. "Would you like some tea?"

"No, thank you. Not sure I can keep it down."

Tess pulls up the chair and sits beside the bed. "You think your trouble is dysentery?"

"Yes," I say without looking at her.

"Any diarrhea?"

"No. Only puking. I'm tired, and that's not like me. I'm usually vigorous to a fault."

"Yes, I've noticed."

Tess is silent for a minute with her hands in her lap, as if she's waiting for me to say something.

"Are your breasts swollen and tender?" she asks.

"Yes. How did you know?" A certain dread is starting to circle over me.

"When was your last bleed?" Tess asks, as if inquiring about the weather.

"I don't remember." The dread is descending.

"Was it more than a month?"

"Maybe two months. I didn't keep track."

Tess rolls her eyes. "Try to remember."

"Yes, two months," I say with hesitation.

"Could it be possible—"

"Yes, it could," I say. "But highly unlikely."

The story of Tom Jordan pours out of me like the morning's porridge. Our time together in New York. Those two deliciously passionate days and nights, hidden in the attic of a kindly couple while the British scoured the city for us.

"I love him, and he loves me, and it was only that one time."

Tess gives me a pathetic look. I'm such a fool. Anyone else would have known immediately, at the first sign. And me, the daughter of a midwife. How could I be so mindless?

"What am I going to do?" I wail. "I can't marry…" As soon as I say it, I wish I could take it back. Too late.

"What do you mean? You *are* married… to Tom Jordan. Isn't that what you told Amos?"

"It is. And that was a lie. A little lie. I thought people in Philadelphia would be more accepting of a married woman, especially a woman whose husband is away fighting for the patriots. It seemed proper somehow."

"I didn't know you cared that much for propriety," Tess says.

"Well, I do, a little."

"Maybe it's not so awful," she says. "You said Tom loves you.

Wouldn't he marry you now, especially with a baby on the way?"

"He would, but I fear he's dead. I haven't heard from him since we left New York. Nor has his family."

Tess is trying to put it all together. "So, if you're not Sarah Jordan, who are you?"

"Sarah Barrett."

As shameful as I feel, it's a relief to finally tell the truth. "How can I provide for a baby—or, as the child would be known far and wide—a bastard? Rachel would throw me out. I'd have to find another home."

It sounds too selfish for me to say it, but what would happen to my dreams of becoming a famous writer? How could I keep working for Amos? He'd never allow it. He'd brand me an idiot for letting it happen in the first place.

"Seems you have some serious thinking to do," Tess says. "At least you're not dying of dysentery."

"I could die in childbirth," I point out.

"True."

"True! That's all you have to say?"

Tess just stares at me until I feel ashamed.

"I'm sorry, Tess. But I just can't have a baby. Not now, maybe never."

"Why is that?"

"I don't know the first thing about caring for a baby. And I'm clumsy. Some women, like my best friend Emma, are born to be mothers. Whatever that magic might be, I don't have it and don't think I'll ever get it."

"Is that so?"

"Tess, the awful truth is, I don't think I even like babies."

I feel like a monster. Who doesn't like babies? No one. Except maybe someone terribly flawed. "No, I have no business bringing a child into the world."

For a moment, we're wrapped in a cocoon of silence.

"There is another way," I say, avoiding Tess's eyes.

"Another way? What are you thinking, Sarah?"

I tell her about my mother offering her midwife services to prostitutes working the dingy brothels in New York. They sought her out not for help with a birth but for help to avoid one. Mother prepared a special tea that brought on a bleed—but only if they weren't far enough along to feel the baby kick.

Tess doesn't seem horrified at all when I relate all this.

"I'm not saying I would do it," I add quickly. I don't know that I could, that I'd have the stomach to do it.

Tess clears her throat. "I know of what you speak. It's called 'taking the trade.' I read all about it in Benjamin Franklin's book, *Every Man His Own Doctor: The Poor Planter's Physician."*

"From Amos's library?"

"Yes. Franklin even includes a recipe for the tea."

"Tess, did *you* do this?"

She looks me straight in the eye. "Yes."

"Then you could help me do it."

Tess doesn't answer and gets a faraway look in her eyes. "Saddest day of my life," she finally says. "I don't regret it, but I wonder every day what might have been."

"But you did it."

"Yes."

"Who was the father?" As soon as I say it, I know I crossed a line.

"That is not your concern, nor anyone else's." The softness in her eyes is replaced by a cold stare.

Why do I feel compelled to blurt out every thought in my head?

"Tess, please forgive my rudeness."

Suddenly, a wave of nausea overtakes me, and I break into a sweat. In a flash, Tess has a basin at the ready, and she's pulling my hair back from my face.

I gag, but nothing comes up. In a moment it passes.

"I'll never eat breakfast again," I moan.

Then I tell her about Rachel and Gertrude and how they were concerned I wasn't eating enough.

"They made me sit down to a bowl of porridge topped with a hunk of last night's fish." The mention of fish triggers a flutter of nausea.

"They *made* you eat it?"

"I tried to politely decline, but they were too much for me."

"I doubt that." Tess chuckles.

For some reason, tears well up and suddenly I'm a weepy mess. "I don't know what's happening to me. I'm so tired of feeling sick," I burst out. "I have to work. I can't be puking every five minutes."

Tess smiles. "The puking will pass, and you'll feel much better."

"How do you know so much about being pregnant? I thought you took the trade, Benjamin Franklin's cure."

"I have a child. I had a child." Her eyes pool, and she looks away.

I want to know what happened, but I just wait patiently in the silence of this dark, dank basement.

"I gave birth to a girl 10 years ago on the first day of July, during a violent thunderstorm," Tess begins slowly. "Dinah."

She wipes away a tear with the back of her hand.

"It was before I had my freedom. When I worked for a tobacco farmer in Virginia."

"You must have been quite young," I say, looking at this waif-like woman with delicate features who comes up to my shoulder.

"I was 17. Dinah was my joy. There was nothing else to be joyful about at that time, except my husband Ben. We worked our fingers bloody, weeding and hoeing from morning until night. Dinah was born, and I was back in the field a week later."

Tess is silent. She's somewhere else. I'm afraid to ask, but I must know.

"Did Dinah… die?"

"No," she answers quickly. "When she was five years old, they came to take her away."

"Take her where?"

"Williamsburg. To be sold like a sack of flour." Tess spits out the words. Her eyes blaze with anger.

I gasp. I can barely picture the horror of it.

"Ben tried to stop the men who came to take her. He loved that child so."

"What happened?"

"He swung a hoe at them. He was like a wild man. They shot him dead in front of the child and me."

Tess is sweating and breathing fast. "Dinah was screaming hysterically as they pried her from my arms and took her away."

"Do you know where—"

"Never laid eyes on her again. Don't know where she is. Or even if she's alive."

"How did you end up here in Philadelphia at the *Sentinel*?"

"A month later, I was sold at auction. I was still crazy with grief, barely able to dress myself."

"Amos *bought* you?" I say, abandoning all courtesy.

"Yes." Then a glimmer of a smile emerges. "For $250, in case the journalist in you has a yearning to know."

"I wasn't going to ask that," I say.

Then Tess looks at me and just shakes her head. "I've never told anyone all that, Sarah. You're the first. And I'll tell you one more thing."

She leans in toward me. "I have never stopped looking for Dinah, and I never will."

CHAPTER 12

Tess agrees to keep my secrets. She even tells Amos I ate a foul oyster and can't stop puking. He's so disgusted by the idea of vomit anywhere near his house, he orders me home immediately.

The walk back to the Porters settles my stomach and clears my head. British soldiers are everywhere. Now there's a mad scramble to find housing for them. Patriots left homes vacant when they fled, but not nearly enough for Howe and his officers.

On top of all that, Washington's men are blasting British supply ships as they try to make their way up the Delaware River. Already the city is reeling from food shortages. Molly can't find flour for her rock-hard biscuits.

Walking up the steps, I dread the prospect of telling Rachel my troubles. But she rushes up to greet me with news of her own.

"Sarah, you're just in time. I was about to read Charles's latest letter to the family."

My plan for a nap and a good wallow in self-pity, dashed.

Everyone is gathered in the parlor, where a fight has broken out over Jack's alleged cheating at checkers.

"Children, settle down so you can hear what your mother is saying," Gertrude orders. The room quiets, and Rachel begins to read:

Dearest Rachel and children,

We finally arrived in Winchester, Virginia, after a bumpy 18 days on roads barely more than a footpath in places. Only 800 people here in this frontier town, and none of them happy to see us.

We are comfortably housed in a small inn, four men to a room. The three others in my room say I snore like a bear in winter.

The children giggle, and even Gertrude emits a little chuckle.

We're drafting a new appeal. We must convince our captors that the allegations against us are a lie. We never gave the British military secrets. Hogwash!

The latest insult is that the patriots insist we pay for our food and lodging. We're prisoners! It's outrageous!

Rachel stops reading. "How could they! First, they take our dear ones without just cause. Then they expect payment."

"Disgraceful," Gertrude echoes.

I silently salute the patriots for their shameless nerve. For most of these men, it won't be a hardship.

Rachel scans the rest of the letter. "Your dear father asks that you keep him in your thoughts and prayers, just as he does all of us. And he is so pleased Henry is on the mend."

Though still pale and thin, Henry is out of bed for the first time in weeks.

"I want to write to Father," Abigail says.

"I'm sure he would appreciate that, my dear," Rachel says. "Please be cheerful. No need to trouble him about the paucity of food. He has troubles enough."

Troubles? I would never say it here, but their "incarceration" barely sounds discomforting. It's barely imprisonment compared to the misery Tom endured on that decrepit British prison ship in New York Harbor.

At least Charles isn't fending off starvation, beatings, and smallpox. Tom might be there still, if I hadn't concocted an outrageously dangerous scheme to rescue him. And now, months later, I get not even a letter, not even a hasty note to let me know he's still alive.

Rachel's Quaker friends arrive for tea. Now that my stomach has settled, I sneak an apple from the kitchen and head up to my room to ponder my dismal future.

I start a letter to Mother, intending to tell her about my… predicament. I can't even say baby. But I end up telling her about Amos and the arrival of the British and the Porters' new cow—anything but the awful truth. I don't know what I fear most: her disappointment, her anger, or her shame. As a midwife, she's seen plenty, and I try to imagine what she'd say if I were one of her mothers-to-be. I've seen her dote on them with infinite compassion and tenderness. But she was never much for doting on me.

Would she be horrified that I thought for one minute about "taking the trade" as Tess put it? Fine for prostitutes, she'd say: Not ladies.

I'm still tormenting myself when the tea ladies leave. I change into a fresh dress, comb my unruly hair, wash my face and head downstairs to see Rachel. But there's a sharp rap on the front door, and I open it to face three British officers standing ramrod straight in their spotless red and white uniforms.

"Mrs. Porter, I presume. I'm Lieutenant John Gray with His Majesty King George's British forces."

"I'm not—"

"By order of Commander-in-Chief William Howe, you are required to house soldiers under the Quartering Act of 1774. We have run out of space for our men, and we respectfully ask you to designate rooms for us in your home."

"But I'm not—"

"We're asking the same of others, especially those with roomy houses, such as yours."

"I'm not Mrs. Porter, but I'll fetch her for you."

When I return with Rachel, I hang back to see what she does.

"Come in, gentlemen," she says as if they were church folk.

Lt. Gray leads the men into the parlor. They take stock of the home as if it were already theirs.

"I understand the need for housing," Rachel says. "But my husband is a prisoner of the patriots, and I know not when he'll be released. Meanwhile, I'm left with five children to care for, and scant food for all those mouths. Without my husband's presence it would be unseemly for me to board gentlemen. And, as you might know, our religion forbids us from assisting in the war effort."

Then she rises—a clear signal the matter is closed. But the men don't budge.

"Mrs. Porter, I don't think you understand the seriousness at hand. We are in dire need of accommodations. The law is very clear—"

"Gentlemen, I don't think you understand. The answer is no. You'll have to look elsewhere."

I'm stunned and elated. I want to cheer Rachel in the name of all womanhood. But Lt. Gray is clearly not of the same mind.

"Mrs. Porter, this is most distressing," he says. "We have the authority to take over your entire house by force, if necessary. I don't want it to come to that. Won't you please change your mind?"

"My answer is still no," Rachel says with no hesitation. "Do what you must."

"This is most irregular." Sweat is beading on his upper lip and forehead. As he rises to leave, he says, "I'll need to report back to my commander. You haven't seen the last of us."

"Good day, gentlemen," Rachel chirps, as if they'd just come by for tea.

Once they're gone, I take her aside. "May I have a word with you? In private?"

"Of course, Sarah," she says looking alarmed. "Why are you home in the middle of the day? I hope you're not ill."

"That's what I need to talk with you about. Shall we go to my room?"

In a tangle of tears and shame, I tell her I'm pregnant.

"Why are you crying? Aren't you happy about this blessed event? It's all part of God's wondrous plan for wedded couples."

I should confess the whole truth. I ache to spill the whole sorry story about my made-up marriage. It's on the tip of my tongue… But something holds me back. Maybe it's my own shame in the presence of a woman who's never had a wicked thought.

"Yes, this is happy news," I say with limp enthusiasm. "I just didn't expect it so soon. And with my husband away and no word from him in months. I fear he may not even be alive."

Rachel takes my hand. "We'll pray for him. We all will."

She's so excited that all I can say is, "Thank you."

Of course, Rachel—ever calm, never confused—has a plan for my immediate future.

"I expect you'll be giving up your employment at the newspaper and moving back with family to await the birth."

"No!" I respond more forcefully than I intend, and Rachel is taken aback. "It's impossible. As you know, my mother is living in the wilds of Canada, and my father is dead."

"What about Tom's family? Surely, they would be happy to have you."

"They're struggling as it is." Another lie. "I couldn't impose."

Rachel is puzzled. "Then what do you propose?"

"I'd like to stay here, if I may...and continue working at the newspaper."

She's stunned. "Continue working? That's highly unusual."

"These are unusual times, and I need the money."

Rachel doesn't need to know that a part of me would die if I couldn't write, if I could do nothing but wait for this child I can't warm to.

"I hope you'll give this some serious thought," she says. "As will I. At the least I'll ask Charles for guidance."

I have no arguments left. "If Charles finds it indecent or decides that I'm a bad influence on the children, I'll understand. I'll leave if he wants. And I know he'll have the final say."

"Don't be so sure, my dear. In the eyes of God, men and women are equals, despite what others might believe."

Rachel—and more to the point, Quakerism—continue to surprise me.

"Let us pray on this, and that your husband will reappear safe and sound," she says, bowing her head.

How can I tell Rachel—pious, sweet Rachel—that I have my doubts about God? I don't see that prayer has ever done anyone the least amount of good. And if she knew I might still rid myself of this problem by "taking the trade," I fear she would see me as wicked to the bone.

But is it just as wicked to bring an unwanted child into this world?

CHAPTER 13

Amos has done a complete turnaround. Gone are his rants about the pompous, wrong-headed British and their attempts to squeeze more money from the colonists. Now Howe and his men can do no wrong. His editorials urge residents to open their homes to British soldiers seeking housing. He praises them for their swift, clean takeover of Philadelphia.

His reversal has paid off. In the weeks after their arrival, the British have rewarded him with orders to print their documents and handbills. I've never seen him in a better mood. When I arrive at the *Sentinel*, he's mulling his next editorial.

"It's an appeal to the good people of Philadelphia," he explains. "The British forces need blankets, woolen stockings, and now flour because of this bloody blockade. Lt. Gray came to see me today with a long list of his needs. I could use your assistance, Sarah."

"Happy to oblige," I say, though I'm perplexed. It's Washington's men who are in dire straits. The British soldiers seem well fed and handsomely clothed. But I'd be a fool to point that out.

Tess has been true to her word and hasn't let on to Amos about my condition or my lack of a husband. After a few weeks, the sickness has let up, and my dashes to the privy are less frequent. I'd pray for a bleed if I thought prayer would do any good. Still no letter from Tom, though Rachel has urged her network of friends to pray for him. It's embarrassing that so many people are praying on my behalf.

Amos dispatches me to Lloyd's for a meat pie, but only if they were baked fresh this morning, and only if they're not too salty, and only if they contain no onions. And it must be wrapped properly in paper and preferably not touched by my hands. It matters not to him that the price for such an obscene luxury in these straitened times is sky high.

Ethan greets me with good cheer. "Sarah, you have a glow this morning."

"And you're looking well." I give him Amos's order.

"The man is as fussy as an old hen. Do you have time for a coffee?"

"I'd like that, and I hope you'll join me."

"I'd be pleased. Not as busy as Father would like. The British still favor their tea over coffee."

When we sit down, I notice that his hands are steady, and he's relaxed. "You seem better," I say. "Have your war troubles eased up?"

"Not entirely. But I do have spells where I feel like myself again. Father and I miss Rip terribly. I hope they catch his killer soon."

"Is there any news about that?"

"Not that I've heard. I'm sure Sam Parsons and his militia pals think I had something to do with it. 'Crazy Ethan. Sick in the head from the war.' But I haven't seen Sam since the British took over."

"You don't seem crazy to me, Ethan," I say between sips of coffee.

"You're too kind." His cheeks flush, and he looks away.

"I think about Rip's death a lot," I say. "Why would anyone do that for some coins?"

"I don't think it was for the money," he says. "The receipts that day were slim."

"It doesn't make sense that someone would kill him over a pittance," I say.

Ethan looks me square in the eye. "I think he was killed because he knew something." Then his eyes squeeze shut as if he's willing himself to stay calm. But his hands begin to tremble, and his breathing is fast.

"I've upset you. I'm sorry, Ethan. I'll go." I push my chair back to stand as Mr. Ripley strides over.

"Son, pull yourself together." Turning to me he says, "What have you done? You'd best go now, Mrs. Jordan."

Back at the *Sentinel* Amos is still fiddling with his editorial. "Sarah, I need your help on this. Read what I have and see if you can organize it better. I'll be in my quarters consuming this meat pie, if it is, indeed, edible," he says, sniffing it.

An hour later I've managed to rewrite his words in some semblance of order and added a few clever touches of my own. I'm certain that people will now happily donate their blankets, stockings, shirts, coats, even their whiskey to the glorious British empire and its brave soldiers.

I look all over the building for Tess. I have a volume of poetry to slip her from his library. Sometimes I sneak books out and pass them on to Tess, and no one is the wiser. I even check the basement. Nothing.

Finally, Amos comes downstairs from his third-floor quarters looking satisfied. The pricey meat pie must have met his picky standards.

"I'll have a look at what you've done, Sarah," he says, taking a seat.

Out of the corner of my eye I see Tess slip down the stairs from the third floor. She straightens her gown and mashes her hair under her cap and looks up to see me staring. She looks away. Then, Amos draws me in.

"This will do just fine, Sarah," he says, meaning that my words will go in the next issue, but the world—at least Philadelphia—won't know they're my words. His name might not be attached to the essay but Amos, as the paper's owner, will still get the credit—or the blame.

When I arrive home, there's a letter for me on the mantle. I know straight away it's from Emma. No one else has her precise handwriting.

Dearest Sarah,

I have the worst possible news. Mother and Father received a letter from Israel Hampton, one of the men who served with Tom's battalion at the Battle of Brandywine near Philadelphia. He wrote that Tom is dead. He saw Tom go down with a bad head wound and never get up. When the fighting was over, the patriot deaths were so catastrophic the bodies were buried on the battlefield. Israel searched for Tom's body, to no avail.

I know this news will be devastating for you. I wish I could be there to provide some comfort. Mother, Father, and the whole family are grief-stricken.

I am so sorry to be the bearer of this awful news.

Your friend forever,
Emma

I feel dizzy and grab the mantle. How could Tom be dead? He survived the Bunker Hill massacre. He survived torture aboard a prison ship. How could he expire on some battlefield just 25 miles away? Sobbing, I slump to the floor, where Abigail finds me.

"Has something happened to Father?" she screams. "I'll fetch Mother."

Rachel half-carries me to my room, where I pour out the devastating news. "Oh, my poor child," she says, stroking my arm. "You've had quite a shock."

I show her the letter, and she reads it slowly.

"Is it certain he's dead?" Rachel asks.

"I'm certain. Emma wouldn't have written to me with such awful news if she didn't believe it herself. It makes sense. No one's heard a word from Tom."

"Nonetheless, I shall continue to pray he's alive."

"Waste of time," I snap.

"Prayer is never a waste of time."

Sobs overtake me again, my whole body shaking with grief. If Rachel is shocked by my doubts about prayer, she doesn't show it. She sits silently with hands folded while I let the pain wash over me.

The next morning I drag myself out of bed, dress halfheartedly, and force myself downstairs. Everyone greets me at breakfast with pleasant smiles and kind words. Rachel has told them about Tom's demise, and about his child that I carry.

"Sarah, I've made you pancakes with maple syrup," Molly says. "I know it's your favorite."

How she managed to secure enough flour when the blockade has virtually choked off the city's entire supply—well, I don't ask.

Henry hands me a picture he's drawn of the new milk cow he's named Blacky for her color, and I'm surprised at how accurately he's captured the likeness.

"Well done!" I crow with as much enthusiasm as I can muster.

I make it through breakfast without tears and leave for the newspaper, despite Rachel's plea that I stay home. Walking to work, I'm glad I put on my wool cloak. The fall air is brisk and helps clear my head of the awful news about Tom. I hope that I don't fall to pieces at the first sight of Amos. I stop at Lloyd's to fortify myself.

Ethan bids me good morning but then takes in my puffy eyes and flushed face. "What's wrong? Are you ill?"

"No. Just some bad news."

He fills a cup with steaming black coffee and hands it too me. "Whatever it is, I'm sorry. If I can do anything to help—"

"Thank you, but you can't. I lost a dear friend in the damned war."

"Must have been a close friend, indeed, to cause you so much grief."

"Yes, closer than you'll ever know." He takes my hand and squeezes it, and I dissolve into a blubbery mess.

"It's no use lying to you," I say. "It's Tom. He's dead."

"Your husband. Oh, I am so sorry."

I don't have the strength to correct him. Nor can I tell him about the baby, for whom I feel no love, especially now.

CHAPTER 14

THE ONLY THING THAT takes my mind off Tom is Tess. The last time I saw her she was slinking out of Amos's quarters in a state of quiet disarray. The look on her face told me everything. Can it be true? I wouldn't have thought so, but I can't dismiss what I saw. That, and a tender moment or two I've witnessed between them. I wonder how she'll react when she sees me.

More importantly, I'm desperate to tell her about Tom's death. She's the only one here that I've been completely honest with about my sorry state. If anyone will understand the mess I'm in, it's Tess.

But Tess will have to wait. As I walk into the *Sentinel*, Jacob, the head apprentice, takes me aside. If he notices my red, puffy eyes, he takes mercy and doesn't say so.

"Prepare yourself: Amos has had a complete turnaround. Now he's fed up with the British. Says the city is a mess since the takeover," Jacob says. "He's out there right now, seeing it for himself."

This is startling: Amos going to the scene of news is a news story in itself! For a moment, I put that delightful inconsistency aside and focus on his apparent change of heart.

"But he *loves* the British," I point out to Jacob. "He says they can do no wrong. He supports every move they make."

"Until now."

"What caused this upset?" I ask.

"He went to saddle his mare to go to church on Sunday morning, and someone had stolen her in the night."

"His precious Buttercup?"

"Yes, and five bags of feed."

"He must be blind with rage," I say. "He'd sleep with that horse if he could."

Jacob is pacing. "For weeks I've been trying to tell him what's been going on all over the city since the British took over. With the blockade, people are desperate. They're stealing fences for firewood. They're slaughtering horses like precious Buttercup for meat."

So it took a cruel slap in the face to wake Amos up. Figures.

"Did he calm down?" I ask.

"No. When he finally arrived at the Presbyterian Church, he found the British had crammed it with their wounded. It's now a hospital. Their blood is soaking the pews."

The heavy oak door flies open with a crash and Amos charges in. His shirt is sweat-stained and untucked. His wig, the one he now wears to conform with the almighty British, hangs precariously.

"Do you know what's going on out there?" he demands.

It's clear he doesn't want an answer.

"The damned British promised they'd bring civility, order to the city when they took over. It's chaos out there. It's not safe on the streets. Their soldiers are stealing sacks of flour from the good people of Philadelphia—at least those that are left. They even stole some widow's goat—just grabbed the poor, skin-and-bones creature from her yard."

I dared open my mouth. "What are you going to do about it?"

"Do about it?" he thunders, most unlike Amos. "I've demanded a meeting with Howe or at least Cornwallis."

Even I know that's not likely. With the Americans blocking the Delaware, supply ships can't reach the city. Rachel complained just this morning about the scarcity of butter and mutton, fearing they'd have to go without. Ethan is down to a few sacks of coffee beans.

"Tess!" Amos yells. "Where is that woman? I can't meet with Howe looking like this. I'll need all fresh clothes and the wash basin."

Tess appears from out of nowhere, carefully avoiding my eyes. "Yes sir. I'll tend to it." In an instant she's gone.

Amos isn't finished. "Sarah, go to the Statehouse. I hear they've turned it into prison for captured American soldiers. A travesty!"

I walk into the Statehouse and find that the British have converted the first floor into barracks for their men. I wonder what the signers of the Declaration of Independence will think about their beloved hall, the building where they cut ties with Britain, being overrun with redcoats.

"Miss, you can't go in there," a guard yells as I wander down a corridor.

I'm prepared for this. "I'm looking for my husband. I'm sure he's here among the wounded prisoners. Please let me have a look."

A lie, though not far from the truth. Tom is dead, but for a fleeting moment I imagine him here among the wounded.

The guard nods. "Go up to the long gallery on the second floor. Mind you, it's not a pretty sight."

I make my way up the stairs wondering what hell awaits. Even though it's fall, it's sweltering hot. All the windows are nailed shut—a heartless move to prevent escapes.

The long hallway is a scene right out of *Dante's Inferno*, with bloodied men, some missing arms or legs, crammed next to each other. The moaning and screaming is a constant din. The stench of rotting flesh makes me nauseous. There's not a doctor or nurse in sight.

"Is no one seeing to their injuries?" I ask a sneering guard.

"We tend our own first," he says. "Besides, it was the Americans started this damn war."

The men are laid out all over the long hallway. Not a bed in sight. As I make my way among them, a boy no more than 15 reaches out. "Mother? Is that you?"

His leg is but a bloody, jagged stump, partially covered in a filthy bandage. I shake my head and wonder what I could possibly do to ease his pain. Flies are everywhere. I half-expect to see vultures perched in the doorways.

I look from face to face for a glimpse of Tom's laughing eyes. Nothing.

At the end of the hall, I see an older man who looks familiar. As I get closer, he looks my way but there's no sign of recognition. A bloody rag covers his shoulder. His arm hangs limp.

"Sam Parsons?" I ask.

"Aye, who's asking?"

"Sarah Jordan. I board with the Porters."

"I remember you. You were there when we rounded up those Quakers. Pompous loyalists hiding behind their Bibles while men like me take the fire."

I swallow my outrage. "What happened to you?"

"Germantown." He winces and gasps for breath. "I was there at dawn with my unit. We surprised them—Howe's men—and pushed them back. Would have succeeded but for the fog. Couldn't see a bloody thing. Our men were shooting every which way. I got hit by one of our own. Then everything went dark and now, all I can make out are shadows. Don't know if I'll ever see proper again."

"I hope so," I offer. It's hard not to feel sorry for him. "Can I bring you anything?"

"Yes. You can bring a doctor. If you can find one. They've abandoned us here to die. I'm not ready to go." He sits up as if to prove he's still fit. "I got a family, and some unfinished business."

"Would that include solving Rip Ripley's murder?" I ask.

"Could be."

"His brother seems to think he was killed because he knew something," I say.

"What?" He starts to laugh but it devolves into a coughing fit and spitting up blood. "What could a coffee seller know? No, it was the brother that did him in. Wanted to get the coffeehouse after their old man dies."

I'm stunned but hold myself together. I leave as quickly as I can, working my way back through the maze of wounded. Finally outside, I take a deep breath and allow myself to ponder Parsons' accusation. Could Ethan have killed his brother over the coffeehouse? I don't believe it.

At the *Sentinel*, Amos is waiting for me. It doesn't look like he's written a word since I left.

"Are you going to meet with Howe?" I ask gently, hoping his mood has improved.

"No. He hasn't responded," he says glumly.

"He is fighting a war." My attempt at levity doesn't help.

"Maybe I'll try Superintendent Galloway." He looks forlorn in his crisp white shirt and royal blue waistcoat. His wig is dusted with lavender, a nicety for meeting with the high officials who have brushed him off.

With the British in control, devout loyalist Joseph Galloway is handling all matters related to the city. It's a humiliation for poor Amos, whose family can trace its Philadelphia roots to the 1680s.

"Have you written the article you were fired up about this morning?" I ask. "The city in chaos?"

"No. I was waiting for you. See what news you've found."

Just what I suspected. He's waiting for me to write the whole piece with a few tiny insertions by him.

"All right. Let's get started," I say, looking around for Tess.

I labor over the article for an hour, and then Amos labors over it for another hour before he deems it fit to run.

Finally, I track down Tess pretending to dust in the library.

"Are you hiding from me?" I ask.

"No, ma'am." Her eyes are focused on an imaginary bit of dust on a book cover. "What is it you're needing?"

"I need you to explain something to me, Tess."

Finally she glares straight at me.

"I know what you want to know."

"Is it true?"

"Yes." She puts down her dust cloth. "I suppose you're going to lecture me now on the proper decorum of ladies."

"Tess, I can hardly do that. Given my own woeful condition. I just want to understand why."

"It's simple, really. Amos bought me at auction, then he allowed me to secure my freedom by working here for three years."

"Meanwhile, servicing his every need, whenever he feels the urge?"

"It's not like that!"

"That's what it looks like." I know I sound shrill, so I try a softer approach. "Tess, you don't owe him anything. You're a free woman."

"Free! You think I'm free?" Her eyes are huge and filled with anger. "You try being me for a day and see how free you feel."

"I only meant—"

"I know what you meant. You couldn't possibly understand, so don't pretend you do. And don't pretend to be my friend. I don't want it. I certainly don't need it. Go away and leave me alone. And for once, try minding your own sorry business."

CHAPTER 15

Dearest Emma,

The news about Tom was a shock. I've been distraught since I heard. I can only imagine how devastated you and your family must be. My heart aches for Tom, his laugh, even his passion for this insane war.

I do have news of my own: It seems I am with child, Tom's child. I don't know what to do. I wish you were here to help me sort it out. Since the news, I've felt nothing for this thing residing inside me. I wish it would just go away. Am I awful to think that? Rachel has been most kind, though she's struggling since her husband was banished to Virginia.

She's looking for a tutor for her children—the war has made it too dangerous to go to school. I told her about you, and she was quite intrigued. Would you consider moving here? The pay is good, and you'd have a place to live. In case you're wondering, the city is filled with British officers, some of them quite charming and pleasing to look at. You'll never find someone in Essex unless you settle for a toothless old codger with garlic breath. Is that what you want?

Write soon!

Sarah

I omit what's at the top of my mind—my falling out with Tess—and finish the letter in time for supper. I take my usual place at the table beside Abigail. Molly is serving corn porridge and turnips again. If I were a better person, I'd be grateful.

Abigail says what we're all thinking. "No! I'm sick of porridge, and I hate turnips. Why can't we have chicken and potatoes and cornbread?"

"Abigail, dear," Rachel begins. "We are far more fortunate than the wounded soldiers crowding the city. Let us give thanks for what we have."

Rachel's self-righteousness is wearing thin. I'm sure she's as sick of turnips as the rest of us.

"And let us thank Molly for her ingenuity," she says. "She provides us with wonderful meals, and she's even hidden the chickens in the carriage house, beyond the reach of thieves."

A sharp knock shortens the accolade. I open the door to a tall, bewigged redcoat with a gleaming sword at his side.

"Good evening, Miss. I'm sorry to interrupt your supper. I wish to see Mrs. Porter. I'm Major John Hammond."

"May I tell her what it's about?"

"Lodging."

"I'll tell her, but I doubt she'll allow it. Being a Quaker, her religion forbids aid to either side in war."

By then Rachel has come forward. "Who's calling at this hour?"

"This is Major John Hammond, and he'd like to take up lodging here," I say, hanging back to watch Rachel put him in his place.

"Major, I'll tell you what I told the last two British officers seeking lodging. My husband is away. It would be unseemly for me to take in another man. Furthermore, my husband would not approve. So goodnight."

Smiling broadly, he puts his foot in the doorway. "Begging your pardon Mrs. Porter. I'm an older, respectable gentlemen. Not like some of the ruffians taking up residence with your neighbors."

"That may be, but—"

"Forgive me Mrs. Porter if you think I'm forward. There is good reason for you to take me in. The city is not safe for women and children. Thieves are lurking everywhere. I can provide some protection for you and your family."

The Major is polished, polite and friendly. I wonder if Rachel will be swayed.

"You make a convincing argument, Major," she says. "But I must say no."

The Major looks grief-stricken. "I see. I'll try again in a few days."

"I'll not change my mind," Rachel says, but he's already down the front steps.

I'm pleased Rachel didn't back down. With Charles gone, she almost seems comfortable in her new role. I wonder how he'd feel about his wife taking over his duties once he returns. I wager it wouldn't sit well.

Back at the table, Gertrude is launching a tirade about the redcoats.

"You know what happened to the Johnson family," she says. "The British came to the door with swords drawn demanding room and board. Their language was foul, and they shattered the front door when they were turned away."

"I doubt our Major Hammond will be back," Rachel says. "I made myself clear."

Gertrude prattles on. "And there's the widow Mrs. Gleason. They barged into her home and took it over, confining Mildred to one room. They wouldn't even let her use the front door, forcing her to come and go through the alley."

Rachel seems untroubled by it all. "There are plenty of vacant homes in the city since the patriot families left."

"None as nice as our house," Abigail says. "And they want the best for themselves."

I don't want to darken the mood, but a question is eating at me. "Rachel, how can you get around the quartering law? Can't the British simply take the house if they feel like it?"

"That's British law during wartime," Rachel calmly explains. "But I believe God's law carries more weight."

Three days later the Major is back. This time he talks his way into tea with Rachel in the parlor. Molly even presents him with a plate of ginger cookies—a precious treat when butter is so hard to come by.

He's a handsome man with a splash of gray in his hair when he's not wearing his wig. With his perpetual smile, and soft green eyes, how could Rachel not find him attractive? Especially compared to stoop-shouldered, sickly Charles.

"His manners are perfect, and he assures me he neither drinks nor smokes. Nor does he keep late hours," she tells me after he's left.

He's back the next evening, this time with a bundle of firewood.

"How thoughtful of you, Major," Rachel gushes as she grabs my arm. "You've met our Sarah, Sarah Jordan. She boards with us and we're all so pleased to have her here."

"How nice to make your acquaintance—formally, that is," he says, bowing slightly.

"Sarah, I've decided to let the Major quarter with us. He's convinced me he's a respectable gentleman. We could do much worse."

"Welcome," I nod to the Major. "I'm sure you'll find it to your liking."

I can't help but wonder if Charles, banished to confinement 200 miles away, will find it to his liking.

Later, as I head upstairs, I see Rachel penning a letter, no doubt to Charles. He'll receive it and the wool stockings Abigail just knitted, via the tight circle of Quaker friends who make occasional trips through dangerous territory to see the imprisoned men.

"I'm sure he'll be pleased about the Major," Rachel says. "With a man in the house, Charles needn't worry so much about our safety," she tells me.

I doubt that will ease his mind.

The Major wastes no time. The next day, Sunday, he arrives while the family is at the Friends Meetinghouse. Molly and I are in the kitchen eating a leisurely breakfast of pancakes that she had managed to squirrel away from the rest of the family.

"Good morning, ladies," the Major says, striding in as if he owned the place. He's trailed by two soldiers.

"You're *all* moving in?" I ask.

"Yes, we'll take the parlor and two bedrooms on the third floor," he says. "I'm sure Mrs. Porter will find it acceptable."

"I'm not so sure," I say. "Might you wait—"

"Can't. We're fighting a war, in case you aren't aware."

"I'm quite aware," I say, wondering what happened to the oh-so-polite gentleman who wooed Rachel.

"Then you won't mind showing my men to the livestock quarters," he says. "We'll also board three horses, a cow, and two sheep."

When Rachel returns with the children, the Major has settled in and already cajoled a grumpy Molly to prepare a meal for him and his men.

"They've eaten the last of the beans and rye bread I was saving for your dinner," Molly tells Rachel.

Rachel marches into the parlor to confront Major Hammond.

"Ah, Mrs. Porter." He stands and bows. "We've taken the liberty of settling into your beautiful home. My men and I want to thank you for your gracious hospitality. I assure you, you'll barely know we're here. And General Howe sends his personal thanks to you and your family for stepping up so generously during these trying times."

If Rachel intended to dress him down, it must have been a fleeting thought. And nothing I could say would make any difference.

"Please, let me know if you need anything else," she says, all the fight gone from her voice. "I trust you'll not stay up late. My children have school in the morning."

CHAPTER 16

Tess has avoided me for days, and that suits me fine. I feel no need to apologize. She should apologize to me for her rudeness. She was clearly out of order.

But after four days, I'm tired of playing cat and mouse. I miss our clandestine talks. Aside from Ethan, she's really my only friend here, and I sorely need someone to talk to about Tom and my…condition.

Amos is off at his parents' estate looking for a horse to replace Buttercup. If he finds one, he'll have to pay a king's ransom. The British are plundering whatever they can get their hands on—horses, cattle, grain, hay, wood, clothing.

He left me instructions to find out more about the redcoats' seizing the city's almshouse for barracks, forcing destitute men, women and children into the street.

As I walk over there, I yearn for my previous employer, the cantankerous Jonah Livingston. At Jonah's *New York Loyal Gazette,* my account of the wretched British prison ships was good enough for my own name to be attached to it, an uncommon honor for men and unheard of for a woman.

It's almost winter and I'm bundled up in my wool cape and scarf. How will we survive the coming months without more firewood? Many a poor soul in Philadelphia is having to burn their furniture just to stay warm. I hope we won't be among them.

Outside the almshouse, children are crying and someone is

passing out chunks of bread.

"We'll have some broth for you soon. Please be patient." It's Agatha Nelson, whose Quaker husband was banished along with the others. She marches over as soon as she sees me.

"If it's news you're looking for, write about this disgrace," she says. "British soldiers evicted some 200 of the city's neediest, throwing them out without the most basic protection from the cold."

"Where will they go?" I ask.

"Our Friends Meetinghouse opened its doors to as many as would fit, but we can't take them all," she says gesturing to the ragtag collection of families and homeless elders left shivering on the street.

"Perhaps the theater?" I offer, desperate to be of some help.

She shakes her head in disgust. "Howe's men have taken it over for their wounded." She takes a deep breath. "This war has no paragons of decency. The so-called patriots, the righteous British—they're all selfish and uncaring."

Her tirade is drowned out by a horse-drawn wagon that pulls up with Rachel and a handful of her Quaker comrades. They've brought a steaming vat of broth, and the motley crowd gathers around for the handout.

I marvel at Rachel, directing the distribution into cups and cracked bowls. The irony strikes me: The Quakers won't take up arms to fight, but they're at the ready to aid anyone the war has left in need. They play no favorites; Rachel and the others have brought food—what little they can scrape together—and bandages to the wounded on both sides.

When the soup line thins, Rachel strides over, her cheeks flush with excitement.

"Have you heard? Everyone's talking about it: A delegation of Quakers is on the way to see General Washington," she says breathlessly.

"Why? What can they possibly do?" I ask. "And are they sure they'll be let through enemy lines in the middle of a war?"

My skepticism doesn't dampen her enthusiasm.

"It's a dangerous mission, no doubt," she says. "The men feel they can convince Washington that the Spanktown Papers are false. And Washington certainly can stop this insanity." In a move so unlike

Rachel, she grabs my arms in unabashed excitement. "Our men could go free very soon. I can't wait to have Charles home again!"

Her excitement is infectious. "The people of Philadelphia need to read about this," I say, hopeful Amos will allow it in print.

He returns without a horse. It seems even Amos Tinkleton of the prestigious Tinkleton family lacks enough money and sway to secure the one thing he wants most: another lovely Buttercup. The armies have bought—more likely stolen—every horse in Pennsylvania and the surrounding colonies.

He's in no mood to give me free rein on my article. "Washington will never free the Quakers, no matter what evidence they have. He despises Quakers! They won't fight. Won't use the Continental money. Won't even give up a damn blanket."

And on the almshouse takeover, he's more heartless. "What did you expect? It's war. Soldiers are shot. They need hospitals, barracks."

I don't tell him about the young mother and baby I saw there, desperate for a hunk of stale bread. In a few months, I thought, that could be me.

I write what I can and shove the paper in front of him. "Here's my version. I suppose you'll tinker with it, add a word or two, then print it as yours."

He looks at me with cold eyes. And with his precise, slow diction he says: "Have you forgotten who owns this newspaper?"

"No."

"No sir!" he fires back. "Now go find Tess and tell her the library floor needs a good polish."

"Yes sir." I hate the man, and I'm glad his mare was stolen.

I find Tess hauling armloads of firewood from the shed into the storage room behind the press.

"Why are you doing that, Tess?"

"Mr. Tinkleton wants it inside so no one can steal it," she says dumping the wood next to a stack of paper and vats of linseed oil and pine rosin for printing.

"I'll help you," I offer.

"No need."

"Tess, I want to." I pick up a few splintery logs, haul them inside and go back for more. Minutes go by without a word between us. Finally, I break the awkward silence.

"I'm sorry. I had no business passing judgment on you the way I did. In fact, what you do and with whom is none of my business."

That's not exactly how I feel, but I'm tired of the wall between us. Also, I've learned that apologizing is not the bitter pill it used to be. Maybe it's just another part of growing up.

But Tess isn't quick to let bygones be bygones. She says nothing for an interminable stretch.

"And you're right, I couldn't possibly understand your situation. I'm not you."

Actually, I'll never understand letting a man have his way with me against my wishes. I imagine Amos forcing Tess to his bed whenever he feels like it. What choice does she have?

Finally, Tess drops a load of wood with a clatter. "I accept your apology. I've missed our talks."

Relief floods me, but she's not done.

"I may have been too hasty with my words, and I'm not surprised you didn't understand. Amos is not the heartless master you picture. He doesn't drag me by the hair to his bedchamber like my last owner did. Have you stopped to think that I might have needs too? Or are you the only one who's ever experienced pleasure with a man?"

Her last words sting, and I can't stop the flood of tears.

"What's wrong?" Tess asks.

"It's Tom," I cry. "He's dead."

"What? Why didn't you tell me?" Tess grasps my hand. "How—"

"I received a letter from Tom's sister, my good friend Emma."

Tess guides me to a dark little nook. "He died in battle, a dreadful battle that took many lives," I say between choking sobs.

"I am so sorry, Sarah. I know only too well how painful that is. Does Amos know?"

"Not yet."

"You need time to mourn."

"I don't see how. I've gotten myself into a terrible fix by pretending to be Mrs. Tom Jordan. And now this baby…" More sobs. It feels good to let it all out in one big, awful flood of misery.

"What will you do?" Tess asks. "I'll help you any way I can."

I reveal what I've been thinking since receiving the news about Tom. It seems the only course—unless I want to raise a bastard child.

"I'm ready to take the trade," I say in a small, shaky voice. "Will you help me?"

CHAPTER 17

Tess doesn't answer immediately, and I begin to worry. Not only do I need her moral support, but she knows the formula for the tea that will bring on a bleed.

"Will you help me?" I ask again, a little louder. "You've been through this."

"Yes, and I told you I regretted it," she finally says. "Are you certain this is what you want?"

"Yes! The sooner the better," I say without hesitation.

"But this is Tom's baby," Tess says, "and you loved Tom."

"I don't love this baby. This thing in me makes me tired and sick and now my clothes feel tight. It's a constant reminder of what I've lost."

I look for signs on Tess's face that she thinks me despicable. I must be. No decent woman would feel this way. But I see no shock or outrage.

"I know the law, Tess, and I can do this in good conscience," I say. "I can take the trade legally for the first few months until—"

She cuts off my lecture.

"Until you feel the baby move—the quickening. I know the law too! I may be a poor charwoman but I'm not ignorant."

"I never said that, and I don't think it either." In fact, the extent of her knowledge stuns me constantly.

"Have you felt the baby kick, Sarah? Be honest, because if you have felt that flicker, no matter how slight, what we're about to do is illegal and we could both go to jail."

I smile with relief. "No, I haven't felt a thing, and that I'm sure of."

"Then I'll help you," Tess says. "I'll prepare the tea, and you can take it here in my quarters."

"You'll need the recipe, the one you used before," I say.

"I remember it word for word. I'll go to the apothecary for the necessary herbs. We'll do it tomorrow night."

"Yes, tomorrow night," I say, handing her some coins. I feel both light and heavy, liberated and depressed.

At home Rachel is all abuzz about the prospect that Charles could come home soon. At supper she chatters about all the things they'll do when he's free.

"We'll roast a turkey with potatoes and turnips and apple pie," she gushes. "Poor dear is probably thin as a rail."

I'm not worried about Charles's girth. He's likely eating better than all of Philadelphia, where melted butter might as well be liquid gold.

"Best not to get your hopes up, Rachel," Gertrude says. "It's not even certain that Washington will meet with our delegation. And even if he did and he was moved to let our men go, there's no guarantee the Continental Congress will agree."

I pick at my food. Molly has managed a chicken soup from scant leftovers. The children argue over the last piece of cornbread. I can't wait for supper to end so I can retreat to my room and think about my decision.

I'm just about to excuse myself when the front door bursts open and in stride Major Hammond and three of his men.

"Good evening Mrs. Porter," he says removing his hat. "I hope we're not interrupting your supper. I see the hour is late," he adds, glancing at his pocket watch.

"Not at all," Rachel says rising from the table. "We're finished. Have you had your supper, Major?"

"No ma'am."

"I'm sure Molly can find something that will satisfy you," she says, gesturing to Molly, who looks dumbstruck.

"But Mrs. Porter—"

"Do the best you can for our guests, Molly," she says with a stern look. Molly whirls around and storms into the kitchen.

"Major, you met our boarder Mrs. Jordan."

"Yes, I had the pleasure."

I remember it well, and there was nothing pleasurable about it.

Both Rachel and I excuse ourselves and head up to our bedrooms but not before she hands me a letter that arrived earlier. It's from Emma!

In my room I tear it open.

Dear Sarah,

The news that you're having a baby lifted my spirits so. It's like a piece of my brother living within you, and that brings me such joy. That must bring you some comfort, though raising a child alone is a frightful prospect. I couldn't do it, but I'm certain you can. I know only too well what happens when you set your mind to something. And I feel certain that eventually you'll come to love this child.

I only wish that Tom were alive to hear the news. He'd be over the moon. I think he'd be tickled you've taken his name without benefit of a proper wedding.

I'm not a little bit jealous that you'll be a mother before me. You never wanted this, and it's all I've ever wanted.

You're right about the lack of eligible men in Essex. It's dismal here. So I'm taking you up on your urging that I move to Philadelphia. (Not just to find a husband, though it will improve my prospects.) I can help with the baby, and if Mrs. Porter is still looking for a tutor for her children, I would gladly accept the job. I can make haste to get there.

I hope this news makes you happy. It certainly won't please Mother and Father, but I can't tolerate another week under their roof. I'd sooner marry the toothless butcher who reeks of garlic, the one Father favors.

Affectionately,
Emma

PS: Ezekiel dragged a dead squirrel into the house and left it on Mother's new sofa. He's been banished to the barn.

The letter falls to the floor as I slump on the bed. I hear laughter from Major Hammond and his men in the dining room. They're probably on their second bottle of wine after consuming every scrap from the kitchen. Rachel will be livid but will say nothing.

I would gladly change places with any of them. I thought my way was clear when I came home: Drink the tea and let it do its work. The herbs would bring on a bleed, and all my problems would end.

Emma's letter has given me pause. As I lie on my bed, I imagine Tom there with me, his touch, my touch. His laugh. His dark, wavy hair. I ache to hear his voice, teasing me about my wild, red curls. He liked me just as I am. I can't stop the tears. I miss him so. Maybe this baby would have pleased him, luring him from the battlefield he loves so much. Now I'll never know.

On my way to the *Sentinel* in the morning, I stop at Lloyd's to fortify myself before seeing Tess.

"Morning Sarah," Ethan greets me. "The usual?"

"Strong as you can make it."

"Mourning your husband can't be easy," he says softly. He lowers his eyes, and a blond lock falls across his face. "If I can do anything—"

"No, you can't," I say a little too curtly. "I'm sorry, Ethan. I'm a little jumpy."

"No apology needed."

I look into what may be the kindest eyes I've ever seen.

"Any news from the Quaker contingent trying to meet with Washington?" I ask.

"Only that the general treated them to a grand midday meal, listened to their case, then chastised them for not using Continental money."

"It doesn't sound promising. Poor Rachel Porter will be disheartened."

Ethan leans in closer, inches from my face. "Have you any news about Rip's murder?"

"Not really," I say slowly, avoiding his eyes.

"If you've heard something, tell me, please Sarah," he pleads.

I ought to keep my mouth shut, but I've never been good at that. Especially when I'm curious myself.

"Well, I saw Samuel Parsons. He was shot during the fighting and is holed up in the Statehouse with other wounded patriots."

Ethan's face tightens immediately. The kindness is gone. "What did he say?"

"He still thinks you had something to do with the murder. He said you had a motive."

I watch his face for any reaction. He looks at me puzzled.

"What motive? Rip was my brother, for God's sake."

His hands are starting to tremble, and I wish I hadn't said anything.

"Tell me!"

"He said your father had changed his will recently and left the coffeehouse to Rip."

Ethan lets out a deep breath and smiles. "He did just that."

"And?"

"He was going to leave it to both of us, but I told him Rip is better suited to it. I have other plans."

"Plans?"

"Yes, though you might think me foolish." A shy smile creeps over his face, making him look boyish and handsome at the same time. "I want to learn shipbuilding."

"That's not foolish at all," I say.

At the *Sentinel*, Amos is steamed up about the British surrender at the Battle of Saratoga in New York—or at least he's acting the part. I can't tell any more what he really thinks.

"It was a terrible loss, a humiliating surrender," he tells me. "I must tell readers just that, but I know Howe and Cornwallis and the others won't like it. I hope they won't withdraw their printing jobs."

Out of the corner of my eye I see Tess straightening a pile of papers. She nods toward the privy, and I slip away from the men. My hands are sweaty, and my stomach is giving me fits.

"I have the herbs," she says. "Are you still determined to go through with this?"

"Yes...I think so."

"I'm sensing some hesitation." Tess does not mince words. "Sarah, you don't have to—"

"Yes, I do. I don't have a choice." I turn to go so she won't see my tears.

"Then, come to my quarters after work," she calls out.

CHAPTER 18

THE DAY DRAGS ON as I help Amos write an account of the British surrender at Saratoga that makes it sound like the patriots barely eked out a victory. Of course, most other accounts describe it as a colossal win for the Americans and an embarrassment for the Brits. As usual, he leaves it to me to turn his muddled wording into intelligent prose.

"You have a way with words, Mrs. Jordan," he tells me in a rare moment of praise. "You're a great asset to me."

I seize the opportunity to make my case. "Mr. Tinkleton, would you consider letting me write under my own name?" I hold my breath and wait.

"What? Are you saying you want your name right up there in the masthead next to mine? How would that look: 'Publisher, Amos Tinkleton…Hired Help, Mrs. Jordan'?"

Clearly he's amused but I persist.

"I just want to be known for my writing. Everyone assumes you write every word in every edition. I'm just asking for a bit of recognition."

He takes an eternity to light his pipe. "A woman writer? My newspaper would lose all credibility. I'd be a laughingstock."

I can't disguise my disappointment. "But in New York, Jonah Livingston wasn't afraid to let readers know what I'd written."

"And look what happened to him—beaten, jailed, his newspaper in ruins."

"That wasn't my doing," I say, though clearly it was. "The British couldn't stand any criticism."

"Exactly! I'll not risk it. Grow up, Sarah. You're lucky to be here."

I can tell Amos won't entertain any further discussion on the issue. He's back to straightening his quill pens and ink bottles so that they line up perfectly—a clear signal for me to leave his office. His words are a bitter pill, and I know he won't change no matter what I do or say.

I take out Emma's letter again. Precious Emma! She perceived the very essence of Tom. He loved me just the way I am. He believed in a cause, no matter how futile it sometimes seemed. And I have a piece of wonderful Tom inside me. The hell with Amos. The damn article about Saratoga will be forgotten in a week.

At the end of the day, I head down to Tess's quarters.

"I'm here," I announce. Tess is ready. She has a heated kettle, her one beautiful china cup, and a small pouch of that fateful tea.

"But I've changed my mind," I say.

"What? What brought this on?"

"Something I read in a letter from Tom's sister, Emma. It brought up all my feelings for Tom and how much I miss him. I still harbor a tiny sliver of hope that he's alive, against all odds."

"I think that's a fine reason," Tess says.

"Also, Emma likes to point out that I'm stubborn as a mule. The more hopeless the challenge, the more I dig in. They can't jail me for having a bastard child, right?"

"They'd be fools," she says drolly. "The water is still hot. Would you like some raspberry mint tea?"

The mention of tea takes me aback. Tess laughs, a hearty belly laugh that ends with a snort. "It's harmless tea. I took it from Amos's private stash."

"Yes, thank you." As she pours it, a wonderful aroma fills the dank room.

"This is a much happier time than when I took the trade," she says handing me the cup and sitting on the bed.

"Did someone help you?" I ask.

"No one even knew."

"Not even Amos?"

"How did you know it was Amos's baby?" she asks, eyes wide.

"I didn't. I guessed." I take a sip, hoping Tess will open up.

"No, I didn't tell Amos. What good would that do? Did you think he would jump at the chance to marry a charwoman, a former slave, and raise a mulatto child? I knew that fairy tale would never happen. So, I thought, why trouble him? He's an important man, and this was one complication he didn't need."

A baby is a bit more than a complication, I muse over my tea. "So he doesn't know, to this day?"

"That's right. And I aim to keep it that way." She gives me a hard look.

"Your secret is safe with me. As I hope mine is with you."

"Of course." She smiles again, and I'm struck by her beauty. I want to know more about this intriguing woman, but I don't want to offend.

"Do you and Amos talk about books?" I ask politely.

"Certainly not! He still doesn't know I can read."

I'm astonished.

"I know my place," she explains when she catches the look on my face. "That won't change."

"How can you hide something like that?" This little woman with the colorful kerchief wrapped around her head flabbergasts me at every turn. Another smile.

"We don't talk much."

I finish the tea and realize it's well after dark.

"I should go home before Mrs. Porter starts to worry. She might send out the British cavalry, as long as they're bunking with us anyway."

Upstairs, I see Amos still at his desk, working by candlelight.

"What keeps you here so late, sir?"

"The books. War is not as profitable as I'd hoped," he says.

I edge toward the door.

"You're here unusually late yourself. Is everything all right?" His face shows something I'd interpret as concern if I didn't know better.

"Everything is fine," I say and slip out the door.

As I walk past Lloyd's, Ethan is just locking up.

"Mrs. Jordan, how nice to see you. It's late. Should you be out alone?"

"I'm not afraid. I can take care of myself."

"No doubt. But there are ruffians and thieves and scofflaws afoot who are only too happy to relieve you of your valuables."

"They would be wise not to tangle with me," I laugh, my first good hearty laugh in many days.

"You seem in good spirits," he says.

"Can you keep a secret?"

"Of course."

"I'm going to have a baby." There, I said it, and it feels right to confide in Ethan.

He gropes for the right words. "Congratulations! Oh, but you're in mourning. I just don't know—"

"It's all right, Ethan. I have mixed feelings."

"Well, I insist on walking you home," he says, taking my arm.

I don't resist. Really, it feels like the most natural thing in the world as we stroll arm in arm past the lamplighters making their rounds. A cold drizzle starts to fall, and I fasten the hood of my cloak.

"Why must it be a secret?" he asks. "You aren't the first wife who's had to give birth after her husband's death on the battlefield."

I know I should be completely honest and tell him the whole sorry truth. But it feels so good to bask in the warmth of this caring soul. The truth would ruin the moment and everything thereafter.

"I must keep working at the *Sentinel* if I am to pay for my room and board. But Amos would sooner cut off his big toe than employ a pregnant woman for all to see."

Ethan is silent, and who could blame him for not knowing just the right thing to say?

"I'll need to conceal it as long as I'm able. Maybe another two months."

"And then?" he asks.

The boom of cannon fire interrupts our conversation. I was grateful for it, as I had no ready answer to Ethan's logical question. Fortunately, the distant thundering distracted him.

"Mud Island on the Delaware, most likely," he says. "They've been fighting over it for weeks."

I wonder whether Ethan is troubled by the din of battle. Instead, he seems animated.

"Of course you know about our blockade on the river?"

"I know it's impossible to get butter, meat, and flour," I say.

"The patriots were clever," he says. "They built these underwater contrivances with spears that pierce the hull of ships that try to pass. They're hidden all through the river. This genius named Robert Smith designed and built them."

I glance at Ethan's red cheeks and see a faint grin.

"How do you know all this?" I ask.

"I learned about it when I was fighting in New York with Sullivan's troops. They tried it on the Hudson River. It worked until the damn British discovered our secret course through the obstacles."

"General John Sullivan?" I ask.

"Yes, I was with him when we tried to take Staten Island from the British. That's where I was wounded."

"General Sullivan, wasn't he—"

"It's not something I talk about much," he says with finality.

At the Porters, I say goodnight. "Thank you for shepherding me home. Who knows what horrible fate I've escaped?"

He tips his cap. "Happy to oblige. I'll see you tomorrow, I hope."

As I bound up the steps, all I can think of is Ethan's quick mention of the patriots' General Sullivan. He's the one who turned the Spanktown Papers over to the Continental Congress. He's the reason Charles Porter and the other prominent Quakers were banished to Virginia.

I wonder why Ethan clammed up after dropping his name.

CHAPTER 19

As expected, Rachel is pleased that Emma is arriving to tutor the children. Emma will be equally pleased to learn about Major Hammond and his men, who seem to have taken over the house. They settle into the parlor nearly every night with boisterous talk and whiskey and cards. Rachel is not pleased but doesn't complain. They expect hearty suppers from Molly, who is less tactful.

Molly told me she'd quit if she could find other employment. Whenever it seems Rachel is about to put her foot down, the Major manages to sweet talk her into even more household privileges. She even joins him for tea in the late afternoon in the parlor, just the two of them. Gertrude thinks it's indecent, but it's hard for me to get worked up. I doubt Rachel has ever had an indecent thought.

Every day she inquires about my health, offering tips about childbirth, whether I want them or not. The whole idea terrifies me. It brings back memories of Mother dragging me to the birthing bed of some poor mother-to-be, where I fainted or puked at the sight of what she always called the "blessed event." How something that large can emerge from such a small crevice, I'll never understand.

"It's one of God's miracles," Rachel told me recently, for the hundredth time.

I don't think God has any idea what an ordeal this is, or he would have made it easier. He certainly wouldn't put up with the morning sickness, exhaustion and breasts so swollen they feel close to exploding.

Even the spinster Gertrude feels compelled to weigh in on the matter.

"It gets easier with every baby," she confided to me in her know-it-all manner. How Gertrude would know this confounds me. And why anyone would endure this more than once is just madness.

I still have little feeling for this thing growing inside me, this constant reminder. When I confessed this to Tess, all she said was, "Give it time."

I wish I could tell Mother everything. Once again I take out my pen and ink tonight to spill my soul out to her in a letter. But instead, I tell her all about Major Hammond and his cohorts. I can picture her smoothly excusing his brutish behavior—the British, of course, can do no wrong.

Before I finish, Abigail knocks on my door. "Supper is ready. Are you coming down?"

"Yes, I'll be right there." I'm not the least bit hungry, but it would be rude not to make an appearance.

Major Hammond is sitting at the head of the table when I arrive.

"Good evening, Mrs. Jordan," he says as I take my usual seat next to Abigail.

"Please call me Sarah," I say. Anyone present would have thought that I was merely putting him at ease, but in fact, the formal title—Mrs. Jordan—is a chafing reminder that I'm an imposter.

"Mrs. Porter has told me that you work for Amos Tinkleton at the *Sentinel*," he says. "A fine publication that takes great pains to report the news accurately."

I nod, suppressing the urge to set him straight about Amos's decidedly biased reporting.

Molly arrives at the table with a kettle of watery potato soup and a tiny loaf of bread sliced thin. "I'm afraid we're out of flour," she says, eyeing the Major with loathing. "I used the last of it for this paltry loaf."

The children groan. Gertrude hushes them with a sharp look.

"We'll make do," Rachel says with a pleasant nod toward the Major.

"As soon as we can get our ships through the Americans'

blockade, supplies will be plentiful." He gives her a dazzling smile. It's sickening.

I dabble at the soup and decline the bread, leaving more for the Major to mop up from his bowl.

It's a somber meal until Rachel announces she's received another letter from Charles. The children raise a cheery ruckus but she quiets them immediately.

"He doesn't say much that's hopeful," she says. "Our lawyers' visit to General Washington accomplished nothing. There's no sign our dear men will be freed any time soon."

"But the law is on Father's side," an indignant Abigail says.

"Clearly, young lady," the Major says. "But Washington despises your people. He's made that very clear."

"I'm afraid there's even more bad news," Rachel says. "Your father is ill, afflicted with fevers that give him a fierce headache. And stomach pains keep him abed."

Worry lines etch Rachel's forehead. She talks about herbs and potions that might help but knows that even the heartiest traveler will soon find the roads to Virginia made impassable by snow.

The Major is clearly tired of the talk.

"Mrs. Porter, I'm sure your husband is strong enough to weather a headache."

He chuckles, and Rachel smiles uneasily.

I can't let it rest. "Charles and the others have not had an easy time of it, Major Hammond. They're certainly not as comfortable as you and all the other British quartered in our city's finest homes."

An awkward silence settles on the room—I have a way of doing that—until Rachel asks the Major if he'd enjoy more soup.

"No, thank you. My compliments to the cook. Now if you'll excuse me."

"I, as well," I say. "I must finish a letter to Mother. She wrote that she delivered twins to a mother with six children."

"Praise God!" Rachel exclaims.

I would sooner praise my mother's bedside skills.

As I'm about to climb the stairs, Major Hammond stops me.

"Sarah, I feel we got off on the wrong foot, you and I," he says softly. "For that, I apologize and hope we can be friends."

He seems sincere, and I can see how Rachel has fallen under his spell.

"Of course, Major," I say.

"I have great respect for Amos Tinkleton and his writing. He certainly has a way with words. I suspect you may have something to do with that." Though his hair is graying at the temple, his shy smile makes him seem younger.

"Yes, I do assist him," I say. If only he knew how much.

He moves in closer. "In fact, I have a bit of news you might want to pass on to Amos."

I move in like a cat eyeing a clueless bird. "I'd be delighted to pass it on."

"I have learned the authorities arrested someone in the murder of that barkeep—Ripley is his name, I believe," he says. "Mrs. Porter told me that you knew him."

"Yes, I often stop for coffee at Lloyd's," I say, anxious to know who did it.

"I met with Joseph Galloway, the new superintendent of police," the Major says. "He told me the killer was Ripley's brother."

I grip the banister tightly. "No, he couldn't possibly—"

"Well, it seems the brother can't explain his whereabouts that night. In fact, he was so agitated by the questions, he clammed up and won't talk to anyone. Seems a sure sign of guilt."

"Where are they holding him?"

"Walnut Street Jail. He can wither away with the rest of the damned Americans crammed in there."

I ignore his harsh words. "I'll certainly let Mr. Tinkleton know about this. Thank you, Major."

"Glad to oblige," he says. "Goodnight, Sarah."

In the morning it's sleeting. Rachel pressed me to stay home by the fire, but I worried all night about Ethan and I'm anxious to find out more. Can this kind, understanding man be a monster who would kill his own brother for control of a coffeehouse?

I declined Rachel's heavy coat, trudging out instead in my wool cloak. Now I wish I'd listened to her. I feel sorry for her, having to manage the house, the children, and the Major and his entourage of perpetually hungry men.

In the kitchen this morning, Molly filled me in on Rachel's latest burden.

"I heard Mrs. Porter and Gertrude arguing," she told me as I gulped down some soupy porridge and the last of the bread. "Seems Mr. Porter wrote that Mrs. Porter never should have allowed the Major to quarter here. Says it's unseemly and sets a bad example for the children."

"So it wasn't quite a love letter," I said.

"No! And when Miss Gertrude said Mr. Porter was dead right—well, Mrs. Porter said they should both mind their own business, that the Major provides protection from thieves and drunkards, and the fact that he's pleasant company is all the better."

I'm so proud of Rachel I could hug her, though it would fluster her beyond words.

My shoes are soaked, and my cloak is soggy when I finally walk into the *Sentinel*. As I peel off the cloak, Joshua is stoking the fire.

He warns me that Amos is in a fouler-than-usual mood. Seems he found a new horse—but someone stole that one too.

"Nobody's safe these days," he says.

As he clatters down the stairs, Amos agrees.

"Nobody's safe gossiping when they should be working," he practically shouts. "You—young lady—I have an assignment for you."

I hope my news puts him in a better mood. "It may interest you to know that your friend Galloway has arrested someone for Rip Ripley's murder."

"Do tell."

"Rip's brother, Ethan. But I'm certain they've made a mistake, and the real killer is still out there."

"That's hardly news."

He yawns, cracks his knuckles, and proclaims that Ethan has no alibi.

"It's him. He killed his brother to get the family property.

It's obvious."

"I'm sure that's not so," I insist.

"We'll do a brief news item on the arrest," Amos says, lighting his long-stem silver pipe. "Make it part of a larger article on the lawlessness throughout the city. Maybe it will spur Galloway and his minions to find the thieves who stole my new horse."

"We should at least get Ethan's side," I say. "I'm sure once everything is in the open, the charge will be dropped. I can try to talk with him at the jail."

Amos is balling up his fists on his desk.

"No! I need you to do something more important," he says.

"Whatever could be more important than a man's life?" I say, perhaps somewhat theatrically.

He takes a puff from his pipe. "I don't find your sass amusing."

"Sorry."

"If you can find the time," he says through clenched jaws, "I need an item about the shortage of hairdressers for the ladies. Mrs. Galloway tells me she's had a devil of a time finding someone to arrange her coiffure in the current style."

I can't contain my dismay. "You mean those towering hairdos with feathers, ribbons and jewelry? The ones that go up two feet or more as some poor rich lady beneath is trying to balance this massive construction on her head. Is that what you want me to write about?"

"Mrs. Galloway says she's tried it herself without success," he says. "For someone of her station, it's a hardship."

"Does she know there's a war going on," I practically scream. "People don't have enough to eat. And you want me to write about this coiffure calamity, this hair hardship?"

"Yes, I do," he says, showing a flash of temper. "I hired you as a favor to Jonah Livingston. He warned me you could be…difficult. He didn't tell me you would wear my patience down to a nub."

I'm so incensed that I hunt down Tess to complain some more. "The man is impossible," I sputter. "What can I do?"

"Just do it," Tess says with an air of exasperation. "If that's the worst thing you're ever forced to do, count yourself among the fortunate."

Chastened, I go back to my desk and write about hair.

At the end of the day, I glance at Amos's item on Ethan's arrest. As I expected, it convicts the poor man without a trial. But if Tess's example has taught me anything, it's the power of quiet persistence.

I have a plan that might just give Ethan a fighting chance.

CHAPTER 20

If Amos knew what I was about to undertake, he'd brand me insane. Maybe I am, but I must try.

As night approaches, a freezing rain lashes my face, and my shoes are still soaked from this morning. Nonetheless, I head for the Walnut Street Jail instead going straight home.

On the way, no one is about. Apparently, even thieves take time off on nights like this and these days, that's rare. Yesterday our neighbor Mrs. Fisher saw a man snatch the underthings that were drying on her line.

The solitude gives me time to think. Soon my clothes will be too tight to hide the growing lump in my belly. I don't know how much longer I can keep my condition secret. For the first time today, I found myself rubbing my stomach, but mercifully Amos didn't notice. It wasn't intentional, and it felt completely natural. Tess said I'd soon feel the baby move—the quickening—and surely warm to it by then. Weeks ago, I would have scoffed. Now, I'm not scoffing.

Emma will help me make sense of it all. It will feel good to be around jolly Emma and laugh like we used to. She'll have something irreverent to say about Rachel's plain clothes and pious speech. Fancied up in one of her brightly colored gowns, she'll be flirting with Major Hammond in no time.

The jail is behind the Statehouse in a three-story brick building built only two years ago. It's an overcrowded rat's nest crammed with crooks, vagrants, and now a slew of prisoners from the war.

When I finally arrive, a cluster of women are loading scraps of food into a basket the prisoners lower from a second-story broken window.

"The British don't feed them enough to keep a bird alive," one of the women tells me. "They'd be eating vermin if we didn't offer what we could."

She tells me that her husband, Jeremy Wright, was arrested last week for stealing biscuits from a bakery on Chestnut Street. "He did what he had to," she says.

I allowed that hogs are treated better than that and she agreed. Privately, I vow to expose the horrific conditions if I can talk my way into the forbidding structure.

As I head for the entrance, Mrs. Wright calls out. "They'll not let you in."

"We'll see," I answer, more determined than ever. After I knock on the door for a full minute, a guard opens it a crack. "Yes? What do you want?"

"I'm here to see a prisoner, Ethan Ripley."

"Ah, the murderer," he says studying me up and down. "No one's allowed in, Miss."

"I am," I assert. "I'm from his attorney's office. I have a message for Mr. Ripley."

"Give it here," he says. "If you're nice to me, I'll see that he gets it."

I expected this, and I'm prepared. "It's a verbal message, so I'll need to see the client personally."

He gives me a long, annoyed look, and I'm beginning to think my ruse has failed. Finally, he shrugs, "Suit yourself. I'll bring him down, but you'll have to be swift."

I wait and wait and listen to the never-ending racket from hundreds of prisoners. Finally, I see Ethan being led down the hall with his hands tied behind his back, his legs shackled. His shirt is ripped.

He's stunned to see me. "Sarah!"

"Give him your message and be quick about it," the guard says.

"Ethan, we're fighting for your freedom and won't stop until you're exonerated." I hope I sound lawyerly.

"Sarah, I'm ashamed for you to see me like this. You shouldn't be—"

"We haven't much time. We need to know where you were that night so we can get this straightened out," I say.

Ethan looks uncomfortable and doesn't answer right away. "I can't say."

"Ethan, I can help you, but you have to help me."

He shakes his head no. I see the pain in his eyes as they fill with tears.

"All right Miss, you've had your time. Let's go, Ripley," he says pushing him toward the hall.

"Sarah, know that I didn't do this. I swear to God I'm innocent," he shouts out to me.

It's not what I was expecting.

When I leave, the women outside are gone. But a few prisoners are at the broken window.

"Have you a little bread?" one calls down. "A warm scarf? Stockings? How about a little kiss?"

I berate myself for not bringing something, anything. I remember how desperate Tom and the other men were on the prison ship in New York. An apple core was a treasure.

The rain turns back to sleet as I walk toward the Delaware River and home. Streetlamps are scarce, and I wish I were dry and warm, tucking into supper with the Porters. Rachel will worry if I'm not there soon.

I'm blocks from home when I hear voices behind me. When I turn to look, the voices get louder. A couple of redcoats, likely fresh from a tavern.

"What's a young lady doing out by herself?" the tall one with a pock-scarred face calls out, slurring his words.

"Maybe you'd like us to accompany you," the other adds.

"No, thank you," I say, picking up my pace.

"That's not very friendly," the younger, red-bearded one says.

"I'm not in a friendly mood," I say, irritated and a little anxious.

The pair also pick up the pace. "I wager she's one of those fancy ladies of pleasure," Pockface says.

"I assure you I'm not. Now leave me be."

"A saucy one," Redbeard says. "I like that."

Pockface agrees, "I say we all get to know each other better," he says. "Give us a kiss."

They're catching up to me, and now I'm truly frightened. I start to run but my soggy shoes make it difficult and I'm gasping for breath. I can hear them grunting to keep up.

"Dammit, you whore! Stop! Stop by order of the King!"

I'm running as fast as I can toward the river, hoping I'll see someone, a dockworker, anyone. But no one is out on this frigid, wind-blasted night. The sleet hits my face like a knife. The river is in turmoil, the waves slamming into the docks. The clanging of masts and rigging is deafening. Suddenly, I trip on a branch blown down by the wind and crash to the ground.

"We've got you now!" Redbeard yells as he pounces on me.

The full weight of his body takes my breath away. But I fight with my hands, trying to gouge his eyes. His breath stinks of ale, and his body isn't any better. With strength I didn't know I had, I try to rip his ugly beard from his flesh. I scream but he stuffs his gloved hand in my mouth, muffling any sound.

"I'll get her hands," Pockface yells as he slams his knees onto my arms. "Feisty one, this whore."

"Best not to fight it," Redbeard says. "You might even like it."

I kick harder but it does no good. I manage to free one hand and with all my strength I double my fist and smash his nose. It might be the first time I ever hit anyone, aside from playing around with my brother when we were kids. I hear a loud, satisfying crack.

"Damn you, bitch," he moans. "You broke it." He slams my cheek, then throws a series of hard, mean jabs right into my belly.

"Please, no, not there!" Then again and again, punch after punch. Finally, Redbeard and Pockface decide they've had enough.

"Not worth droppin' my breeches," Redbeard grunts.

With blood pouring out of my mouth, I manage to let loose one final scream. In the freezing wind and driving rain, it seems I've managed to ruin their fun.

"Leave her, man. We better get out of here."

I feel a terrible pain. Everything goes dark. My head is spinning. I try to scream again, but nothing comes out. I hear only muffled sounds.

"Help me dump her on the rocks…tide will wash her out, if she don't freeze first…no one will know."

Then the effort to hold onto consciousness becomes too great and I give in.

CHAPTER 21

"Oh my God! Get help! Is she alive?"

Voices from somewhere. Can't make sense of it. Where am I? Am I dreaming?

"Is it her? The one missing from the Porter house?"

"Never mind. Get blankets and a wagon, quickly!"

"Mother?" I hear what sounds like my voice. Each breath is a jab to my chest, a razor slitting my heart. I try to open my eyes and can't.

"Don't try to talk, Miss. We'll help you."

"No! Get away!" I scream. I writhe and try to kick, but the pain in my belly is too great.

A man is saying something.

"So much blood. What beast would do this? I hope they hang him."

I manage to open an eye but can't focus. They lift me onto a wagon, and every jolt sends searing pain through my body. I'm so thirsty. Is that sand in my mouth?

"Found her on the rocks between the wharves."

"Miracle she didn't get washed away."

Now the wagon is rolling. Shivering. Someone covers me with a thick wool blanket.

"I think she's coming around."

"Where am I?" I croak as the wagon creaks along.

"We're taking you home. To the Porters' house. They're worried sick about you. Everyone in the neighborhood has been poking through sheds and calling your name for hours."

Finally, the wagon stops. I hear more voices.

"Bring her inside and be careful. Let's get her out of those wet clothes. Gather all the blankets. Fill the bed warmer with coals."

A familiar voice. Rachel? Then children's voices.

One of the men lifts me over his shoulder and gently carries me like a baby up the front steps. Then blackness again.

"So thirsty." I can barely get the words out.

"Put the cup to her lips." I hear an unfamiliar voice, soft and sure.

Warm water trickles down my raw throat. I open an eye and see Rachel's worried face give way to relief.

"You're safe now," she says, removing the cup. "You gave us quite a scare."

Somehow I'm in my bed, nestled in piles of pillows and blankets. I'm confused and anxious.

"What happened?" I rasp.

"Let her sleep. She needs to rest." The voice comes from a stocky woman I've never seen before.

"No. I want to know."

Rachel moves closer and takes my hand. "Someone attacked you last night. Happened near the river as you were walking home. Alone."

My mind struggles to clear, but I pick up the disapproval in her voice.

"Whoever it was beat you badly about the face and broke some ribs. That's why it hurts to breathe. You have a gash on your scalp that the doctor stitched up. And your left eye should open just fine when the swelling does down, God willing."

"Is that all? The baby?"

"That's all you need to deal with now," Rachel says. "It's best that you sleep."

Suddenly, a cramp grips my belly, and I cry out.

"There's more, isn't there?" I cry out. "Tell me."

The other woman nods.

"All right," Rachel says. "This is Mrs. Pollock. She's a midwife."

Her grim face tells me everything, and a heavy sadness overtakes me.

"I'm afraid you've lost the baby, my dear," Mrs. Pollock says. "I'm so sorry."

I barely hear the rest.

"The worst is over, but you'll bleed some for a few days. I'll be here to help you."

My one good eye tears up, and a sob rises in my chest, but it hurts so much I can't let it go.

"Sarah, I lost a baby once," Rachel says. "The grief is unbearable, but it subsides. I was able to go on and have three more. For you, the blessing in all this is that you're alive."

"God must have been watching over you." Mrs. Pollock says.

My memory is clear though the pain is unrelenting. God had nothing to do with what happened last night, I want to tell them. Now I remember the two redcoats, the stink of ale and sweat, and what they did. And the baby…

I'm so overtaken by grief and anger, my sobs come out in wrenching yelps that hurt my chest. But I can't stop. I sound like a dog that got too close to the fire. Rachel grips my hand.

The baby, Tom's baby, is gone. And I want it back more than anything. How strange that this thing I didn't want has become so precious. I feel guilty that I couldn't protect it from those two animals.

The sobbing finally lets up. "I'm going to give you a potion to help you sleep," Mrs. Pollock says. "Your body needs to recover from this…abuse." She puts the cup to my lips, and I swallow as much as I can.

I drift in and out of a dream-riddled sleep. There are cascading images: a snowball fight, Seth's dog Molly chasing a skunk, our old house in the woods, a gunshot, my mother crying. They weave in, they weave out.

When I awake, I'm hit by waves of pain and a pounding headache. I see a pile of bloody bedding in the corner. I have no idea what day it is, and Tess is sitting in the chair by my bed, her hair wrapped in a bright purple kerchief.

I start to sit up. "Tess, how—"

"Shhh! You must rest."

"We heard about the attack," she says. "Amos is frantic. He's ready to personally hang whoever did this. He asked me to check in on you."

"I'll live," I say.

"No doubt," she says. "You wouldn't die with the account of a gruesome crime yet to finish."

That makes me feel good.

"Do you remember anything? Was it a stranger, or a man you knew?"

"A stranger," I say immediately. "No, wait—it was two strangers. They were drunk."

"Sarah, you don't have to go on. Maybe we should speak of other things."

But the terrible memory has lumbered out of the fog, demanding that I put it into words.

"They were redcoats. One had pocked cheeks and the other a red beard. One of them is sporting a freshly broken nose."

"Your doing?"

"Yes."

"Excellent."

"I fought them as much as I could."

"I'm sure you did," Tess says. "I brought you a copy of *Robinson Crusoe* to busy your mind while you recover."

"From Amos's library, no doubt." I examine it with my one good eye.

She nods. "How are you feeling?"

I shift in the bed and wince. "Like I've been trampled by an elephant."

I can't keep up the small talk. "Tess, I lost the baby."

She sighs deeply. "Yes, I know. Mrs. Porter told me."

"Aren't you going to say it?"

"Say what?" Tess looks confused.

"Tell me: 'Isn't this what you wanted all along. To lose the baby. Problem solved.'"

“I would *never* say that—nor think it,” she says. “But now that you’ve brought it up…”

“I don’t know what I feel.” I choke up, and my chest feels like someone slammed it with a heavy book. “A month ago, I might have been relieved to have it gone. But lately, I’ve felt different. It’s hard to explain. Protective.”

“I understand,” she says, her voice softening. “It’s an attachment, a bond that grows.”

The sobs gush out. “Did I cause this to happen? Did I miscarry because I couldn’t love my own baby enough? You do remember, I nearly took the trade.”

Tess leans forward and practically hisses in my face.

“No! Those men, those brutes, those monsters took away your baby. And they beat you mercilessly.” She lowers her voice. “And they would have raped you if you hadn’t put up such a fight. We will find them and make them pay.”

I’ve never seen her so fierce. I feel better already.

CHAPTER 22

It's been a week since the attack. My ribs are beginning to mend. The swelling in my face has gone down, and I can finally see out of both eyes. I can't stand being bedridden one more day. I finished reading *Robinson Crusoe* and would have gone batty if Tess hadn't returned with a copy of *Moll Flanders* that kept me up late at night. Moll's wayward life makes mine seem straitlaced.

This morning, I dress myself with some effort and gingerly venture down the stairs to take my seat at the breakfast table.

"Sarah, come sit by me," Henry says.

"No, me," his twin insists.

"Boys!" Gertrude exclaims.

"It's so nice to see you up and about, my dear," Rachel says. "And lucky for you, Molly has found the only butter and flour for sale in all of Philadelphia, and she's made johnnycakes."

"Had to pay a king's ransom for it," Molly says, flipping two onto my plate.

I've eaten little in the last week, but the johnnycakes smell so good I dive in with abandon.

"Slow down," cautions Gertrude, ever the killjoy. "Give your body half a chance to digest your food properly."

"You look like you've been kicked by a horse," Jack says.

Rachel is aghast. "Jack! What a mean thing to say!"

"Feels that way too," I say stuffing my mouth. "You should see the horse."

Everyone laughs.

Rachel has told the children that a couple of thieves knocked me down, but she left out the brutal details. I appreciate her discretion.

"Have you heard from Charles?" I ask her.

"Yes, he asked that I send him cash to pay their lawyer, and for room and board. I exchanged some gold coins for Continental money."

"How can you get it to him? It's 200 miles and two armies away."

"Yes, it's a risky trip," Rachel replies, keeping her typical silence on how her Quaker network manages to get essential business done even in the heat of war.

And then there's the matter of Quaker doctrine.

"You sent him Continental money?" Gertrude asks indignantly. "That money is tainted. It's the currency of war! We shouldn't even touch it."

"These are desperate times," Rachel says. "I hid it in the lining of a shirt that I sent along."

"And also in the stockings I knitted," Abigail adds.

"Thank the Lord there are people risking their lives to help our men," Rachel says. "And hundreds are flooding government offices with letters on their behalf."

"Does Charles have other news?" Gertrude asks.

"Only that he and the others are allowed to attend Quaker Meetings and see any visitors able to make the trek," Rachel says.

It doesn't sound like much of a hardship to me. Rachel must have read my mind.

"I fear he's not sharing all their suffering," she says. "Our letters must go through censors from both armies."

I wonder how much Rachel isn't telling him—or us.

I'm deep into *Moll Flanders* and her many husbands, when Gertrude knocks on my bedroom door.

"Amos Tinkleton is in the parlor. Are you well enough to greet him?"

"Yes, certainly."

I bound down the stairs forgetting about my sore ribs.

"Mr. Tinkleton, how nice to see you. Please sit down."

Molly appears out of nowhere and asks if we'd like coffee.

"Only if you have enough to spare," Amos answers. My first coffee in a week, and I'm practically drooling with anticipation.

He takes off his pigskin gloves, one finger at a time, and places them just so on the table.

I take a sip of Molly's steaming brew and thank God for coffee beans.

"I heard all about the attack, and how you somehow managed to cheat death," he says.

"Yes, I survived," I smile.

"I would expect nothing less," he says. "I'm glad to see you're on the mend. You gave us quite a scare."

I can't picture Amos being scared that a thorn in his side at work would be plucked out forever, but he seems genuinely concerned and I'm touched.

"If it's not too painful to talk about, what were you doing out alone that night?"

"I went to the Walnut Street Jail to see if I could talk with Ethan Ripley," I say.

"Why didn't you tell me?"

"You would have said no. Am I right?"

"Probably. I would have told you no one is allowed in, especially a young woman. And that no young woman should attempt to navigate the streets at night—not in these brutish times."

"But I wanted to get Ethan's side of the story."

"What makes you think his 'side' of the story is worth our time?" Amos sputters. "Besides, he's not talking—to anyone."

"I thought he would talk to me," I say, suddenly embarrassed at my self-important tone.

"Did the guards usher you in on a red carpet? Did you even get inside the door?"

"Yes, I did. I talked my way in."

"I might have guessed," he says. He sounds put out, but I detect an iota of admiration. "And did he tell you where he was the night of the murder?"

"No."

"There! The boy doesn't have an alibi. If he did, he'd talk."

"I'm not so sure. Something about the way he told me he 'couldn't say.' I feel there's more to it."

"I commend you for trying," he says. "But I wish you'd asked me before you went. I care about your safety." He sounds protective, and it makes me feel good.

Though I don't need anyone to protect me. Or so I used to tell myself.

"So the attack was after you left the jail to walk home?"

"Yes. Near the docks."

"Lucky they found you in time," he says reaching for his gloves. "Well, I should be going. Don't want to tire you out. You should know that the entire city of Philadelphia is looking for the bastards who did this to you."

"Good. Tell them to keep an eye out for a bearded redcoat with a broken nose."

"I heard you managed to inflict some damage. Good girl."

He puts his hand on my shoulder, a warm gesture he's never attempted before. "I want you back at the *Sentinel* as soon as you're able. Among your many other duties, I'd like you to follow the Ripley murder story."

It's snowing when I wake up. Big, wet flakes that melt almost as soon as they land. The children are outside trying to have a snowball fight, scraping up the scant amount on the ground.

It reminds me of home, though the snowdrifts in New Hampshire ran to six feet instead of six inches. Last night I wrote a letter to Mother and told her everything. Almost everything. I left out the part about the baby. The last thing I need is Mother pleading with me to move to Canada for my own well-being.

I also had time to think about what Amos said: He *needs* me back at the *Sentinel*, and he wants more on the Ripley murder. I've thought of little else since he left, aside from losing the baby.

At breakfast I make my announcement: "I'm going back to work tomorrow."

"Too soon," Rachel says. "You need more rest."

The children chime in. "Too soon. Too soon."

"It's been more than a week," I say. "If I rest any more I'll go mad and dress the cat in breeches and a wig."

The children laugh, but Gertrude doesn't.

"You could relapse, you silly child! You're lucky you didn't catch pneumonia!"

"She right," Rachel adds. "And your injuries aren't all on the outside."

I wonder how she always seems so on target in assessing my inner life. But I remain unswayed.

"Mr. Tinkleton needs me, and I have business I need to attend to," I say, hoping my voice sounds firm and final. "So tomorrow it is."

The rest of the day I race to finish *Moll Flanders*. She's just taken her fourth husband when I hear a commotion downstairs.

Then Emma's voice. Can that be?

I rush downstairs, though my chest is still wrapped in the heavy plaster bandage the doctor wrapped tight.

"Emma! I wasn't sure you'd come!"

Emma rushes to hug me but Rachel shouts at her to be careful.

"I know, I know," Emma says, holding back. "On the way over here, the apprentice Joshua told me all about your latest mishap."

Rachel, ever the mother hen, steps in to correct her. "It was more than a mishap."

"Rachel, this is Emma Jordan, the tutor I told you about for the children."

"Welcome," she says, taking in Emma's bright yellow dress. "We're so glad you've made it. It's not safe out there."

"Don't I know it!" Emma says with her big, jolly laugh. "I had the devil of a time getting here."

"Well, come into the back parlor and have a cup of tea and a biscuit," Rachel says.

Rachel, Gertrude, Abigail and I excitedly usher Emma into the smaller parlor, where the women do their sewing. Except me, of course. I lack any needle wisdom.

"Emma, how did you get here all the way from New Hampshire? You do know there's a war raging all around us?" I joke.

"What war?" she quips with a straight face.

It feels so good to have Emma here.

"Mr. Bascomb was making a trip to New York for supplies for his store, so I went along. Mother didn't think it proper, but I convinced her."

"And your father too? That must have been tough," I say, remembering the tight rein he kept on Emma.

"From New York, I rode a stagecoach called The Flying Machine to Philadelphia," Emma says. "Took only two days."

"Imagine that!" Rachel says.

"Two days felt like two weeks on my poor derriere," Emma says.

"What's a derriere?" Abigail asks.

"It's French for my *arse*," Emma laughs. "Something you'll learn when we start French lessons."

Eyes huge, Abigail breaks into a wide smile. Gertrude is not amused.

"Thought my teeth would rattle loose," Emma says. "They told me springs under the seats would make it painless. That's not what my...derriere says."

Abigail is beaming. Emma has already worked her charm. I can't say I'm not a little jealous of her ease with people.

"Where did you stay overnight on your journey, my dear?" Rachel asks.

"Princeton, New Jersey. At the College Inn. A raucous group in the taproom kept me awake half the night so I finally joined them for an ale and made some new friends. Woke with a screeching headache."

This bit of news surprises me. Not her eagle eye for available men, but her boldness. I've always been the bold one, daring to take risks, no matter how insane.

"You must be fatigued," Rachel says. "Molly is making up a bed for you in Sarah's room for now. We're a bit crowded, temporarily.

Major Hammond is quartering with us in the front parlor, and his men are in the attic."

Emma's eyes light up, as I expected.

"I'll show you upstairs," I say. I can't wait to get Emma alone so we can talk more freely.

"Tell me about this Major Hammond," she says as we climb the stairs.

"He's a bloody redcoat. Not your cup of tea." I'm a little miffed that she hasn't asked about me.

But once we're out of earshot, she hugs me gently. "Tell me everything."

I open up for the first time about the attack and losing the baby. The pain, the shame, the anger.

"You have every right to be angry," she says as we sit on the bed. "I hope those men hang for what they did."

"Me too."

"At least you're lucky you weren't raped," Emma says, which gives me scant comfort.

"Emma, they wanted me dead! They almost succeeded."

"And they did kill the baby," she says.

That stirs the emotions I thought I'd gotten past.

Emma throws her arms around me, and I cry, letting it all drain out of me.

CHAPTER 23

IN A WEEK EMMA has set up a classroom in the back parlor for the older children and the twins. I don't know how she keeps order, but it may have something to do with the peppermint candies she keeps hidden in her sleeve.

As expected, she's worked her charms on Major Hammond. Last night they talked for hours after supper. The Major fought with the redcoats on Long Island, and she told him about tutoring the children of Captain Pendleton in British-held New York City. I could hear giggling and raucous laughter all the way up in my room—our room. I can't help but feel that Emma has already replaced Rachel in the Major's charm offensive.

I'm finally back working at the *Sentinel,* though Amos treats me gingerly. I've told him a thousand times that I've recovered but he insists that excessive self-confidence is just another tell-tale sign of how badly I was shaken up. I have to say I find his attention beguiling. I'm beginning to understand how Tess is drawn to him.

Ethan is still in jail and I worry about him, perhaps too much. I feel in my bones that he's innocent but proving it is impossible without his opening up. Emma thinks he must be guilty, probably because the Major told her a man without an alibi is a guilty man.

At Lloyd's this morning, I'm waited on by Ethan's father, who's unaccustomed to working the counter. He spills coffee on my cloak and apologizes by giving me an apple tart, fresh from the oven.

"What do you hear from Ethan?" I ask.

"Not much. Won't talk to me. Damn fool won't talk to anyone." His sad eyes have huge, dark circles under them. I'm sure he feels he's lost two sons.

"I'm certain he's hiding something," I say, hoping to draw him out. "Maybe trying to keep someone else out of trouble."

Silently, he busies himself sweeping some crumbs off the counter.

"Lucy Nelson," he says so softly I can barely make out his words. "They were keeping company before Rip was killed."

I'm surprised. Ethan seemed too traumatized to have an interest in courtship, or most anything else.

"I don't know Lucy Nelson," I say.

"Her dad is Andrew Nelson, one of the Quakers they kidnapped and sent to Virginia."

I'm not sure how to proceed but Mr. Ripley fills in the blanks.

"She's the youngest daughter," he says. "Quite a flirt if you ask me."

Two days later I call at the Nelsons' elegant three-story brick mansion. Befitting the home of a respected businessman, the house is massive and set off by white columns at the entrance.

An elderly servant ushers me into the parlor, where Agatha Nelson sits perched on a dark maroon velvet sofa. Beside her is Lucy, a petite young woman, pretty even in her plain gray Quaker dress. It's Lucy I really want to see, but I keep that to myself.

"Rachel told me you had something to tell us," Agatha says. "I hope you have news—good news, that is—from our dear husbands and they'll be home soon."

"Not good news, I'm afraid."

I tell them what I know: Reacting to some minor offense, Virginia officials want to move the men to a jail even deeper in the colony. And that jail—in Staunton—is known as a filthy, hellish spot.

"That's awful," Agatha says. "They delight in our misery."

I tell her that Rachel and the others are trying their best to spread the word about this latest outrage with a flurry of letters.

"We won't stand for it," Agatha vows. "Will we, Lucy?"

"Yes, Mother. Whatever you say." Lucy seems miles away and is clearly at odds with her mother.

"I was saddened to hear about your accident," Agatha says. "Seems you've made a full recovery."

It was no accident, and I may never get over it. However, I keep that to myself. The Quaker community is tight, and no doubt the full story of my "accident" has been passed around.

"Thank you. Yes, I'm back working at the *Sentinel*." I can tell by her face that my employment is barely above whoring. "I had to return sooner than I would have liked because of Ethan Ripley's trial."

Suddenly, Lucy starts to pay attention.

"It starts next week," I say, "and it doesn't look good for him."

Lucy is flushed, fidgeting with her hair.

"Unless he can account for his whereabouts that night, he doesn't have much of a chance," I say.

Mother and daughter exchange looks. Agatha's eyes penetrate like a hot poker. Lucy looks terrified.

"Maybe he was with one of the prostitutes from Shipley's Tavern and is too embarrassed to admit the truth," Agatha says, eyes still locked on Lucy.

"Maybe," I say. "But I imagine embarrassment is an easier burden than death by hanging."

"The boy is still troubled by what happened in battle," Agatha says. "Maybe his brain is scrambled, and he can't remember that night."

Lucy looks anguished but she says nothing. Agatha gets up, signaling our talk is concluded. I have no choice but to leave without gleaning a thing to help Ethan.

When I return to the *Sentinel*, Amos and Joshua are ecstatic. The first British ship has made it through the blockade on the Delaware. More are on the way.

"This is big news," Amos proclaims. "All the supplies we've all needed for months will finally arrive."

"We'll get ink and paper just in time," Joshua says.

"This could be a gold mine for us," Amos says. "More advertising. Merchants will have more stock to sell—more pots and pans, fabric, coffee, rum—and they'll need to let the public know."

Rachel will be thrilled. She'll no longer have to send Molly out to scrounge up what she can from markets stripped to the bare bones. Emma will be over the moon. She's been wanting new hair ribbons since the Major took notice of her. And I'll finally get the boots I need for the coming winter. My shoes are in tatters.

"I suppose you'll be writing something about it," I say to Amos.

"Yes, and I'll need your help," he says, almost gleefully. "I've missed your clever way with words."

Blatant flattery. I cringe but I love it and, for once, shut up. I'm learning the benefits of patience.

Tess walks in with a worried look. "Excuse me. Mrs. Jordan, there's a young lady to see you."

Standing by the front door is Lucy Nelson, who looks as if she might turn and run any second.

"Come in Lucy," I say.

She doesn't move. "Can we talk…privately?"

"Of course."

Upstairs in the library, she lets loose.

"I couldn't speak freely in front of my mother," she says. "She watches me like a hawk, everything I do and say." I see the eye roll and realize I'm talking with a girl fighting her way to womanhood and independence. It wasn't so long ago that I chafed under my own mother's all-too-keen observation.

"I understand," I say, hoping I convey the sympathy I feel.

Lucy takes a deep breath and relaxes.

I see why her mother keeps her close. She's every bit as pretty as Emma was at that age. Boys were drawn to her as if under a spell.

I think I know why Lucy is here, but she's quiet and I worry that she's getting cold feet. I take a chance and prompt her.

"You know where Ethan was that night, don't you?"

"Yes."

"Did you see him behind the Statehouse, waiting to ambush Rip? Did he kill Rip?"

It's my deepest fear—that this gentle man became enraged and attacked his own brother.

"No. He couldn't have," she says, her voice shaking.

"Because?"

"He was with me."

I want to scream "Hallelujah!" but I control myself.

"Where?"

"We were at the coffeehouse," she says. "It was late. Rip had left earlier. We were alone."

I have a million questions. Were they lovers? And if they were, why am I bothered?

"Did you have feelings for Ethan?"

"Sort of."

"What does that mean?"

Her story comes out in sobs and gulps.

"Mother insists I marry a Quaker and practice the faith, just as she did, and her mother before her," Lucy says with dramatic but earnest flourishes.

"But that's not what you want, is it?"

"No. I'm tired of the rules. I don't want everything mapped out for me—and the Quaker boys, to be honest, are boring. I can't have even a little fun," she says.

I understand her defiance. I've been there.

"If I marry outside the faith, I'd be expelled from the church and my family," she says.

I haven't seen that happen, but I know it to be true. The comfort of faith can come at a high price.

"So let me see if I understand this," I say. "You thought you'd flirt with Ethan and eventually marry him to escape the binds of your mother and your faith."

"That makes it sound so..."

"Cold?" I ask.

"You make it sound like I didn't care a whit about Ethan," she fires back. "I did care. We talked a lot that night. He understood my frustrations with Mother. He listened to me—no one else does."

"So you talked for hours?" I ask.

"Yes. He kissed me more than once. I liked it and asked for more, much more."

"Did he oblige?" I ask, fearing the answer.

"No. He wouldn't, though I pressed him."

I finally exhale. I'm not sure why I've been holding my breath.

"He told me to go home and grow up before I make any more big decisions," she pouts.

I smile at this and want to cheer Ethan's fortitude. But she has one more big decision to make, and I'm sure she knows what it is.

"Lucy, if you want to help Ethan, you'll need to tell the truth about where he was that night," I say. "He's protecting you by not speaking out. He doesn't want to ruin your good name. But he could be hanged for murder if the truth doesn't come out."

For the first time, Lucy surveys the thousands of books in Amos's library. "These are all important books, aren't they?"

"Most are. Some are just stories about ordinary people who do extraordinary things," I tell her.

Lucy is awed.

"Telling the truth will upset your mother," I say. "I wouldn't want to be in your shoes for the tongue lashing you'll get. But freeing an innocent man will set you free, too."

I'm not sure she knows what I'm talking about, and I'm not even sure I quite believe it. Yes, maybe she can free Ethan, but she may also be shunned for being with him in the first place. It's a huge choice for anyone, no less a confused girl.

Miraculously, she looks as if she might just come around.

"I'll do it. But it must be today before I lose my nerve."

CHAPTER 24

Lucy was true to her word. She marched straight to the office of Joseph Galloway, the keeper of Philadelphia's peace under British rule. She told her story, then wrote it out and signed it as her sworn testimony. Within a day, a gaunt Ethan was released and enjoyed his first real meal in weeks. In another day, he was back at the coffeehouse.

When I walk in, he smiles broadly and hands me a big mug of steaming coffee.

"You deserve this," he says. "Actually, you deserve much more. Father told me what you did."

"No, it was all Lucy's doing," I say. "That took courage. She had to tell the authorities *and* her mother. I'm not sure which was worse."

Ethan smiles shyly. "I'd like to thank you proper if you could stop by tomorrow night at closing time."

"What do you think he has in mind?" Emma asks me later when we're undressing for bed.

"I haven't even thought about it," I say, knowing that Emma immediately recognizes a lie in the name of love.

"I bet it's hair ribbons or a comb or perfume," she says, brushing her hair vigorously.

I laugh. "That's what someone would give you."

"I'd certainly put it to better use than you," she snickers.

She's right, but it stings. Lately, I've put more effort into making myself look good. I'm not sure why. Maybe it's Emma's influence. She dresses every day as if she's going to a ball.

Maybe it's seeing how the Major eyes her at supper that makes me wish that someone would ogle me like that. Tom always said he liked my slapdash attention to appearance, but I think he was just trying to make me feel good.

"Major Hammond asked me to accompany him to Sunday dinner at the home of Joseph Galloway," Emma crows. "But I haven't the appropriate gown for such an affair."

"Don't look to Rachel," I say. "Quaker women are partial to dull, shapeless dresses, and she's no different."

Emma looks thoughtful. "I could never be a Quaker."

"No, you're too fond of daring gowns that expose your breasts clear down to the nipples," I say. "It's a wonder they don't flop out like fish."

"Ah, the green-eyed monster, jealousy! That's what I detect," she says, quoting a phrase from Shakespeare that my father liked to spring on us from time to time.

"Not so." Obviously, she's right.

"The Major has lived in New York," she says. "He's accustomed to sophisticated ways."

"I bet he kept company with your old boss, Captain Pendleton," I say. "Both bloody redcoats of distinction. Probably liked the same rum."

"Fortunately, he didn't recall meeting the good captain," she says. "I don't need the Major to know about that dark chapter in my life."

"You mean when you were a spy in the captain's household?"

"I was *not* a spy," she snaps.

"And it wasn't a dark chapter," I say. "We freed Tom, *your* brother, from that wretched prison hulk anchored in the harbor. Saved his life."

"Nearly lost ours in those wild seas," she says, climbing into bed. "That's the last time I help in one of your wild schemes."

"We'll see," I laugh.

The next day I run into Tess as she's coming out of the privy.

"Amos is fit to be tied," she whispers. "He found one of his books hidden in my quarters behind the chimney."

"Which one?" I ask.

"*Tom Jones.* Apparently, it's his favorite, and when he couldn't find it in the library, he went on a rampage searching for it."

Tess looks terrified. I'd be too.

"He has the book back in his precious hands, right?" I ask. "Problem solved."

Tess rolls her eyes. "You have so much to learn about being a poor, ignorant charwoman."

"But you're not ignorant."

"In his eyes, I'm an illiterate Negro," she says, her voice filled with anger. "He thinks I was going to sell the book so I could quit this job."

"Did you tell him otherwise?"

"I tried. But he wouldn't listen. When I tried again, he slapped me."

I feel my anger building.

"Why didn't you just confess and tell his royal highness you can read? That you've read half the books in the library. And *Tom Jones* was just another."

Tess looks at me as if I'm the village idiot. "The man was in no mood to hear that I've conspired for two years to read every one of his books. No one wants to hear they've been made a fool of."

Surprisingly, I see a ray of sunlight in the storm. "At least he didn't fire you," I say.

"Yet," she says, grabbing a mop and pail.

I watch the clock the rest of the day, anxious to see Ethan when I leave. To amuse myself, I rifle through stacks of yellowing newspapers for an item, something to fill out the *Sentinel.* I find it: A London sleuth has determined the true author of *Common Sense*, that stirring call for independence, is none other than John Adams. Tell that to Thomas Paine!

Amos is not amused. His dark mood hovers, and he spends hours cleaning every one of his quill pens without saying a word.

I venture into his office eventually to show him the article he wanted on what residents can expect to purchase once all the ships arrive.

"I don't give a damn that perfumed soaps will be on sale at Anderson's Apothecary," he seethes, enunciating each syllable precisely. "I want to know when I can buy eggs, and will they cost an arm and a leg?"

"Sorry, Amos," I say barely above a whisper. "I'll work on it some more."

I dip my pen and glance at the clock. Five o'clock. I'll have to hurry.

The next version isn't much better. I worry that Ethan will give up on me and go home. But finally Amos deems my words fit, if barely. "This will do." He sighs heavily. I want to heave the ink bottle at him, but I leave before he can find fault with anything else.

It's beginning to snow as I dash to the coffeehouse. The streetlamps are lit but Lloyd's looks completely dark. I bang on the front door like a madwoman.

"Ethan? Ethan, are you still here?"

Finally the heavy oak door creeks open, and Ethan peers out. "I was just about to leave," he says. "I thought you forgot."

"No, no, not at all," I say breathlessly. "Amos kept me late."

He lights a lantern, takes my arm and leads me to a table where he's laid out a loaf of bread, a hunk of cheese, two glasses and a half-full bottle of rum. I'm surprised and pleased.

"It's a paltry supper, but that's all I have until the ships arrive," he says.

"Don't apologize! It's a banquet."

"Hardly," he laughs, pushing his sandy hair back from his forehead.

I didn't realize how tall he is, towering over me. He's a leaner version of Rip. I'm not sure what's happening here, and I'm a little wary. He seems to sense that.

"My father is upstairs in his office working on the books," he says.

I relax and take a sip of rum.

"I wanted to thank you again for what you did," he says. "With Lucy." He hands me a small package wrapped in paper and tied with a string.

"What's this?"

"Open it."

I tear off the paper. It's a book: *The Further Adventures of Robinson Crusoe.* I hug it to my chest and squeal with delight, something that would shock Emma.

"It's the sequel," he says. "I heard you were fond of the original."

"How did you know?"

"Tess told me. We chat when she comes in for Amos's coffee."

"What else has Tess told you?"

He laughs but then gets serious. "What you did for me was courageous. I like that."

"Not as courageous as what you did in battle," I say. "Someday I hope you'll tell me about it."

"Maybe," he says, smiling shyly. "Someday I hope you'll tell me what happened the night you were attacked." Then he adds quickly, "But only if you want to."

He takes my hand, and immediately I yank it back. What else does he want? Am I a fool to come here, alone?

"I understand," he says. "Maybe my time with Lucy made you fear that I'm something of a rake—after one thing, and one thing only."

I laugh.

"No, it sounded more like she was after one thing, and one thing only."

He lets loose a big hearty laugh, and I relax again. His agitation, the tremors, are all gone—or at least held in check for my benefit.

We finish the bread and cheese, all the while chatting about Rip, the scarcity of coffee beans, George Washington's favorite horse Nelson, and why the moon doesn't fall out of the sky. It's easy, and I could go on all night. He's a good listener.

"This has been a lovely time, but I must be going," I say.

He jumps up. "I'll walk you home."

Ordinarily I'd have pointed out that I don't need a chaperone, but not tonight. I don't know if I'll ever shed my fears, but his pleasant company helps.

When we leave the coffeehouse, the snow is coming down harder. He takes my arm as we stroll.

"I don't want you to fall," he says.

"I won't fall," I laugh. "You know I really can take care of myself—most of the time."

He holds me just a bit tighter.

We walk by the Statehouse, near where Rip's body was found. I know he's thinking about that night.

"I won't sleep soundly until I know who murdered him," he says. "I'm sorry—it does no good to talk about it."

"No need to apologize, Ethan. I think about it all the time too, and it's frustrating because I think the answer is just so close."

"Galloway and his men won't lift a finger to find him," he says.

"Samuel Parsons won't either. He was so sure it was you."

As we approach the Porters', he stops and faces me, eyes big. "I say we do our own investigation, you and I. Between us, we're a good team."

"Yes! We could," I say, excited about diving in wholeheartedly. "But you must be more forthcoming. You told me a while back that you didn't think the killer was motivated by money."

"I still don't," he says as we walk up the front steps. I hear voices just inside.

He takes both my hands. "We'll continue this, Sarah."

Then he kisses the top of my head. I want so much to wrap my arms around him, kiss him on the lips. But I do the sensible thing and say goodnight.

CHAPTER 25

THE SNOW FALLS FOR three days, blanketing the roads and sidewalks. Magically, it hides the garbage, manure, and other debris I dodge daily on my walk to the *Sentinel*. But it makes me homesick for New Hampshire, where my brother and I would ice skate on the pond until our fingers and toes, hands and feet were numb from the biting cold.

It doesn't help when Major Hammond invites Emma to go on a sleigh ride through the city at dusk. Other British officers and their ladies, all wrapped in cozy furs, join them in a procession of sleighs that wind up at the stately home of Joseph Galloway.

"Mrs. Galloway served us steaming bowls of turtle soup," she tells us at breakfast, still in a near-swoon from the luxuriousness of it all.

"Where in heaven's name could she find live turtles?" Rachel asks as she spoons watery porridge into Baby Mary.

"The British have no shortage of fineries now that their ships can unload," Emma says. "That's what the Major told me."

"I wonder when the rest of us will benefit," Rachel mutters.

Now I know how it is that Emma has mysteriously acquired a bolt of satin for a new gown and bonnet. I'm not jealous, I swear.

"The broth was seasoned with sherry, hot pepper and anchovies," Emma goes on, as if she's a longtime connoisseur of turtle soup.

"I suppose the Major will no longer be interested in tea and biscuits in the parlor," Rachel says wistfully.

If Rachel's imprisoned husband knew that the dashing officer now has someone else to dote on, I've no doubt he'd be pleased. Still, I can't help but feel sorry for her. She's had no letter from Charles for weeks. I know she's worried sick, almost nightly taking to her bed with a terrible headache.

Emma has won over the Porter children. Today she's promised them a snowball fight after they've done their lessons, unless Rachel finds out and makes a fuss.

As I slurp the porridge, I try to sort out why Emma so irritates me. She's my best friend. I've confided my secrets to her, most of them anyway. When I told her about my evening with Ethan, she reacted as if I'd virtually invited him into my bed.

"It's too soon. You were beaten, nearly raped, and you lost a baby—Tom's baby. *My brother's baby,*" she said.

"You've got it wrong, Emma," I patiently explained. "He just wanted to thank me, nothing more. Nothing else happened."

"I saw the look on your face when you came in," she said.

That's when I finally lost my temper.

"Tom is dead! I can't bring him back, and I can't bring back the baby. I wish I could. You have no idea how much I wish that."

Tess corners me at the *Sentinel* even before I've brushed the snow off my cloak.

"I don't know what to do," she whispers. "Amos is still mad as fury. Avoids me like a wet dog."

From the corner of my eye I see Amos watching us as we head downstairs. He doesn't move a muscle. The basement is dark, and Tess lights a lantern.

"Let him stew," I say. "He's impossible!"

Tess just rolls her eyes.

"I know what I'd do," I say. "I'd quit. Let him find someone else to clean the privy."

"I can't quit, and I don't want to."

"Why on earth not?"

"Look at me Sarah! I'm a poor charwoman. I can't just find another job with quarters—especially one with the benefits I have here."

"What benefits? You bed down with a man whenever he snaps his fingers. You live in a windowless basement."

"That man bought my freedom, and pays me a regular wage," she says. "And I have feelings for him that you'll never understand."

"That man doesn't know who you really are!" I practically scream. "Are you going to continue this charade just to get back in his good graces?"

"Right now he thinks I was going to sell one of his most valuable books and make off with a pile of money."

I'm beginning to see a way, however murky, out of this ungodly mess. "I have an idea. I'll tell Amos that it was me! I snatched the book and took it home because I've always wanted to read *Tom Jones*. When I brought it back, I left it in your quarters accidentally when you and I were deep in discussion of intimate female matters."

"You would do that for me?" Tess asks incredulously.

"Of course. Amos will be furious with me, but he'll get over it. Besides, he needs me to go through his miserable stacks of papers. And without me, who's going to pretty up his prose?"

"How can I ever repay you?" she says.

"There is a way," I smile. "Tell Amos that you want to learn to read. That I've offered to teach you."

Tess churns out objections like a seasoned lawyer. "He won't like it. If I can read, he'd figure I could leave. He did buy me out of slavery—but not to see me up and leave him! He'll never allow it."

"Reading is not against the law in Pennsylvania," I say. "Besides, as even Amos would admit: You're a free woman."

"I know the law! I know Amos!" she hisses. "And I know my place."

"Then as I'm sure you also know, there's a move right here in Pennsylvania to abolish slavery. If Amos believes he's had a hand in helping you climb the ladder, maybe we could get him to publicly back it."

Tess is dubious. "You're asking a lot of the poor man."

"Poor man?" I laugh. "He'll be dumbfounded when he sees what a fast learner you are."

I wait patiently for the right time to tell Amos what I want him to hear about his first-edition copy of *Tom Jones*. When he returns from a rum-soaked meeting with Joseph Galloway, I make my move.

"How did it go with Galloway?" I ask as he plops down at his desk.

"Exceptionally well. He's pleased with our coverage of the war. Circulation is up. Advertising is up. If this continues, we can publish more than once a week."

"Congratulations," I say enthusiastically. Then I take a long breath. "Amos, I must tell you something."

"Are you ill?"

"No." I proceed to tell him one lie after another, absolving Tess of any blame in the book debacle. He looks puzzled at first, and I fear he doesn't believe me. I expect him to interrupt with a tongue-lashing that leaves me gasping for air.

"So you see, it's all my fault," I conclude, waiting forever as he finishes lining up his papers just so.

"Why didn't you simply ask me if you could borrow a book?" he says, not looking up.

"I didn't think you'd allow it," I say. "I know how important your book collection is to you." I remind myself not to sound too reverent, but I do admire his passion for books.

He finally looks up, smiling. I see kindness in his eyes, and I'm taken with how handsome he is. He's sworn off the ill-fitting wig, and his black wavy hair frames his high cheekbones.

"From now on, just ask me if you wish to borrow a book," he says. "I trust you to return it properly when you're done."

"And Tess?"

"She has no use for books. Couldn't read her own name in large type."

"What about an apology?" I say as gently as I can. "You did accuse her of thievery."

"I'll consider it. Now back to work. We have much to do," he says, flicking his finger as if to brush me away. "What I learned from Galloway will go nicely on the front page."

“What’s that?”

“Washington and his troops have settled in for the winter barely 20 miles from the city,” he says. “A godforsaken place called Valley Forge. They’ll be sitting ducks.”

“Won’t be that easy,” I say. “Just two weeks ago, your mighty redcoats failed to wipe them out at the Battle of White Marsh.”

He looks at me with disdain. “What you don’t know is something else I learned, and Galloway heard it direct from Cornwallis.”

“I give up.”

He leans forward and whispers what we’ll soon have in the headlines. “Washington and his troops are in such dire straits they can’t survive much longer.” Amos is practically rejoicing.

“What do you mean?” I panic at first, thinking of Tom. It must be a reflex in war wives, even fresh widows like me.

Seeing the stricken look on my face, Amos tones down his excitement.

“The Americans are starving. Washington can’t get his hands on grain and meat. The men are in rags, freezing to death.”

Suddenly, the question of who snatched *Tom Jones* seems not to matter a whit. My clever little strategies make no difference in the greater world, and little enough even in my own.

“They won’t survive the winter,” I say, wondering if this is how the war will end—for want of bread and breeches.

Amos, for once, is silent.

CHAPTER 26

A WEEK LATER, WE'RE eating a sparse supper of potato soup when a neighbor bangs on the front door, screaming.

"Fire! Fire!"

We rush out into the cold and see flames shooting up along the outskirts of the city. Young Jack scrambles up through the attic to the rooftop and calls out: "At least a dozen homes ablaze."

The smoke is thick, blown by fierce gusts. My eyes burn, but I can't stop watching.

For hours we wait and watch, wondering if we should pack up and flee to God knows where. By midnight, the wind dies down. We're safe, more or less, but we don't have to be told just how awful the destruction must be.

"Most of them are large country estates," Rachel says. "Don't Amos Tinkleton's parents have a home out there?"

"Yes. I hope it's been spared," I say. I know it's filled with antiques and fine art. Their stable has the best horses. Maybe one day I'll get to see it, but I'm not holding my breath.

Emma is unusually thoughtful. "I'm sure these fires just came from a kitchen accident gone terribly bad on just the wrong night," she says. "I'm certain the Major will know exactly what happened."

Within the hour he bursts in with his entourage, all in a joyous mood.

"Did you see it?" he asks breathlessly.

"How could we not see it!" Emma says.

"Our men had no choice but to torch them," he says.

"It was deliberate?" Rachel says, incredulous.

"The rebels were using them to hide in and regroup," he says, pouring whiskey for his men. "A toast! To King George!"

I don't believe it and go to bed in disgust. Emma stays up for another round. She doesn't seem to notice Rachel's disapproving look—whether it's the liquor, the late hour, or her children's teacher carousing. Could be all of it.

At the *Sentinel*, I'm working on an article about the fires—thankfully the Tinkleton estate was spared—when a note arrives for me.

Sarah,

Meet me after work tonight at the coffeehouse if you're able. We have much to discuss.

Ethan

I spend the rest of the day wondering what he means. Of course, I hope it's me he wants to discuss. I think he fancies me, and I find myself strangely attracted to him. As for Rip's murder, I haven't heard any news. I don't even know if anyone is looking into it.

At Ethan's door, I smooth out the wrinkles in my dress. He opens as soon as I knock.

"Sarah, I was afraid you might not come."

There's no big smile or cheery greeting, no candle-lit spread on the table.

"Come up to my quarters," he says, gesturing to the stairs. "We can talk there. Father is gone."

I'm a little apprehensive but follow him up the dark mahogany stairs. There's something reassuring in his directness.

He leads me to a nicely furnished parlor with floral wallpaper, and we sit down on the small couch, our knees practically touching.

"My parents first lived here when they started the coffeehouse," he says. "Father still has an office here."

He suddenly turns to me with a worried look.

"Sarah, I owe you an explanation. About Rip's murder."

"You mean you know who did it?"

"No, not that," he smiles shyly. "I told you the killer likely wasn't motivated by money, but I never explained why."

I see a slight tremor in his hand and worry he'll lose control. "You don't have to—"

"No, I want to. Before I lose my nerve. It has to do with the Spanktown Papers that the *Sentinel* wrote about back in September. The scandal that led to Charles Porter and the Quakers being banished to Virginia."

I'm puzzled. "What does that have to do with Rip?"

"It has more to do with me," he says.

"You?"

"Yes. Let me back up to the beginning."

In slow, careful sentences, he tells his story. He was fighting with General John Sullivan's American troops on Staten Island last August. The battle was a humiliating loss for Sullivan.

"I came away with a shoulder wound and bullet fragments grazing my head." He pulls back his hair, and I see the scars on his temple.

"Awful," I say. "But what does that have to do with Rip?"

"I'm getting to it."

Sullivan, a big blowhard of a man, was disgraced by his loss, but quickly attempted to play the hero. Going through the belongings of a soldier who had defected to the British, he came across papers that relayed secret information about the numbers, armaments, and movements of American troops.

"They were supposedly papers from an annual Quaker meeting in Spanktown, New Jersey," Ethan says. "Sullivan knew he'd elevate his low standing with his superiors, so he got the papers to Congress as soon as he could."

I'm beginning to wonder where all this is going. "Ethan, we

printed news of the Spanktown papers last year. It was because of the Spanktown papers that the Quaker elders were banished to Virginia."

"The thing is," he continues in an increasingly excited voice, "none of it is true."

He jumps up. "None of it! I swear on my mother's grave that those papers were forged. It was all just to make the Quakers look bad and make Sullivan look good for foiling their supposed plot!"

"Forged? That's what the Quakers have been saying for months, but without any proof."

"I was a witness," Ethan says hoarsely. "I was a courier at Sullivan's headquarters when he supposedly 'found' the papers in the baggage of a so-called deserter."

My head is spinning. "I still don't understand how this ties into Rip."

"I know it's confusing," he says, pulling out a bottle of whiskey and two glasses. "I made the mistake of telling Rip it was all made up. He wanted more than anything to expose it and free the Quakers."

I'm incredulous. "Why would he care so much? So many people around here think the Quakers are secret loyalists anyway. Rip couldn't have expected you, just back from the war, to put yourself on the firing line once again."

Ethan took a deep breath. "I figured it was too dangerous and I told him so. Besides, no one would believe Rip over Sullivan. We argued, nearly came to blows. He told me I was a coward, and he would do it anyway."

"And someone made sure he didn't," I say.

"It should have been me instead of him," Ethan says. "I'll regret it always."

"It's not your fault someone killed Rip."

"But that's the mystery," he says pouring himself another shot of whiskey. "Not knowing who killed him is killing me slowly."

He seems just as tortured now as he was when he came home from the fighting. I want to do something, anything, to ease the pain.

"That's what *we* have to figure out." I pick up my glass and offer a toast. "Here's to us—the Spanktown investigators."

"To us," he says, finally smiling. "We make a good team."

He edges closer to me, and I expect him to make a move for my hand, my leg. He doesn't. There's an awkward silence. We each sip our whiskey.

"You must know by now that I have feelings for you, Mrs. Jordan," he says, reminding me just how much about me is a lie. Would he still have feelings if he knew that I'm not—and never have been—Mrs. Jordan?

"I have feelings for you too," I whisper. "But it's so soon."

"I know," he says, taking my hand. "I understand. I'm in no rush."

We just sit there holding hands for at least a minute. Then he kisses my forehead tenderly.

I can't hold back. I pull his face down to mine, and my lips, as if obeying their own will, seek out his lips. Passion floods me, and I don't want to stop. I press my body against his. He presses back harder. His tongue caresses mine.

Suddenly, he pushes away. "Sarah, I'm sorry. I forgot for a moment. You're not ready for this."

"Yes, I am!"

After a moment, he pulls me close again, and his hand moves to my breast. Suddenly, my mind flashes on that night, those two men, their hands all over me. I recoil.

"You're right, I'm not ready."

He tenderly takes my hand and kisses it.

"I understand," he says. "If you ever are ready, I'll be right here."

CHAPTER 27

Two days before Christmas, Rachel finally receives a letter from Charles.

"They are no closer to being freed," she tells everyone at supper. "And it seems certain they'll be dragged farther away from us and locked up in less hospitable quarters."

I suspect Charles is putting the best face on everything for the family's sake, and the "less hospitable quarters" are cold and rat-infested.

"He says one of the Quakers escaped and fled by horseback," she says. "Their captors fear others will do the same, though Father says he has no intention of skulking away."

Rachel's voice cracks. "He thanks you, Abigail, for the stockings you knitted. Jack, he's grateful for the picture you drew of the ships in the river. He sends his love to you all and asks that you keep him in your prayers."

Emma and the Major exchange looks, and I wonder what's going on. She's always had trouble keeping a secret, though I'm certain—relatively certain—she's held onto mine.

Finally, the Major clears his throat. "Mrs. Porter, Christmas will be here in two days. I think it would be splendid if we celebrate the day with a big dinner for everyone, my men included. I'll supply the goose and whatever else we need. I'll even pay Molly to help serve."

Emma chimes in. "I could teach the children some Christmas carols."

"What do you say?" he asks Rachel. "Shall we have ourselves a feast?"

Dead silence fills the dining room. Even the children are quiet.

"Major Hammond." Rachel's voice is stern and direct. "We don't *celebrate* Christmas. Every day is holy; Christmas is no different."

Emma is crestfallen. The Major is stunned. And I'm disappointed too. I don't know why Rachel can't loosen her pious reins and let everyone enjoy the day.

"We've all made it through a tough time, Rachel," I say. "A day of celebration seems justified. We could all do with a hearty meal after doing without—"

"Father would not allow it," she says with finality. "Nor will I."

Supper is a somber affair after that. Once the children are in bed, Rachel retires to the back parlor to read her tattered, leather-bound Bible. The Major and three of his men move into what is now *his* parlor for cards and rum, a snub to Rachel and her strict ways.

Emma is miffed that she's excluded. And miffed about Christmas. It seems as if she and the Major had it all worked out.

"The British have all the food they want. We're left with scraps," she wails to me before bed.

"The price of everything is so high," I say. "You can't really blame Rachel. Without a husband to bring in—"

"I know, I know," she snaps. "I don't need a lecture."

I want to talk to her more about my night with Ethan but she's too prickly. I haven't told her about my hesitation when I thought I was ready for his touch, but that's just as well. She'd lecture me on eternal fidelity to Tom.

Instead, I focus on her.

"Has the Major kissed you yet?" I ask, knowing the obvious answer as soon as the words are out of my mouth.

She gives me a pathetic look.

"Do you know anything about him? He's older, does he have—"

"I don't know, Sarah, and I don't care," she says. "He doesn't talk about himself, unlike every other man I know. It's refreshing. Now go to sleep."

A pall hangs over breakfast. I try to bring up Christmas dinner, though I make a point of calling it the Major's "dinner offer" to avoid the dreaded word "celebration." Rachel doesn't budge.

"You and Emma are welcome to join us at our meetinghouse on Christmas for a day of silence and prayer," she tells me.

I would sooner pluck feathers all day, but I manage to politely decline.

At the *Sentinel*, Amos is obsessed with a tip that Washington's men are planning an attack on Philadelphia.

"It came directly from Galloway, and he got it from his good friend and comrade General Howe," Amos says. The man never tires of pointing out his connections with the well-connected.

"How can Washington mount an attack when he can't even clothe his men?" I ask. "They're starving to death at Valley Forge."

"I'm not so sure about that," Amos says. "The crafty bastard wants that lie about his ill-equipped troops to spread far and wide. All the better for a surprise attack."

Seems far-fetched to me but it would certainly be an ingenious strategy. Major Hammond hasn't hinted that anything is afoot. On the other hand, he's so consumed with Emma, his latest conquest, that maybe military affairs have taken a backseat.

Sitting in his favorite leather chair, Amos is in full command. "Joshua, build up the fire. Tess, get me some tea. I'm parched.'"

Then he gets to me: "Go to Galloway's office and pick up a parcel."

Not 'Sarah, *please* pick up a parcel' or 'Sarah, I'm sorry to make you brave the cold but I need a favor'....No, none of the niceties for Sarah. The man is insufferable.

It's bitter cold, and I bundle up. Thankfully, I have my new boots, though they cost double what I expected.

Given Amos's ingratitude, I decide to take my time and stop for coffee. I want to see Ethan. I've thought about him constantly—not so much our passionate kisses, but the comfort of his presence, his arm around my shoulder.

Once at Lloyd's, I seat myself at a table, and a bewigged gentleman beckons Ethan over. Gesturing toward me and practically hissing, he seems to resent my presence.

"Sir, we're open to all here," Ethan tells him. "We think the presence of ladies enhances our establishment."

"How can we talk comfortably with women in earshot?" the idiot grumps.

I can't help but join in on the fun.

"Are you afraid we don't possess the wit to keep up with your pompous prattle?" I ask him. "If you care to engage in a friendly debate about any topic of current interest, I'm sure I can convince you otherwise!"

"Hmmph!" He strides away to a far corner of the coffeehouse.

Ethan beams. "What can I get you, Mrs. Jordan?"

"Your strongest coffee, maybe with a dash of humility," I laugh.

"Where are you off to in this weather?" he asks.

"A place where I'll need all my wits. Joseph Galloway's office. Amos needs me to pick up something."

I draw closer and lower my voice. "Have you thought more about the other night—that is to say, about the Spanktown papers and Rip?"

"It's all I've thought about," he says. "And you, of course."

I smile and feel a blush coming on. "I could tell Galloway what we know. Could lead to something."

He takes a sharp breath. "Not a good idea. I don't trust the bloody loyalist."

I know I'm just stalling to avoid the frigid cold, so I head out once again. Before I go, I give Ethan what I hope is a look of smoldering fondness.

As I trudge to Galloway's office, I imagine snuggling up with Ethan on a sleigh ride at twilight. I'm puzzled by his reluctance to tell Galloway everything. Maybe it's his war nerves.

At Galloway's office, I bang the brass knocker, and an elderly doorman in formal attire guides me into the front parlor. A portrait of a young Mrs. Galloway hangs over the fireplace above an ornately carved mantle. I sit down carefully on a red satin sofa with a crown carved into the walnut frame.

From behind the closed office door, I can hear raised voices. "Your men are out of control. Today, an old man was beaten and robbed in broad daylight. There's continuous pillaging. Every day, it's something."

"Mr. Galloway, we're doing what we can. We've warned our

soldiers that there will be heavy penalties."

"They should hang!" he thunders. "The citizens of Philadelphia won't tolerate it, and neither will I. Do you understand?"

"Yes, sir."

"Then good day." Two redcoat officers walk out grim-faced, and the doorman ushers me in.

As flames crackle in his fireplace, Joseph Galloway sits at the biggest desk I've ever seen.

"You must be Sarah from the *Sentinel*," he says with a tight smile. Well-coiffed and dapper, he's smaller than I imagined.

"Yes, Mr. Galloway. Do you have something I'm to bring to Mr. Tinkleton?"

"Yes, I do. Your employer has the finest library in Philadelphia, except for that of the rebel rat Franklin," he says. "But Amos doesn't have this."

He hands me a volume with a beautifully embossed cover: *Candide*, by Voltaire. "One of the original English translations, from 1759."

"I will see that he gets it," I say, wondering why I've been sent on this odd little mission when a messenger could do the job.

He dispatches me briskly. "Thank you, ma'am."

Outside, I can't resist leafing through the novel I'd heard so much about. It was a scandalous satire when it came out, and I'd love to see if it still has its bite.

But as soon as I open it, a folded note sealed with wax falls out. I'm so tempted to peel it open, but Amos would certainly know, and I can't risk any more lies.

I put the note back in the book and stuff it under my cloak. War makes odd bedfellows. What exactly is going on with Amos and the most powerful loyalist in Philadelphia?

As soon as I return, Amos confronts me. "Do you have it?"

"Of course. For your library," I say not hiding my puzzlement as I hand him the book.

He immediately pulls out the note and tosses the book on his desk.

"So it's to be Christmas Day!" he mumbles to himself, just loud enough for me to hear.

I suppose it's one of Galloway's invitations for dinner—another sumptuous affair that doesn't include me. But why the secrecy?

CHAPTER 28

I COME HOME TO find Major Hammond and Rachel huddled over tea in his parlor. Rachel is giggling. I can't believe it.

Upstairs, Emma is sitting on her bed knitting mittens for Jack, and she's not happy.

"Why is he spending time with her," she grouses, knitting needles clacking away. "They've been in there for an hour. Must have sipped an ocean of tea by now."

"They're probably just talking about the high cost of butter," I say. "They're at least an arm's length from each other. What could happen with bug-eyed Gertrude lurking about?"

"I just don't like it," she says. Then she looks up at me. "You're hiding something. I can tell."

"No. I don't think so." I suppose I'm unsettled by Amos's odd secrecy, but I don't let on.

"I don't trust you," she says. "You've kept things from me before, and it never ends well for me."

True. When I blew up the patriots' ammunition depot in Essex, I almost blew up Emma too. When I rescued Tom from the prison ship, she almost drowned.

"You're acting *so* crazy," I say.

But trying to jolly Emma out of a dark mood is near impossible.

The Major stays for supper, and Molly makes scrambled eggs, a favorite with the children. There's also fresh cornbread, a dish the

Major has praised to the skies. I cautioned Emma to sweeten her mood and she did, making a big show of sitting next to him and warmly greeting Rachel.

"I have news," Rachel announces as she dishes up the eggs. I figure it's another letter from Charles until she looks fondly at the Major.

"Major Hammond and I have come to an agreement about Christmas," she says. "The children and I will spend the day at the meetinghouse and then join Gertrude and others for an evening of quiet reflection. And the Major will honor the day in the style of his faith. The Quaker religion teaches us to be tolerant of different—"

"What Mrs. Porter is trying to say," he interrupts, beaming at Sarah, "is that I'll be hosting a Christmas dinner with my men, and of course Emma and Sarah, and all who wish to join us for this glorious day."

Emma is her jovial self again. "Splendid! I'll make a pumpkin pie—I'll make three pies. What about you, Sarah?"

I can't breathe, much less talk. I've just figured out what Amos meant: The patriots will attack on Christmas Day. Of course. We'll all be eating pumpkin pie when the cannons boom and Philadelphia goes up in flames.

"Sarah, what's your contribution?" Emma asks again. She's needling me because I'm as familiar with the workings of a kitchen as she is with a printing press.

"Bread. I'll make bread," I stammer.

"Bread!" She's incredulous. "This will be a miracle. A Christmas miracle."

It's still snowing on Christmas Eve, and the Major, deep into his port wine, revels in the grim details he's heard about life for the patriots at Valley Forge. From his sources, he's learned that men are half frozen, sickly, and infested with lice. They have not one cow to slaughter, and their flour stores are almost gone. Dressed in rags, they're scrambling to finish a slew of crude log huts before more severe weather sets in.

Of course, if you listen to Amos, it's all a crafty ruse by the greatest deceiver of all time: His Excellency George Washington. "He and his men are eating hearty," he assured me yesterday. "His favorite is roast lamb, and his boys have pillaged the countryside for the tenderest specimens."

Emma is up to her elbows in flour. After making two pumpkin pies, she's throwing together a mince pie using venison Molly found while scouring the city for humbler ingredients. The Major comes into the kitchen often to steal kisses, and Emma obliges.

They ignore me as I struggle to make one edible loaf of bread. That suits me. I'm in no mood to witness their cuddling or even to talk—not with the patriots swooping in tomorrow with their military might. Of course, I'm hoping the rebels prevail in this damnable war, but it's sure to be a bloodbath.

The Major is true to his word and arrives with a squawking 20-pound goose that Molly is happy to silence with her butcher knife. By the time I go to bed she has it defeathered, seasoned, stuffed with onions, apples, and nuts, and ready for the spit on Christmas Day.

Tonight, Emma is in the parlor alone with the Major. The door is closed when I head for the stairs. I wager she'll spend the entire night there. I lie awake for hours, on high alert as I listen for a muffled shout, a rumble of wagons—anything that might signal the patriots' imminent descent upon the city.

In the morning, I awake to another four inches of snow and complete silence. I expect to hear church bells calling worshippers—until I remember the patriots hid so many of the big, heavy bells months ago to keep them from the redcoats.

When the children rush outside for a snowball fight, I throw on my cloak and mittens. The snow is just sticky enough for the perfect snowball, but before I can let loose, Jack lands one right on my neck.

"You won't get away with that," I yell at him, just as if I'm back in Essex fighting my brother Seth. "Abigail, you and I will take on the boys!"

For the next little while, snowballs fly back and forth furiously, and I cease to care about the patriots' attack. For the first time in months, I feel giddy.

Then it's over, and we all traipse inside wet and exhausted, leaving tracks through the house.

Rachel is not amused. "Be ready to leave for the meetinghouse in 15 minutes," she tells her children.

When they're finally gone, I roust Emma, who came up to bed sometime before dawn.

"Go away," she mutters, burying her head under the covers.

"It's Christmas. We've much to do," I say. I can't tell her that she should at least be fully dressed when the patriots attack.

Downstairs, the parlor door is open and there's no sign of Major Hammond. Molly, who's peeling a mountain of potatoes, tells me he's gone off to round up some whiskey and rum.

"His men will come with a fierce appetite, and not just for roast goose."

I take a breath.

"What's wrong with you?" Molly says. "You look terrified."

"Nothing. I just want everything to be perfect. Looks like you have it all in hand. I worried for nothing."

The goose is already roasting on a spit over the fire, and it smells heavenly. I wonder how Ethan is spending Christmas, and Tess too. Mother, no doubt, will be sitting bedside, tending some mother-to-be whose child will have the misfortune of sharing a birthday with Jesus.

Emma finally makes an appearance dressed in her new satin gown, courtesy of the Major. Her hair is swept up in a fashionable style. Only her red eyes give away her late-night reveling as she looks over my torn skirt, still soaking wet from my outdoor exertions.

"Is that what you're wearing?" she says. "You know the Major's entire staff will be here for dinner."

"I was having a snowball fight with the children, not attending a ball. Of course I'm going to change," I retort, though I hadn't thought of it until this minute.

Upstairs I take out my best gown, a blue silk that matches my eyes. I brought it from New York, where I wore it to the theater in better times. It goes on over the dreaded stays that cinch my waist to the point of strangulation. The final touch is the locket Tom gave me when we fled New York that day.

A glance in the mirror: My hair is a disaster. I wrestle it as best I can with a tie, but the curls escape and I finally give up, letting it hang loose. Emma will scoff, but that's how Tom liked it.

I catch myself: What does it matter how Tom liked it? He's gone.

One last look in the mirror and the woman staring back is a surprisingly pretty redhead. I head downstairs with a spring in my step.

The Major has just arrived with six of his men, all in dress uniforms and polished to a shine. Are they poised for battle? No one seems the least bit worried about anything. When he sees me, he acts surprised.

"And who is this lovely bird?" he slurs, making it clear he and the men have already dipped into the spirits.

Emma is stunned too, though clearly put off by the Major's eagerness to flirt with a woman other than herself.

"Oh yes," she says haughtily. "Sarah can make herself presentable when coaxed."

"I hardly had to be coaxed," I tell the Major, smiling broadly. "Not when we have the honor of hosting the King's men." My words drip with insincerity.

For hours the goose sizzles over the fire and the men leisurely drain their bottles. They chide each other over this one's poor marksmanship and that one's inability to read maps. But mostly, they ramble on about how Washington and his men are bungling fools.

"He's dug his grave at Valley Force," the Major says. Emma nods in agreement, and I kick her under the table. When did she become such a damn loyalist?

Finally, Molly presents the goose, burnt black and shriveled like a prune. "It was fit to eat an hour ago," she says.

"Molly, you're too modest," I tell her hoping she'll realize with the rest of us that a goose reduced to ash matters not nearly as much as the fun and camaraderie of a good Christmas gathering. "You must take home the leftovers."

"Well said!" One of the men stammers from too much drink.

He reaches for Molly's backside, and she smacks him hard.

I can't help but laugh, along with everyone else. I'll never have another Christmas Day like this one. I pour myself another glass of rum and feel my troubles slipping away.

The Major carves up the goose and doles out chunks of charred meat to everyone. The men don't care, and they dive into it as if it's the last meal they'll ever have.

Emma is at the Major's side, practically in his lap, laughing gaily at everything he says. The baby-faced soldier next to me tries to flirt.

"So you're Sarah," he says. "And you made the bread." He slathers a glob of butter on a slice and takes a bite. "A triumph."

Obviously soused. No one has ever complimented my kitchen skills. But it doesn't matter.

"Thank you, Sergeant," I say.

He moves closer. "Maybe you and I could—"

Boom! Boom!

"They're here!" I scream. "The rebels. Come to take back the city."

Boom!

I rush outside, and the others follow.

"Oh no, what's happening?" Emma asks the Major as he wraps a shawl around her shoulders.

"Nothing is happening," he says calmly. "It's just lunatics setting off fireworks. That's all it is."

He herds everyone back inside. I'm the last, listening in vain as the noise stops. I can't believe it's just fireworks.

"You've had quite a scare, Sarah," the Major says. "Nothing to worry about." He squeezes my arm in a manner that suggests something more than just comfort.

"I was so sure," I say, exhausted from anticipation.

"We picked up a report days ago that Washington was planning a surprise attack on Christmas," the Major says. "But our people checked it out. Discovered the great general changed his mind when he realized his men are dying in droves." He laughs.

"Today they're feasting on vinegar and rice. How could they possibly attack our city when they can't even rustle up a proper meal? This is the end of their little rebellion."

CHAPTER 29

"How DID YOU SPEND Christmas?" I ask Tess as I hang my cloak by the door.

A grin consumes her whole face. "Amos took me to his parents' house."

"The estate in the country?" I can't believe it.

Her grin gets even bigger.

"He presented you to his family?" I whisper.

"Not exactly." She nods toward Amos's office. "Meet me at the privy and I'll tell you everything."

Outside, we shiver as she goes on about their cozy carriage ride to the estate.

"I know what you're thinking, and it's not like that," she says. "He asked me to help with his family's Christmas dinner because their servants had the day off."

I hide my disappointment. "Did you at least get dinner?"

"More than I've ever eaten in my life. They had roast duck, venison, whipped potato, plum pudding, three kinds of pie." She smiles slyly. "I managed to squirrel away two more meals under my cloak without anyone noticing. And there's more."

"What?"

"On the way home Amos was feeling no pain, so I asked him about me learning to read."

"And?"

"I told him you'd offered to teach me."

"Did he get angry?"

"No," she says. "He asked why. Why would a Negro charwoman need to learn letters?"

"Did you tell him you don't intend to clean privies the rest of your life?"

"No. I told him I wanted to read all his books."

"But don't you want to better yourself?" As soon as I say it, I bite my tongue.

"You had to ruin it, didn't you," she storms. "You can't possibly understand. You don't live in my world."

"I'm sorry, Tess. What I meant—"

"I know what you meant. In case you want to know, Amos said yes. He's not the cold-hearted bastard you think he is. And yes, I'm the woman who cleans his privy. That's who I am."

Tess avoids me for days, and it's my own fault. The urge to speak before I think is one of my major failings. Amos is distant too, as if I might tell the world that the young woman he bought out of slavery now cleans his privy and services his needs.

With as few words as possible, he politely asks me to write an article about all the ships in the harbor and the return of trade to the city. He perks up when I tell him about the other signs of prosperity I've seen.

"The Southwark Theater is opening with British soldiers playing the parts, even the women," I tell him. "Smith Tavern is advertising weekly balls on Thursday nights. Restaurants are opening. And concerts and cockfights and horse races—"

"Excellent! All good news for the *Sentinel*," he says.

Of course, for him it's all about money. When I tell Ethan about the theater, he's singularly unexcited. And the notion of men in women's roles—while it used to be the standard for centuries—elicits a disapproving grunt.

But an hour later a note arrives at the *Sentinel,* and I know instantly by the careful handwriting that it's from him.

My Dear Sarah,

It would be my honor if you would accompany me Jan. 19 to the Southwark Theater's first performance of "The Wonder: A Woman Keeps a Secret."

Your friend and confidant,
Ethan Ripley

I write back.

My Dear Ethan,

I would be pleased to accompany you to the play. I hear the actresses are quite ravishing.

Your friend and confidante,
Sarah

I can't bear to sign my so-called full name: Sarah Jordan. Soon I'll tell Ethan everything: I'm Sarah Barrett, chronic liar and impersonator. I don't regret what I've done, but it's a lot to throw at a man who's only fault is being scarred by war.

Days later, I'm daydreaming about what I'll wear to the play when an ear-splitting explosion rocks the Porter house.

"What was that!" I yell, racing down the stairs, just as Major Hammond emerges from the parlor with two aides in tow.

"Couldn't be an attack," he says. "We'd hear more cannon fire."

Emma dashes in from the other parlor with Abigail, who's clutching her French book.

Then the Major looks about, agitated. "Where's Jack?"

Blank looks from everyone. Suddenly, he bursts out the door and leaps down the steps. Struggling to keep up with him, we all see a thunderhead of black smoke over the Delaware.

In the crowd gathered on the wharf, I spot Jack. Someone has wrapped an old blanket around him and he's been crying.

"Boy, are you all right?" The Major puts his arms around him and pulls him close.

"Yes," Jack says, barely above a whisper.

"What happened?" I ask softly.

He pours out his story, pausing only to wipe his nose with his sleeve.

"Sam and his brother Dan and me, we were at the wharves. We were watching the men unload cargo from the ships. The ones that just arrived."

"Yes, yes, then what happened?" the Major asks, urgently scanning the growing crowd.

"Dan spotted something in the water. Looked like a barrel. We thought it might have fallen off one of the ships."

Jack starts to whimper and the Major rubs his shoulder.

"You're all right, son. Go on."

"We thought there might be something valuable in it."

"Like what?" Abigail asks impatiently.

"I don't know! Something worth some money. So Dan said we should get his father's boat from the docks and row out there."

"In this weather?" Emma says incredulous. "The river is raging, full of ice chunks."

"I know. I know," he says. "I was too scared to go, and I was already freezing. They called me a chicken, said I was worse than a girl."

"So you didn't go with them?" I ask.

"No, I stayed on the dock and watched them go." Now he's sobbing.

"You did the right thing," the Major says. "The water is so frigid it would have killed you in less than a minute."

"No, I should have gone with them," Jacks says. "I could have helped."

"Hurry up and tell us what they did," Abigail says.

"When they reached the barrel—it wasn't that far out there—they bumped up against it. And then—well, it just happened. The explosion."

Jack covers his face. I can barely hear him.

"The blast knocked me to the ground. I remember men looking down and telling me my friends were dead. 'Gone,' they said." Tears stream down his face. "Gone," he whimpers. "Like that."

The Major looks disgusted. "Those boys didn't have a chance. Damn, rebels! How low will they stoop?"

CHAPTER 30

Scanning the choppy waters, I see dozens of barrels bobbing down the river amid the chunks of ice.

"What are they?" I ask dumbfounded.

"I'm not sure," the Major yells as he dashes off with his men. "Can't take any chances."

For the next couple of hours, I station myself on the wharf and watch the strangest spectacle unfold.

British soldiers on the shore and on their warships fire guns and cannons at the bobbing barrels. One after another, they explode with a thunderous burst that lights the sky and unleashes thick plumes of black smoke.

I know it sounds risky to be so close to such chaos and destruction, but I can't tear myself away. Besides, Amos will want an article on this mayhem, and I don't want to miss any detail.

Citizens are panicked, fearing Philadelphia is under siege, that the entire city will go up in flames at any moment.

Soon, I expect to see—yet again—frightened families in loaded-down wagons fleeing for safety to God-knows-where. Already, I've seen one rumble out of town with a poor cow tethered to the back. I worry about Rachel and the children, especially Jack, hoping they can flee to a relative's house farther from the waterfront.

As the tide comes in, bringing with it more barrels and explosions, I finally make my way to the *Sentinel*. Amos is at Joseph Galloway's office, no doubt getting the latest on all the chaos.

Joshua and Tess are frantically packing up all the metal type. Soon, it'll be hauled to the Tinkleton estate for safekeeping.

The three of us discuss the likely possibilities. If the patriots come streaming in, they might raid the *Sentinel*, shutting down a pro-British paper and confiscating metal to melt down for bullets.

Or, as Tess points out, they might not be quite as practical as all that. "They might just decide to burn down everything they see," she says.

"What about Amos's books?" I ask.

"No time," she says.

I hadn't even thought about what I'd lose if the Porters' house went up in flames. Maybe *Robinson Crusoe*, and of course, the sequel Ethan gave me. Not to mention the cozy shelter provided me by a family I've grown to care about.

Ethan! I head for the coffeehouse to make sure he's all right. All the noise and tumult could surely send him into a state of nervous collapse.

But when I walk in, there's Ethan serving coffee to a cluster of men all buzzing about the commotion at the river.

"Seems to be letting up," he says, without a trace of anxiety.

I'm relieved. "I was worried about you." He gives me a warm smile.

He leans in closer. "This has all the signs of Bushnell's handiwork," he says.

"Who?"

"David Bushnell," he says as if I should know. "He's a genius. Knows all about explosives. He's the one who secretly built a vessel just big enough for a man to navigate underwater and dispatch a bomb to an unsuspecting target. Damn near blew up a British ship in New York Harbor two years ago. I was there."

"Yes, I remember hearing about it," I say. "The *Turtle*. That's what they called it."

"He's the only one I know who could rig up an underwater exploding barrel," he says.

"But how?" I ask.

"He must have come up with a trigger mechanism to explode

gunpowder underwater and at a precise time. Ingenious!"

When I return to the *Sentinel*, Amos is back, now convinced the spectacle is only that—a spectacle.

"Some moron is spreading the word that rebels are hidden in the barrels to take the city by storm, like the Greeks in the Trojan horse," he says. "It's nonsense. No harm will come to us."

I tell him about David Bushnell and relate Ethan's theory.

"That goes along with what I heard from Galloway. He's scrambling to make sense of it," he says.

By the end of the day, we've gathered enough information to write an article.

"People are clamoring to know what in God's name that was all about," he says. "We need to publish a special edition. Joshua, Tess: unpack the type."

I set to work writing as fast as I can. Seems Bushnell's enthusiasm for blowing up things was only heightened after his near-miss in New York. He then devised a way to stuff a floating barrel full of gunpowder and have it go off when it struck something—like the hull of a British ship.

"Washington thought it was brilliant," Amos says. "So Bushnell built a hundred barrels, stuffed them with bombs, and released them into the Delaware at night."

"Sounds brilliant so far," I say.

"The kegs were supposed to float with the tide until they bumped into the British ships at anchor in the middle of the river."

"And then?"

"The ships weren't there. The damn rebels didn't know that they'd been moved to the docks because of all the ice chunks in the river. Galloway told me that," he says proudly.

It's all making sense to me now. "The ice slowed down the barrels," I say. At night, they would barely be seen. But when they floated by during the day, they were in plain sight for the British guns and those poor boys.

Amos is somber only for a moment. "The British unloaded every bit of ammunition they had. They annihilated a damn flotilla of barrels!"

Amos doesn't often laugh but now he's almost doubled over.

"It's too good," he says. "We'll call it The Battle of the Kegs."

In this week's editions and next, we write about the Battle of the Kegs. The patriots' ingenious plan gone awry, and the redcoats' brave fight against the vilest of foes: kegs. Amos gleefully points out that neither side covered itself in glory.

"The best kind of story," he tells me.

Then Francis Hopkinson, a signer of the Declaration of Independence, pens a delicious poem about it, advising that it be sung to the tune of "Yankee Doodle." Hopkinson takes special aim at General William Howe and his notorious affair with the beautiful Mrs. Loring.

Of course we run the poem in its entirety, making note of Amos's favorite lines:

Sir William he, snug as a flea,
Lay all this time a snoring;
Nor dreamt of harm, as he lay warm
In bed with Mrs. Loring.
Now in a fright he starts upright,
Awak'd by such a clatter;
First rubs his eyes, then boldly cries,
"For God's sake, what's the matter?"

"It's done wonders for morale at Valley Forge," Amos tells me. "I hear the bloody rebels are singing it around the campfire."

For young Jack there was nothing funny about the exploding kegs. After all, his friends died and he very nearly could have gone as well. At dinner, Jack reproaches me for my lighthearted newspaper tales about the "Battle of the Kegs."

"My friends warranted barely a mention. You didn't even

list their names—Samuel Zachary Davenport and Daniel David Davenport, by the way. I've seen you use full names in articles about some poor family looking for their lost dog."

I can't defend myself. "It was a terrible lapse," I say, knowing that will hardly suffice. "I'm sorry."

Rachel has tried her best to help him get over the terrible shock. Emma urged him to write about it in a letter to his father. But Rachel confided to me later that she couldn't bring herself to include the letter in her weekly bundle of goods for Charles.

"Poor dear has enough to worry about without fretting over Jack's terrible news."

Instead, she keeps urging her poor son to thank the Lord for keeping him on the dock when his friends ventured into the river.

"You can make your life a tribute to the boys who weren't as fortunate," she says, though I doubt anyone at the table had the foggiest idea what she meant.

"I should have gone with them," Jack says, fighting tears. "I might have saved them."

"I doubt it Jack," the Major says. "The rebels didn't intend that anyone survive their mischief."

Emma nods approvingly, and I flinch. There's something about the Major that galls me, and it's not that he's a damn redcoat. And it's not that he's Emma's lover.

I glower at him. "I don't think the patriots intended to kill two innocent boys."

He glowers back. "What makes you so sure?"

CHAPTER 31

Ethan keeps his word and takes me to the Southwark Theatre, which makes Emma envious but not enough to deny me her yellow silk gown. Emma and Abigail spend two hours turning the messy lion's den atop my head into a tall nest of braids, curls, feathers and ribbons.

"It's a miracle—a transformation," Emma told Ethan, who picked me up in his father's one-horse carriage.

"You look stunning," he tells me on the ride to the theater.

"So do you," I say, eyeing his white breeches, red velvet waistcoat and royal blue coat.

"Thanks to Rip," he says. "His togs. He was the one with good taste."

"To Rip." I toast him with imaginary champagne.

Rip was handsome as the devil. Ethan's allure is more subtle, quiet and charming. It's Ethan who makes me want to feel his body close. I'm glad I'm not wearing Tom's locket.

There's a cluster of carriages at the Southwark Theater—easy to spot with its red paint and rooftop cupola. The crowd is decidedly British, which makes Ethan uneasy.

"There's General Howe," I whisper, just as the heavily decorated officer helps the infamous Mrs. Loring out of an elegant carriage with elaborate carvings and gold-plated trim.

"That carriage belonged to Andrew Nelson, one of the banished Quakers," I tell Ethan. "Howe helped himself to it once Nelson was carted away."

"Damn redcoats! They're living it up here while the boys at Valley Forge are scavenging for food," Ethan mutters.

Inside the theater, built just 12 years ago, we take our seats under the candlelit chandeliers and oil lamps. In the balcony, I spot Joseph Galloway and his wife Grace, dripping with jewels.

"Handsome couple," Ethan whispers. "Not finding my brother's killer must pay quite nicely."

As the curtain opens on *The Wonder: A Woman Keeps a Secret*, our mood lightens. To my amazement, it was written by a woman, Susanna Centlivre, in 1714. It's a rollicking tale about a young woman who escapes an arranged marriage by jumping out a window.

Ethan turns to me and leans over. "Sounds like something you might do."

"I've done far worse. Someday I'll tell you."

I wish the play would never end. The lights, the laughter, my hand in Ethan's. I feel pretty and enjoy the appreciative looks I get from the men.

Our driver is waiting for us when it's over, and we pile into the carriage. It's cold and damp, but Ethan has thought to bring a blanket and we cuddle underneath. I hope this night never ends.

I want to tell him the truth about my "marriage," but I can't do it, not just yet. I can't ruin his image of me as the brave little widow. His arm wraps around my shoulder, and I resist the maddening urge to guide his hand over my body.

"I haven't told you everything about my time with Washington's men," he says, "but not on this lovely night."

"When the time is right," I say. The closest I've come to the ravages of war was seeing men with missing arms and legs, men out of their minds with pain, in the makeshift hospital at the Statehouse. I'm sure he's seen death up close. How many men has he killed? How many boys?

"Were there some good times?" I ask, trying to lighten the mood.

"Oh, yes," he says, brightening up. "I made some good friends. We had some laughs foraging for watermelons on Long Island in the dead of night. Some of them couldn't read or write so I wrote letters home for them. I had a reputation for heartfelt love letters."

"I believe it," I laugh. "I've seen your masterful penmanship."

"My mother was a Quaker and made sure Rip and I could write a legible hand," he says. "I was 12 when she died of pneumonia. Father did his best after that, but I still miss her, her laugh especially. Because Father wasn't a Quaker, her people shunned her after she wed. She never forgot and joyfully broke every one of their damn rules."

We arrive home, and he walks me to the door. I kiss him tenderly and whisper, "One day we'll tell each other our deepest secrets."

A week later, Agatha Nelson bangs on the front door after supper. Rachel answers with a worried look. "Come in Agatha. What's wrong?"

"It's about our men," she says, clutching an envelope. "I've received word from my dear husband."

"Come sit at the table," Rachel says. "I'll brew some tea. We have some pie left from supper."

"No, don't bother," Agatha says. "This is urgent, I'm sorry to say."

Emma and I share a look and linger over the dishes.

"It's terrible, terrible news," she says.

"Charles?"

"No, not Charles. It's Samuel Morton and Zeke Quimby. Both have died horribly, and we must tell their wives."

Rachel gasps. "What happened?"

"Samuel went first, after getting a violent cold. He lingered for weeks with a fever and grew weak. The men did their best to nurse him, but the Lord finally took him. And now it's just Elizabeth, with nine children to care for."

"Doesn't the Morton family own several mills?" I ask, trying not to seem as if I'm eavesdropping, which, of course, I am.

"Yes," she says, throwing a sharp glance my way. "So at least they'll have the means to go on, but without Samuel..."

"What about poor Zeke?" Rachel asks.

"It gets worse," Agatha says, and I quietly take a seat across from them. "Zeke had a leg wound that festered for weeks and turned black. The local doctor told him he'd die if the leg didn't come off above the knee. Being a pious man, he had faith that he'd survive."

Agatha closes her eyes. She's silent for a few seconds. When she resumes, her voice wavers.

"As I understand it," she says, "this so-called doctor was also the town drunk. He was practically falling down when he took the saw to Zeke's leg."

My stomach is churning at this tale. I picture Zeke, so pious he denies the offer of whiskey, screaming as the blade bears down. Rachel's face has gone white.

"Zeke survived for nine days but couldn't hold on any longer. He was 67 and even a younger man couldn't have endured."

"What will we tell poor Clara?" Rachel asks. "She'll want the truth."

"There's more," Agatha says, lowering her voice to a whisper that I can barely hear. "All the men are sickly in that godforsaken place."

"And Charles?" Rachel presses her hand to her temple. She must have one of her terrible headaches, and I wonder how much more she can take.

Agatha reaches out to grasp her hand. "My dear, it will work out. Charles is not among the most severely stricken but his condition is serious: Fever, a dull pain in his chest, and swelling in his side."

Rachel groans. "The children need not know about this." She shoots me an unmistakable look.

Agatha goes on to talk about her own husband. "He's got the rheumatism. They all have dreadful colds and fevers, and they have no medicines."

"They have to be freed soon or they'll all die," Rachel says.

"What about the appeals?" I ask. "They can't be held without charges forever."

"Sarah, our lawyers have flooded the courts with appeals," Rachel says. "They've even gone to the Continental Congress."

Agatha is more animated than I've ever seen her.

"Let's not forget the great George Washington," she practically spits. "He's rebuffed our men at every turn. He'll never be a friend to us."

I agree, but it doesn't come out that way. "He thinks Quakers are loyalists in sheep's clothing, aiding the British at every turn."

"Whose side are you on, Sarah?" Agatha snaps.

"I'm only citing what's in the Spanktown Papers."

"Lies! All of it, lies!" Agatha says.

"I believe you! I know they're lies!" I hadn't intended to say it, but I did. Really, I'm not sure what I know for sure and, more than anything, I don't want to get Ethan in trouble. Lacking any skill in the subtleties of conversation, I change the subject.

"Is there nothing that can be done for your men?"

"Before they all die?" Rachel says. "No."

I hear the anger in her voice—not something I'm accustomed to. She's always the voice of optimism and goodwill.

"There may be something you could do," I say, tossing out the seed of an idea that neither of them will like.

"Well, what is it?" Agatha says, as if I couldn't possibly have anything useful to say.

"The men's peace mission failed. Right? Didn't they get a chilly reception from the generals on both sides of the war?"

They nod.

"Why not launch one of your own?"

"A women's peace mission?" Rachel says, floored.

"Us, go to General Washington and plead our men's case?" Agatha says.

"Yes!"

There's dead silence for a half minute.

"The men would be against it," Rachel says with finality.

"Not only that," Agatha says. "Washington wouldn't allow it. He's busy with a war."

I rise from my chair, ready to head for bed. "What do you have to lose?"

CHAPTER 32

A FEW NIGHTS LATER, Major Hammond calls out to me when I tiptoe through the front door. It's late. I've been at a violin concert that put Ethan to sleep, and I'm taken aback.

"Sarah, come into my parlor, please." I note how he now calls it *my* parlor, but I choose not to quibble.

I take a seat hesitantly, and he closes the door.

"If this is about breaking curfew—"

"It's not." He takes a sip of rum. "Would you like some?"

"No, thank you. Is something wrong? Is Emma—"

"Nothing to do with Emma. I wanted you to be the first to learn: We've arrested the two soldiers who attacked you that night."

The words send a shock wave through my body. Suddenly, I feel dizzy.

"We'll do our best to make sure they pay mightily," he says, looking away. "British military law doesn't stand for the Crown's soldiers behaving like savages. If I have my way, they'll get a hundred lashes and die, the bloody bastards."

"That's good news," I say. He needn't know that I've imagined all the ways I could make them suffer. "I think about what happened all the time, especially when I'm out alone."

"You shouldn't be out alone, especially at night," he says in a gentle, fatherly tone.

"I can take care of myself," I say briskly.

"These are difficult times," he says.

"How do you know it's them?"

"They made the mistake of bragging about what they'd done," he says. "And what they would have gone on to do if you hadn't made short work of them."

"Swine!"

"Your detailed descriptions helped a great deal. Sam Hopkinson and Abe Jackson are their names. They were already known to us as rowdy drunkards not quite fit for service to the King."

I rise and thank him. "At least other women will be safe from them now."

Upstairs, I undress quietly so as not to wake Emma, who's snoring exuberantly.

With the quilt pulled tight around me, I can't sleep. I should be thrilled that those monsters were finally caught. But I can't summon any joy. I didn't tell the Major that the worst part was losing the baby—the baby I didn't want but eventually wanted more than life itself. For the first time in months, I sob silently into my pillow. I mourn for my daughter, for I'm sure it was a girl. I would have named her Caroline, after my grandmother.

The next day I tell Tess about the arrests, and she barely reacts.

"Aren't you happy for me?" I ask. "Those animals will get what they deserve—likely a hundred lashes, according to Major Hammond."

"I assume you know they have to be found guilty first," Tess says dryly. "The chances of that happening are not in your favor."

"With my testimony and the fact that they were stupid enough to brag about the attack, how could it go wrong? They *have* to be found guilty."

Tess rolls her eyes. "Sometimes your naivete astounds me. Don't you read the newspapers? The word of a woman will never hold sway over that of two men in service to the King."

For the first time, I'm struck by doubt that anything good will come of my ordeal.

"Surely they'll believe the word of an educated lady who works for Amos Tinkleton?"

Tess shrugs.

"By the time they finish with you, they'll have cast you as a wild tart with no means of her own."

Tess's words put a damper on my elation, and in my heart I know she's right. I have only to go to Lloyd's and witness the way men react to women, as if we're all brainless twits.

When I tell Amos about the arrests, he flies into action as if the patriots had just swept into town.

"Of course, we'll run an article about it. People will want to know." I would have felt better if that hadn't been his first reaction. But Amos is a journalist and a businessman before being a mere man.

He puts together an article brimming with outrage about the attack and gratitude for the arrests. He doesn't name me—he calls me a "young maiden"—but he does demand better policing on city streets.

"We can't have brutes and scofflaws roaming free to do whatever they wish," he writes, keeping out most of the bloody details. "Our city should be a beacon of civility and commerce during these difficult times."

I give him the highest praise I can: "Amos, I wouldn't change a word."

When I drop by the coffeehouse, Ethan's reaction is touching. "Are you alright?" he gently asks, taking my hand. "How do you feel about it?"

"I'm glad they're in custody," I say, "though now I'm worried no one will believe me when they go on trial. That's what Tess thinks. If they go free…"

"I saw what they did to you," he says. "It's a miracle you survived. I'll testify to that. Others will too. You won't be alone."

When I arrive home, Emma is hovering over Jack while he stumbles through his multiplication tables.

"I hate arithmetic," he moans.

"One day you'll thank me," Emma says. "We're almost done."

"Sarah, do you fancy a cup of tea before supper?" she says, then lowers her voice. "Or something stronger?"

"Yes, and yes," I answer. I'm still rattled by the arrests and welcome the chance to unleash my feelings.

"Let's go into the Major's parlor," Emma says. "He's gone for the evening, and I know where he stashes his rum."

"Emma, when did you become such a clever sneak?"

"When I started consorting with you," she laughs. "You've talked me into some, shall we say, dubious undertakings."

She pours two glasses.

"To us," I say, clinking our glasses. "May we undertake some more."

"No, thank you! The Major told me all about the charges. I'm sorry you have to go through all that."

"I'm not. I *want* those pigs to go on trial. I want to testify. I want people to know what they did."

"Not me," Emma says. "I'd sooner die than tell the world about it. It's too private."

"You mean you'd be embarrassed?" I ask.

"It's not just that."

"What is it then?"

"Your reputation. It would suffer."

"Oh, I see," I say. "The scandal! My prospects for marriage would be slim to none, right?"

"Well, I wouldn't put it quite like that."

"But that's what you mean. I'd be damaged goods. What man would possibly want me?"

This isn't what I expected from Emma.

"I was hoping you'd support me," I tell her. "Give me some encouragement."

"Of course I'll support you. You're my best friend," she says. "It's just not something I could or would do. And I'm being realistic."

"Emma, I don't give a fig whether I'm damaged goods in the marriage market."

"Well, that's the difference between us. If it's any consolation, I wish I were more like you."

"I'm stunned," I say. "You're the one who's always had boys lined up. It took you less than a week to work your magic on the Major.

He's totally smitten."

"As am I," she says. "I go weak when he touches me."

She laughs her big jolly laugh.

"I guess that means he does more than touch," I say.

"And it will only get better."

I give her a quizzical look. "What are you hiding, Emma?"

"The Major is taking over the back parlor for his men and their war business. That means he'll have one parlor all to himself—or rather, us."

"Does Rachel know?"

"She's not happy. But there's nothing she can do about it, given the quartering law."

"I wonder what the British are really up to..."

"In the winter?" she says. "Nothing! Soldiers don't do anything in the winter. They're busy with their plays and concerts and cockfights."

"Does the Major ever tell you anything?" I ask.

Emma groans. "I'm not going to spy on the man, if that's what you're asking. I'm done with your ludicrous schemes."

I strike a shocked pose. "I would never ask."

"He doesn't tell me anything, anyway," she says. "I've told him everything about myself, and—"

"Everything?" Emma has a loose tongue, especially after a few swigs of rum. "You didn't tell him about us tricking the British and rescuing Tom—"

"Of course not. I'm not a half-wit. I only told him about growing up in New Hampshire, the farm, my family. He knows my parents are patriots, but that didn't seem to bother him. He thinks I favor the British, and I haven't said otherwise."

"And has he told you all about himself?"

"He might be from New York. He talks about fighting there. Thank God he's older, more mature than the boys I've known. He doesn't feel he has to prove anything to me by bragging."

"That's all you know?"

"Yes, and I don't care to know more, so don't ask me to snoop around his quarters."

"I would never ask you to do that, but if you wanted to..."

CHAPTER 33

"My stomach is rejoicing," I tell Ethan.

We're dining at one of the fancy restaurants that's opened since the British took over the city. With goods flowing into the port, food shortages are a thing of the past. I sample turtle soup and Madeira wine and can barely contain my enthusiasm.

"How about dessert?" he asks. "Chocolate truffles, apricot pudding, almond cake?"

"I could easily become used to this."

"So could I—and I don't mean just the food," he says. "I'm very fond of you, Sarah Jordan."

Maybe it's the wine or the crackling fire or Ethan's easy company, but I let down my guard.

"I'm not Sarah Jordan."

Puzzled, he smiles. "What?"

"I'm Sarah Barrett. I've been wanting to tell you, but I was afraid."

"Afraid of what? Who is Sarah…Barrett?"

My tale comes tumbling out in fits and starts. "I'm not married, never was. Though I was in love with Tom Jordan and hoped we'd marry one day. We were planning on it, in a way."

I try to explain that it was easier and more acceptable to come to a new city as a married woman whose husband is away fighting in the war.

That makes all the sense in the world to me, but I can tell Ethan is struggling to understand. "So, the baby—if there was a baby—was Tom's."

"Yes. And there was definitely a baby!" I didn't expect this from Ethan. "When I was attacked, they didn't succeed in killing me, but they definitely killed my child."

I was holding myself together until this point, and now the tears flow. "Tom never knew about the baby, and now they're both gone."

"This is a lot to take in," he says. He reaches for his wine glass, and I see the tremor in his hand. "Do you still love this...Tom Jordan?"

"I do. Rather, I did. It's fading since I met you. I care so very deeply for you, Ethan."

"I love you, Sarah. At least I did, but now—well, now I don't know what to think. My head is spinning. Is there any more you've conveniently forgotten to tell me?"

"No...well, yes, a bit more." I tell him everything about the flaming arrow and my prowess as an archer—blowing up the ammunition stores in New Hampshire.

"That's why I fled to New York."

"Dare I ask what brought you to Philadelphia?"

At this point, there's no reason to hold back. I relate how I managed to rescue Tom and then my escape from the redcoats as I lay hidden in a casket.

"Who are you?" Ethan is completely baffled. "I thought I knew you. Turns out you have this whole other life that you waited until now to tell me about."

I've ruined everything. I should have known he'd react this way. "I can see you're put off by the truth. Shall we go?"

"Stunned by the truth is more like it," he says. "I'll need some time for all this to sink in."

He wraps my cloak around my shoulders, and we go out into the chilly, damp air. It's a solemn walk home, though he holds my hand the entire way. Perhaps all is not lost.

At the Porter house, he kisses me on the forehead. Choking back tears, I barely utter a thank you for the evening.

Inside I hear the buzz of conversation and find Rachel is hosting a few Quaker wives.

"Come in, Sarah," she says. I want nothing more than to slink off to bed for a good cry and now I've lost even that.

"Please, sit down." There's urgency in Rachel's voice as she hands me a cup of tea.

"We've received more bad news about our men," Agatha Nelson says.

"Another death?" I ask with trepidation.

"Not yet," Agatha says. "But our hopes that they'd be freed after the new year have been dashed. In a supreme act of stupidity, Pennsylvania's Assembly has voted to extend their exile by six months."

"I'm not sure Charles can survive that long," Rachel says. "He's not a young man."

"They're all doing poorly," Agatha says quietly. "My husband is nearly crippled from rheumatism."

"Are they still being held without charges?" I ask.

They all burst into angry assent.

"It's illegal," I say. "And indecent."

"All they want is to keep our men jailed without giving them their day in court," Mary Pearson chimes in. "That's indecent indeed."

Rachel, as their unofficial leader, talks about all the letters of protest they've written to General Washington and all the papers their lawyers have filed.

"All to no avail," she says. "Sarah, I told the others about your suggestion that we wives go to General Washington's camp and plead our case."

For the first time, I see the women mobilizing as efficiently as a military unit, with Rachel and Agatha leading the charge.

"We think it's a good idea," Agatha says. "Though it means traveling through dangerous territory in the midst of a war."

"And we've decided not to tell our men about it," Rachel says.

"For fear they'll say no?" I ask.

Rachel looks uneasy. "It's more to spare them the worry about our welfare."

I smile to myself. But I want to cheer for women everywhere.

"You'll need to write an eloquent appeal to Washington," I say. "I can help you with that."

"Good!" Agatha says. "We should do it without lawyers."

After a sleepless night of worry about Ethan, I force myself out of bed and into my clothes. Emma's bed is empty and doesn't look slept in. How long before Rachel notices and raises a ruckus?

My head is pounding so I forgo breakfast and head straight for the coffeehouse. I want to see if Ethan hates me as much as I fear.

I walk in hesitantly, and he seems surprised.

"Oh, good morning, Sarah. The usual?"

"Yes. Strong as you have it."

After a long silence, he leans in. "I hear something is afoot in Rip's murder case. Galloway was in this morning and asked me if Rip was wearing a gold pocket watch that night. Told him I couldn't imagine it. He wasn't the type for fancy baubles."

"How strange," I say. But no stranger than Ethan not mentioning my sudden bout of truth-telling last night.

"Maybe you can ask around," he says, avoiding my eyes.

"Does that mean we're partners again—at least in the business of investigation?"

He smiles slightly. "Yes, business partners."

I leave feeling hopeful that I haven't destroyed everything with him.

At the *Sentinel*, I ask Amos about Rip's murder.

"Haven't heard a thing, and I saw Galloway yesterday about those damn Quakers. Seems they'll be held even longer."

"Yes, I know. Maybe it's time for another article about how wrong it is. Held since September without any charges. It's criminal. Literally."

"Not so fast," he says, lighting his pipe. "Galloway doesn't want an article. And I'm quite sure Washington doesn't either."

Pleading with Amos is a fool's errand, but I forge ahead. "People need to know that it's illegal."

He gives me a condescending look. "Nobody cares except Quakers. Neither side has any use for people who hide under the cloak of religion. They won't pay taxes! They won't even donate blankets. It's pure selfishness. Everyone knows they've got the money."

"But—"

"For God's sake, no one's asking them to carry a musket and march off to war."

I'd rather have a tooth yanked out than agree with him, but he does make sense. Especially when I think of what Tom and Ethan have sacrificed.

"Amos, you don't live with a Quaker family like I do," I say. "They really believe in all this nonviolence talk—they're not pretending. Two of the hostages—that's what they are—have already died horrible deaths. Most of them are elderly and ailing."

"Spare me your tears," he says. "All they have to do is pledge allegiance to the patriot cause, and they'll be released. They can go home to their families."

"You know they won't do that," I argue. "That violates their beliefs."

He draws on his pipe. "Then they'll have to grow fonder of jail in the wilds of western Virginia."

"Not so fast," I say, mimicking him. "The wives have a plan that could bring their husbands home."

"The wives? What could they possibly do?" He puts his pipe down.

Finally, I have his attention. "They're going to pay General Washington a visit."

"They can't do that," he says. "That's absurd. Don't they know Washington is a little busy fighting a war?"

"Don't underestimate these women," I say, smiling.

He smiles back at me. "Don't underestimate their husbands. They would never allow this."

CHAPTER 34

ETHAN'S NOTE IS MYSTERIOUS.

Joseph Galloway has asked to see me and my father about Rip. He wants us to come to his office at 2 o'clock today. And he said you might want to be there as well.

How would Galloway know I have a special interest in Rip? Simply because I went to his funeral? We were friends, nothing more.

Of course, I'm there at 2 o'clock when Ethan and his father step into Galloway's ornate parlor.

"What's this about?" I ask them.

"Perhaps they've made some progress in the case," Ethan says.

"Whatever it is, it won't bring back my boy," old Mr. Ripley says, as he puts on his spectacles and surveys the oil paintings lining the walls.

After a few minutes, Galloway's assistant ushers us into his office.

"Thank you all for coming on such short notice," Galloway says, rising behind his enormous desk. "But I think you'll be gratified." He's dressed as if he's going to the opera—velvet waistcoat with rows of velvet-covered buttons, lacy white cravat, perfectly groomed wig.

Ethan looks uncomfortable in such elegant surroundings. He rubs his hands together, something I've noticed he does when he's ill at ease.

"I wanted you to be the first to learn that we've found Robert Ripley's killers," Galloway says.

Ethan gasps, then smiles.

"That is good news! Isn't it, Father? Who are the savages who did this to my brother?" he asks.

"Sam Hopkinson and Abe Jackson, the two redcoats who attacked you, Mrs. Jordan."

I can't believe what I've just heard. "How can that be?"

"We're certain of it," Galloway says. "And Major Hammond has assured me that those men will pay with their lives. Of course, they'll have their legal rights, but we've got them cold."

"How do you know it's them?" I ask. "What proof do you have?"

"Let us worry about that, Mrs. Jordan," Galloway says.

"We would all like to know the damning evidence you have," Ethan says.

I smile broadly at Galloway, who seems taken aback.

"We found Rip's gold pocket watch engraved with his initials *R.R.* in their belongings after they were arrested for the assault," he says. "Seems they bragged about it, just as they did the beating they gave you, Mrs. Jordan."

"This is certainly welcome news," Mr. Ripley says, rising from his chair. "I can finally put the boy to rest. Thank you for your diligence. We'll take our leave now."

With the matter all but closed, Ethan and I stand as well, though an uneasy look passes between us.

On the walk back Ethan is silent. Finally, he clears his throat. "Father, I don't recall Rip having a pocket watch, much less a gold one."

"I don't either but that's not to say he didn't," the elder Ripley says as we walk. "We didn't know every detail about him. The matter is done. Let's thank God for that."

Despite his father's relief, Ethan can't let it go. "But, if—"

"I said it's done. Not another word, son."

I'm not about to raise my questions. We walk the rest of the way in silence.

At the *Sentinel*, Amos gleefully anticipates running an article about the murder charges against Hopkinson and Jackson.

"I love a good hanging," he says, "and so do our readers. This is much better than yet another sob story about the poor Quakers."

I don't tell him about my reservations. He's in no mood to hear.

Most of all, I can't bear to see another hanging. The last one nearly killed me. That was in New York when the British learned one of their most trusted officers, Dan Pritchard, was a spy for the patriots. Without his help, I couldn't have rescued Tom from the prison ship.

And it didn't help that Emma was in love with Dan. Before Dan, she was infatuated with my brother Seth back in Essex. Now he's dead too. I don't blame Emma for thinking I'm the source of her bad luck.

I help Amos write the article, though he embellishes it beyond anything I would do. He's so excited, he spills ink down the front of his waistcoat.

"Tess!" he yells.

Tess comes running in as if he's scalded himself. "What is it, sir?"

Pointing to the dribbled ink, he barks an order: "Get me a fresh one!"

She dashes out, and after a moment, I follow.

"Tess," I whisper. "If I were you, I'd take my time getting another waistcoat."

She wheels around. "You're not me, are you?"

I see the anger in her eyes and know I've overstepped my bounds, again. "I'm sorry, Tess. I'm an idiot."

Why do I always say the wrong thing? After an eternity, she finally responds.

"No, you're not an idiot. It's that thoughtless tongue of yours. Flapping again."

I laugh, and she smiles ever so slightly.

"Amos asked me how our reading lessons were coming along," I say. "I told him you're a fast learner. That you'd be reading Shakespeare by the end of the year."

"Ha! I've already read *Romeo and Juliet*—from his library." She grows serious. "How much longer do you think we can carry on this ruse? The man is not an imbecile."

"No, he certainly isn't, but it'll be such fun to see his reaction when he realizes you're so much more than the charwoman he beds down whenever he feels the urge."

"No, it won't. No one likes to find out he's been made a fool of," she says, heading for the stairs to fetch Amos his fresh clothing.

Arriving home late, I eat supper in the kitchen with Molly, who shares what's left of a rabbit stew and a hunk of rye bread.

"Delicious!" I say. "I don't know how you do it. Preparing edible food is a complete mystery to me."

"It's all I've ever done," she says. "And it's getting to be a damn sight harder since the Major and his cronies arrived. They eat like they've been starved half to death. And they go through more whiskey than an Irish wake."

I let her go on for a while. Molly knows everything that goes on in this house. Nothing escapes her critical eye.

"Last night there were ten of them, and Mrs. Porter said they kept her awake until midnight. Poor thing is trying to meet with her lady friends. And Emma—the teacher for pity's sake—is carrying on with the Major right under her nose."

"I have some news of my own," I say. "The same men who attacked me also killed Rip Ripley from the coffeehouse. Sam Hopkinson and Abe Jackson. Galloway told us they'll hang for it."

"Those drunken fools?

"Galloway says they found Rip's pocket watch in the men's belongings," I say, taking the last spoonful of stew.

Molly pops a bit of bread into her mouth. "Only an idiot would hang onto a murdered man's pocket watch. Those two had better start praying for God's mercy."

Emma is upstairs brushing her long, blond hair, when I walk into our bedroom. "I thought you'd be with the Major, now that you have your own little love nest."

She gives me a pouty look. "He's huddled with his men—war business."

"What's going on?" I ask.

"No idea, and I don't care," she says.

"I suppose the Major told you they've solved Rip's murder," I say.

"Yes, I heard. I guess we can expect another awful public hanging."

"I'm not so sure."

She gives me a wary look. "What are you up to?"

"I don't know just yet."

"Well, don't even think about dragging me into it."

"You know me too well, Emma."

We laugh like schoolgirls but, as happens so often these days, I ruin the moment.

"But really, Emma," I ask. "How much do you actually know about this Major John Hammond?"

"Can't you leave well enough alone?" Emma says, putting on her nightgown. "Just when I find someone I love, you ruin it for me."

She plops onto the bed. "Well, not this time. The Major is a good man, and I do believe he loves me."

I don't want to start an argument, but I can't stop myself.

"How do you know? Has he told you? Has he asked for your hand in marriage?"

"I just know," she says. "He wouldn't lead me on this way if he didn't have the best intentions."

As I blow out the candle, I bid her goodnight. Emma is so bright but so naïve.

As I lie there in the dark, I think about Ethan, his arms around me, our bodies pressed together, doing all the things I'm sure Emma does nightly with the Major.

But Ethan, I fear, has no interest in rekindling our brief, beautiful romance.

CHAPTER 35

The next morning, I arrive at the *Sentinel* to find another curious note from Ethan.

Sarah,

I wish to discuss Rip's murder with you. Please stop by the coffeehouse after work today.

Ethan Ripley

Cold and businesslike. There's no, *My dearest Sarah*. Not even a *Yours truly, Ethan*. I send back an equally impersonal note agreeing to the meeting.

The day is painfully slow. I'm anxious to find out if Ethan has an ounce of affection for me. And another worry haunts me: What if the two redcoats are wrongfully hanged, and Rip's killer is still out there?

When Amos sees me daydreaming, he orders me to write an article about three new apothecaries in town. It's a nod to the British, showing our readers how prosperous their takeover has made the city. More importantly for Amos, it's a source of new advertising.

I slog through it, though I'm amused to learn that one of the apothecaries also offers home services: bloodletting and tooth pulling. Finally, I hand it to Amos for his inspection.

"This will do," he says, stunning me with faint praise. "I'm pleased you're able to keep up with your chores here while you help Tess learn to read. Won't be easy—teaching a grown woman from her background. Could take years for her to learn her letters."

"Oh, I doubt that," I say. "She's determined."

His words surprise me, but under the kindness I sense a different message: If Tess were white, the job would be easier. I can't wait to see his face when Tess emerges from her cocoon as an articulate scholar.

Mercifully, the day ends and I walk briskly to the coffeehouse. A cold drizzle hangs in the air, but people are afoot and carriages rumble by with smartly dressed couples headed to the ball at King's Tavern. The tavern is one of the *Sentinel's* new advertisers, a feat Amos is still crowing over.

At the coffeehouse, Ethan greets me hurriedly. "I just have to finish closing up. Go upstairs and wait for me."

No *Good evening, Sarah. How are you?* I muse over how rapidly our relationship has soured.

I climb the stairs. In the parlor, I thumb through a book on shipbuilding. It's full of sketches and numbers and details about the world's most durable shipbuilding woods. It seems he's serious about wanting to learn the trade. How long will it be before he leaves the coffeehouse and pursues his dream, forgetting I ever existed?

Finally, I hear his hurried footsteps on the stairs. "Sarah, can I get you some cider?"

"Yes, thank you," I say, keeping up the air of formality.

Finally, he sits down across from me—not beside me, as he would have in happier times.

"I haven't slept a wink since the murder charges were filed," he says.

I nod, letting him continue.

"I've riffled through Rip's old room looking for any sign, like a receipt, showing he ever owned a pocket watch. Nothing. I even stopped by a couple of watchmakers' shops to see if they remembered Rip buying one. No luck."

"Hmm. Rip didn't seem the sort for niceties like that."

"I doubt he'd ever part with that much money for anything but a musket," he says. "What he cared about most was joining Washington's men and crushing the redcoats."

"And he never had a chance to do it."

"Thanks to me," Ethan says. "Me and my troubles." He offers a rueful smile. "So if these two simpletons didn't kill Rip, who did?"

"My question exactly," I say. "You told me a while back that it probably had something to do with the Spanktown Papers and the Quakers and General Sullivan."

"Yes," he says, biting his lip nervously. "I've wanted to talk with you about that."

"You thought the papers were made-up," I say. "Do you have proof?"

"Yes."

"Well, for God's sake what is it?"

He looks at the floor for several seconds and then straight into my eyes.

"I was the one who wrote the Spanktown Papers. I penned them as Sullivan's lackey stood over my shoulder, telling me what to write."

"You?" I start to laugh but he's dead serious.

He nods slowly but I'm still in shock.

"You wrote those documents incriminating the Quakers? The ones that got them ripped from their homes? Did they threaten you with a beating or was it your fine penmanship?"

"It was an order," he calmly says. "I presume it came from Sullivan. Who else? Carried out by his fanatically loyal aide. I've forgotten his name, but I'll never forget that bastard's face. He knew I wanted to go home after my injuries at Staten Island. He told me I'd be branded a deserter if I didn't carry out the order. He hardly had to tell me that the ultimate punishment for deserters was hanging."

Tears pool in his eyes. "I should have told you earlier, but I was so ashamed."

Suddenly I realize he'd been in a life-or-death struggle he couldn't possibly win. I was too quick to judge.

"It's not your fault," I say, reaching for his hand. "You were following an order."

"I wanted to tell the truth and get the poor Quakers set free, but I was afraid."

"Afraid of what?"

"Afraid no one would believe the ramblings of a mere soldier driven mad by his war wounds. Even now, it's my word against Sullivan's."

I stand behind him and rub his shoulders but he's inconsolable.

"It should have been me with my throat cut," he sobs.

I kiss the top of his head. "I'm glad it wasn't you. Carrying this secret could drive a person mad. What a terrible burden."

He wipes his eyes and manages a weak smile. "So, as I think about it, Mrs. Jordan, how can I fault you for concocting a little thing like a husband?"

We sit in merciful silence for a minute.

"No more lies." I say. "Agreed?"

"Agreed!"

We shake hands, smiling. Then he wraps his arms around me and we hold tight for what seems an eternity. Finally he kisses me on the lips—a long, tender kiss that I cling to until he breaks away.

"I almost forgot. You, being a clever one, will appreciate this," he says. "When I penned the letter, I left clues that would tell anyone it wasn't written by a Quaker."

"Clues? Clues that would exonerate the Quakers?"

He nods with a big smile. "Quakers never use actual days of the week or the month by name. They say 9th month, 6th day. Something about not using names derived from pagan gods."

"Of course, you would know that. Your mother was a Quaker."

"I dropped in other inconsistencies," he says. "My way of getting the truth out."

"Aren't you the clever one," I murmur.

"Not clever enough to solve Rip's murder. Now we're back to where we started."

"We're a team, remember?" I say. "We'll figure it out."

"Could have just been a robbery gone wrong," he ventures.

"Enough detective work for now," I say.

We lock in a long embrace. Maybe it's the cider, but I feel such a passionate longing for this sandy-haired man that I press my body against his.

"Is the time right?" he whispers.

"The time is most definitely right."

CHAPTER 36

I DECIDE TO KEEP my silence about Ethan's revelation, for now. Emma would blab it to Major Hammond, who would not be pleased to see Rip's murder case unravel. After all, the Major received high praise from Joseph Galloway for finding the killers and could be in line for a promotion when the pair are hanged.

Ethan and I must work fast, but Amos isn't giving me a moment's peace. He dined with Galloway and his wife at King's Tavern last night, and the city's loyalist leader insisted he knew best how the Brits could win the war quickly.

"Attack Valley Forge, that's what he said," Amos tells me. "With Washington's troops so crippled, Howe should swoop in there as soon as possible. Winter be damned!"

I didn't bother to raise the very points that Amos had made himself in the past few weeks: The winter is hobbling the British too. Supply lines to yet another battlefield would be tough to establish. In some spots, cannon would be virtually impossible to haul.

"So, he wants you to back this terrible idea?" I ask. "With a convincing piece in the *Sentinel*?"

"Yes." He slowly fills his pipe and lights it with a splinter of wood lit from a candle Tess brings over.

"Washington's men couldn't possibly mount a defense," I say. "They're an army without shoes."

"Exactly. It would be a brutal end, but a quick one. And Galloway says that's better than letting it drag on for years with more dead soldiers and more anguish for the families."

I picture Tom at Valley Forge, half-starved and freezing when the redcoats pounce. Of course, I know Tom is dead. But so many others are hanging on. An attack would be a massacre.

Amos is sucking hard on his pipe. I can tell he's torn.

"If Galloway thinks an attack is such a brilliant idea," I ask, "why doesn't he talk to General Howe? He's the one to decide."

"Howe is stalling," Amos says. "He's hesitant to attack in the winter. He told Galloway that attacking in a blizzard would be a waste of gunpowder. He said to just let the winter do its work."

"They're only fair-weather fighters?"

"Something like that," he says.

I remind Amos that the Brits' Howe has not covered himself with glory lately. In fact, I boldly tell him, he's mostly covered himself with the beautiful Mrs. Loring.

"I wonder if he's too busy for battle squiring her to every social event in town," I say, only half-joking. Howe does nothing to hide his affair, and it's the talk of Philadelphia.

"What are you going to do? About an article?" I ask, figuring he'll write whatever twaddle Galloway feeds him.

Amos surprises me. "Nothing just yet."

But then I remind myself: Amos is ever the businessman. I'm sure he's weighing the paper's potential profits should the war end quickly with a British victory.

He surprises me yet again. "I don't like Galloway getting me to do his dirty work."

I wonder if he's letting his true colors come through. Underneath it all, maybe he's a patriot at heart.

I run this by Tess as she's in the library dusting.

"The man is perplexing," Tess says. "You'll never guess what he did last night."

"Tell me, tell me."

"After I made his dinner, I was cleaning up. He came to me and said, 'Tess, this is for you.'"

"What was it?" I ask, intensely curious.

"A book."

"A book?"

"Not just any book. *The New England Primer*. He said it might help me learn my letters."

I explode in laughter. "A primer? For children just learning to read? Wait until he finds out you've devoured Thomas Paine's *Common Sense*."

"Don't you dare laugh," she chides. "I think it's sweet. He's making an effort."

I tell her all about Ethan and our efforts to find Rip's killer. I don't leave anything out.

"You like this young man," she says.

I say nothing, but I don't have to.

"Be careful, very careful," she says. "You can't live on the edge forever. Eventually you'll go over."

"Oh Tess, you're too cautious."

She doesn't seem to appreciate my sudden, devil-may-care attitude.

"I have to be cautious," she says, without the hint of a smile.

Major Hammond and two of his men join us for supper, and we crowd around the table while Molly, grimacing, serves up sparse portions of succotash and rye bread.

"We'll make it stretch, won't we Molly," Rachel says, clearly trying to lighten the mood. "The Major and his men have been good enough to supply us with game whenever they can."

"Yes ma'am," Molly says, forcing a ridiculous grin.

"I think we should help each other as much as possible," the Major says as he turns toward Rachel.

Emma rolls her eyes.

"I agree," Rachel says. "In fact, there is something I'd like from you. It concerns my Charles and the other Quaker gentlemen banished by the patriots."

"Terrible injustice there," he says. His men murmur their assent.

"It's criminal!" Rachel practically shouts. "Captives since

September, and they've never been charged with a crime. All their appeals have done no good. Our dear ones are suffering. They need medicine. Two have already died."

She looks to me, and I silently encourage her to go on.

"Sarah has suggested that we wives travel to Valley Forge and demand to see General Washington. We've tried every other way we know to plead for our husbands' freedom."

"That's quite an extraordinary mission," the Major says. "Especially for a group of women, and with a war going on."

"That's where we can use your help," Rachel says.

I can't help but chime in. "They'll need help with the permits to leave the city and travel through the war zone. Surely you can ease their way."

Gertrude practically levitates with anger.

"This is the first I've heard of this," she growls. "You're certainly not going, Rachel. Not with a baby and young children to tend."

"Yes, I am," Rachel says.

"But it's too dangerous," Gertrude says. "The British are going to attack Valley Forge any day now. Isn't that right, Major Hammond?"

The Major is on his third glass of whiskey and, as usual, wants to demonstrate his cozy connections with the redcoats' top brass.

"I've heard all the talk," he says. "Joseph Galloway is telling anyone who'll listen that an attack will end the war. But I'll let you in on a little secret."

We all stop eating and lean in.

"General Howe isn't going to order an attack on Valley Forge," he says. "The general told me himself. It seems Washington made a brilliant move when he picked that spot. It's high up and treeless, not easy to attack."

"Is that so?" Gertrude says, warily.

"Also, he's certain that Washington has more men in fighting shape than we've been led to believe—that they're not nearly the ragtag, barefoot army we've heard about. And that's exactly the word we get from our spies—that is to say, our agents in the field."

What a relief! As much as I've seen cruelty from the patriots—such as the very banishment we've been talking about—I desire a continuation of British rule far less. But I keep those thoughts to myself.

"That's good to hear," Rachel says. "So you'll help us with the permits?"

"I'll do that," he says. "But I don't think it's wise for you women to travel that far without men to keep you safe. Perhaps they could also help you make your case to Washington."

"No!" Rachel and I blurt out together.

"That's exactly the point," Rachel says, locking eyes with me. "This is a women's mission. That's the only way it can work."

After a moment's silence, she says, simply, "The men have failed. We think we can do better."

Later in our room, Emma makes it clear that she opposes it.

"I think it's a fool's errand," she says. "If the men, the lawyers, can't free the Quakers, what makes you so sure the women can?"

"The women are more eloquent about describing how hard the banishment has been on families. You can't deny that."

"It's not like the men are locked in dungeons with only bread and water," she says. "They're even allowed to go to worship services."

"Rachel doesn't know anything for certain," I say. "Charles's letters have stopped coming. That's another reason she's so desperate."

"Desperate!" She practically spits out each syllable. "Tom fought for his life every day he was on that hellish prison ship, and many of his comrades didn't make it. That's what I would call desperate."

Hearing Tom's name shakes me for a moment. But I have to remind myself yet again that he was Emma's brother and she misses him as much as I do. I try to tread lightly.

"No, it's nothing like Tom's imprisonment. But they're still prisoners of a war they haven't fought. Don't you want to see Rachel and the wives succeed?"

"Of course I do," she bristles.

"Then what is it?"

"All right, I'll tell you. If Rachel leaves for a week, or God knows how long, I'll be here with five children including a baby," she says.

"There's no way Gertrude will stay and help. She's made it clear what she thinks about the idea. It will be me and the children, day and night. I don't know if I can do that, even with your help."

"Hmm. I see your point."

This is no time to tell her that I won't be here either. That is, if I can convince Rachel to let me accompany them. And if I can talk her friends into accepting a much younger woman who isn't even a Quaker. And finally, if I can talk Amos into printing the story of anti-war women braving battlefield conditions to meet with the infamous General Washington.

Sleep won't come easily. Even if Amos grudgingly lets me proceed, Washington could well refuse to see these gentlewomen. They could be imprisoned for even trying.

No, there will be no sleep tonight.

CHAPTER 37

MILITARY OFFICIALS ANNOUNCED THEY'D set Feb. 12 for the hanging of Sam Hopkinson and Abe Jackson.

The men offered no credible defense at their court martial. Galloway summed it up for Amos over a steaming shepherd's pie at his home: "We had the deceased's pocket watch and statements from witnesses in the jail. They're guilty as sin."

The next morning Amos is eager to run an article. "Should be a good crowd at the hanging," he tells me. "Readers will want souvenir editions. Taverns will all do a brisk business. Of course you'll want to be there."

"No, I won't," I say emphatically.

"Why not? I thought you'd be pleased to see the men who attacked you—practically killed you—hanging by the neck," he says with a smile that sickens me.

"I hate them, but I'm not convinced they killed Rip over a pocket watch. If there's the slightest doubt, I can't bear to see them hang."

"There isn't the slightest doubt," Amos says. "Galloway and your friend Major Hammond agree. A pocket watch like that could fetch some money for a couple of fools who don't have any. It all makes sense to me."

"Wouldn't they have sold it right away—not held onto it for months?" I ask.

I can see I've irritated him. He's arranging the ink bottles on his desk in perfect rows. Finally, he speaks.

"If you're so smart," he says, in his precise way, "Who was it? Who killed this fellow with no known enemies and good will toward all?"

"I don't know."

"There. You see? Enjoy the hanging."

I walk away in disgust and join Tess outside. She's sweeping the walkway with such vigor the tiniest grain of sand doesn't have a chance.

I startle her with a simple question: "How can you put up with that man?"

"What's he done now?"

"He has the compassion of a snake," I say. "He finds a hanging entertaining."

"Come inside before you catch your death of cold," she says, grabbing my hand. "I want to show you something."

In the hallway, she pulls a tattered clipping from her sleeve. It's an advertisement from the *Virginia Gazette* for a missing slave girl.

"I'm certain it's my daughter Dinah. She's alive!"

Then she starts to read:

Runaway slave

Girl, goes by the name Dinah, absconded from the household of Doctor Balcom in Williamsburg, Virginia. Small of stature, about 10 years old, may be making her way to Philadelphia. Girl is clever, knows her letters and—

I see Amos walking up behind Tess.

"Tess!" I whisper.

"Hush! There's more," she says, oblivious to his looming presence.

And she is cunning, having run away several times previously. She is light-skinned with a small scar shaped like a half-moon on her right arm—"

"Tess!" I scream. "Amos—"

Tess turns, sees him, and lets out a little whimper.

"So, you can't read!" he jeers. "I heard every word, perfectly enunciated."

"Mister Tinkleton, I'm—"

"Sorry?" he suggests. "Sorry for deceiving me like an old fool?"

Tess is paralyzed, unable to speak.

"I can explain," I stumble, with no idea what to say next.

"And you," he says. "You were part of this fraud. You probably engineered it."

"What are you going to do?" Tess asks softly, terrified.

I know what she's thinking: Her previous owners were quick with the whip. But Amos would never go that far.

"It's my fault," I say. "Don't blame Tess. I talked her into it."

"I might have known."

"You don't have to fire me, Amos," I say. "I'll just go. I'll go right now."

I've never been more ashamed. As usual I've made a mess of things. I have no clue how I'll support myself. But worst of all, I've made everything worse for Tess.

Suddenly the rage on Amos's face turns into an odd smile, and he breaks into a bout of laughter that brings tears to his eyes.

"The look on your faces! You should have seen it."

"What's so funny?" I ask.

"I've known all along about your little game," he says, pulling out a handkerchief to blow his nose. "It was such fun to see the lengths that you two would go to just to pull the wool over my eyes."

My shame turns into confusion. To think, we've been had by the most insufferable man I know. Tess is still in shock.

"Just when did you figure out Tess could read?" I ask.

"Tess," he says, turning to her, his voice softer. "You made a little mistake."

"What mistake?" she asks uneasily.

"I had a hunch. So just before Christmas I asked you to look for a book missing from my library. I believe it was—"

"*The Vicar of Wakefield* by Oliver Goldsmith," Tess says without hesitation. "You thought maybe it was somewhere in the building."

"You located it and brought it to me. 'Found it out by the privy,' you said so proudly."

Tess looks uneasy now.

He smiles. "You found it right where it was supposed to be in the library. It wasn't missing at all. That's when I knew."

"So you let us make fools of ourselves," I say.

"Yes!" Amos is practically dancing, but Tess is still scared.

"What are you going to do with me?" she mumbles.

"I don't know," he says. "I've never employed a Negro who could read. What will you want next? Higher wages? It's a slippery slope, and I'll have to think on it. In the meantime, go back to your chores."

He utters not one word about Tess's daughter. The man has no heart.

"And me?" I ask, wondering what's going through his devious mind.

"You!" he laughs. "The master conspirator. I can't thank you enough for the joy you've given me today."

I'm bewildered. Is he toying with me? Setting the stage for more humiliation?

"I think you've suffered enough recently," he says, brushing a thread from his waistcoat. "I know how much you want to attend the hangings, despite your avowals to the contrary."

"No, I—"

"So as your punishment for this little scheme, I'll go in your place. I'll write it and capture all its glory. It'll be the social event of the season. I want to get a place right up front so I can see their sweaty brows and hear the snap of their necks."

I can't wait to get home and tell Emma everything about my day: the upcoming hanging, the trick Amos played, the newspaper notice about Tess's daughter. If I had even a shred more to convey, I'd burst!

But Emma is in no mood to hear my news. The children are running amok, and I find her sitting forlornly by the window in our room.

"What's wrong?" I ask. Her eyes are red from crying, not a sight

I'm accustomed to, and I'm worried. "Tell me."

"Major John Hammond…is married," she says in a voice dripping with disgust. "He's got four children."

I'm surprised but not shocked. He's always been so secretive, and Emma has managed to brush it off. But now, she's dumbstruck.

"He deceived me," she says. "I thought I had struck gold."

"Did he lie about it to you? Or was it more an omission of pertinent information?" I ask.

"He didn't tell me anything," she says, her voice rising. "I had to find out myself."

"How?"

"I was alone with him in his parlor when he left to visit the privy," she says. "I swear I wasn't spying, but I found a half-written letter to his wife under a book on his desk. It was addressed to *My dearest Mary*."

"Could be his sister," I say, hopefully.

"It's not his sister." She spits out the words. "The first line made reference to *our four young ones and how much he misses everyone*."

I want to congratulate Emma on her intelligence efforts, but I know not to trifle with her.

"How could I be so blind? I thought there was a good chance we'd marry. Who knows, maybe the redcoats will win this damnable war. Then we'd be sitting pretty."

"They can't," I rush to say. "I mean, I don't want them to win."

"You're more of a patriot than I am."

"Well, Tom was a patriot," I remind her. "So was my brother Seth."

"I know all that. But does it really matter who wins? Will day-to-day life really change for anyone?"

"Of course it matters," I say. I give her a big, long hug as she gets up to deal with the wild children downstairs.

"Of course it matters," I repeat to myself as I lie awake hours later.

CHAPTER 38

THE NOTE ETHAN LEFT for me at the *Sentinel* sounds urgent.

Sarah,

I must see you. Could you come to the coffeehouse on Sunday after services? We'll be closed but I'll await you.

Ethan

I write back yes, of course.

Rachel thinks Emma and I go to Sunday services at Christ Church. Emma goes as a ruse to meet men. Most of the time, I veer off before we reach the church, opting for a walk unless the weather is stormy. Then I sit on a hard wooden pew and daydream about Ben Franklin and John Adams hatching revolutionary plans on that very spot.

Today it's cloudy and cold when I say goodbye to Emma at the church steps.

"Don't do anything idiotic," she says, knowing I'll be seeing Ethan.

I feign surprise. "Me?"

"You know what I mean. Trouble finds you like a bird dog on the scent."

"Good luck," I say. "May the church be filled with unattached men seeking salvation and the pleasure of a woman's company."

"That's not—oh, never mind," she says. "You are so irksome at times."

Walking to the coffeehouse, I pass the London Book Shop and spot an advertisement for the latest offering: *Plain Truth*, an annoying twist on Thomas Paine's *Common Sense* that urges readers to stay loyal to Britain. The store also boasts a circulating library, but its catalogue of books is only open to "gentlemen." Is the Bible the only refuge for ladies who read?

By the time I arrive at the coffeehouse I've worked myself into a lather of indignation.

At the door, Ethan lifts my spirits with his warm hug. "I've brewed you some coffee, strong as the devil and hot as hell," he says. "And there's some aging gingerbread."

"Ah, I shall live to see another day."

At the table, he unrolls a document. "My discharge paper from when I was in General Sullivan's command in New York," he says.

"I'm glad you were discharged," I say, "but why have you brought this out?"

"I couldn't remember the name of the skunk who signed it. It says right here it was Captain Rupert Pratt, Sullivan's lackey. He idolized the general—would do anything for him."

"He's the one who browbeat you into writing the incriminating papers," I say, sipping my coffee.

"He's the very one, but I wager the order came from Sullivan," Ethan says. "Pratt told me I was a dead man if I didn't do it. After I did it, he told me I'd be a dead man if I told anyone."

"No wonder you were such a mess when you got home," I say, taking his hand. "Rip was asking a lot of you to spill the beans."

"He paid the price." Ethan says.

"So now you think this Rupert Pratt may have killed Rip to save his own skin?"

"Who knows? Maybe he was afraid for his career. Or maybe he was trying to gain favor with Sullivan. Whatever the case, he knew he was following an illegal order to forge the papers, and it could come back to ruin him."

We still don't have all the pieces, but I hate to throw cold water on Ethan's theory.

"If it's Pratt," I ask gingerly, "wouldn't he have gone after you and not Rip?"

Ethan mulls that for nearly a minute. "It was night, and maybe he mistook Rip for me. We do—did—look a lot alike."

"Maybe," I say hesitantly.

"I know it's a long shot," he says. "But it's all we have."

"You're right," I say. "Do you know what happened to Pratt after you left the army?"

"No idea. Probably Sullivan pinned a medal on his chest."

I smile at Ethan. "It seems you and I must find this Rupert Pratt."

"Good," he says, handing me more gingerbread. "I was hoping you'd see it that way."

"If he's the killer, we must work fast," I say. "And Pratt could be just about anywhere."

Ethan bites his lip nervously. "There's one hitch. My father. He's dead set against all this."

"What do you mean?" I ask.

"I showed him my discharge papers and told him everything. He just kept saying, no, no, no."

"He doesn't want to dredge up all those painful memories," I say.

"Yes, that's it. And he really believes the killers are those two rats who attacked you. Why else would they be charged with murder? The British couldn't possibly get it wrong. And the pocket watch."

"Yes, the pocket watch," I say. "That's a hard one."

His eyes grow wide. "What if we're wrong, Sarah? My father's a smart man."

"We're not wrong." I wonder if Ethan can sense the depth of my doubts.

"You are a most remarkable creature, Miss Barrett," he says. He puts his arm around me, and I nestle into the crook of his shoulder. As I tilt my head up, his lips meet mine and we linger over a gentle kiss.

The door creaks open, and we fly apart. Ethan's father walks in, surprised to see me.

"Oh, hello Sarah," he stammers.

Clearly miffed, Ethan jumps in. "Father and I do the books every Sunday…and he's early."

"And I'm late, I must be going," I say. "Thank you, Ethan, for the coffee and conversation. Goodbye, Mr. Ripley."

Services are over when I walk back to Christ Church in a cold rain. I'm dreading the walk home. Parishioners stream into the downpour in their Sunday finery. The latest fashions are quickly sopping wet, and it seems the newfangled umbrellas of oiled silk aren't meant for a good Philadelphia soaking. Emma dashes out pulling along a portly, bald man at least my father's age. She sees me and waves me over.

"Mr. Waters has kindly offered to give us a ride home in his carriage," Emma says.

"How nice of you, Mr. Waters," I say climbing into the most elegant carriage I've ever seen.

Mr. Waters seems most interested in sitting as close as possible to Emma.

"Did you find the pastor's sermon enlightening, my dear?" he asks, inches from her face.

Emma doesn't hesitate. "It was so long and tedious, I nodded off. Did I miss anything?"

He explodes with laughter. "You're a funny one."

When we arrive at the Porters' house, he clears his throat. "Would you consider accompanying me to church next Sunday?"

"No, thank you. My betrothed will surely be home from the war next week," she says without hesitation.

We're both up the front steps in a flash. We hold back our laughter until we're inside.

"You liar!" I poke her.

"Did you want to walk home in the pouring rain?"

"You could be a very good spy."

She gives me a look that would stop a rabid cat.

For Sunday dinner, Molly and Rachel are roasting a side of beef that Major Hammond provided. Abigail and Jack take turns at the spit, while the younger children shoot marbles until Rachel orders them out of the kitchen.

"The Major and two of his men will be joining us for dinner," she tells Emma and me. "How was church?"

"Most enlightening," Emma says, while I smother a laugh.

"Perhaps you can enlighten us during dinner," Rachel says. "We'll be ready in a few minutes."

Molly is mashing potatoes with milk and globs of butter, which is finally and mercifully available. The ever-present boiled turnip and parsnip dish is on the table. The apple pie Emma made last night is on the sideboard. I'm the only one without an offering.

"Can I help with anything, Rachel," I offer meekly.

"I wouldn't let her," Emma laughs. "Her kitchen skills are sadly lacking. Remember the last time you tried to make bread?"

"It wasn't that bad," I say. "Was it?"

"It could have choked a horse." Emma snorts with laughter.

"Perhaps you could tell the Major dinner is ready," Rachel says.

"Certainly," I say, glad to be out of the kitchen and away from Emma's needling.

When I knock on the parlor door, it takes a few moments for the Major to open it.

He seems displeased with the intrusion, and I wonder if he's finishing another letter to his wife.

"Oh, Sarah," he says, clearly disappointed I'm not Emma. "How lovely to see you."

"Dinner is ready," I say, peering inside. I see the open rum bottle and an empty glass. The Major is already in his cups.

"I'll be right there. Thank you, my dear." The door closes before I can utter a word.

At the table, the Major carves the roast beef with gusto. "Well done, Mrs. Porter!"

Rachel is glowing. "How goes the war?" she asks him.

"Excellent! We'll have this rebellion snuffed out in six months," he says.

"Here, here," one of his men says. "I'll drink to that."

Rachel declines to raise her glass.

"I hear the patriots will soon receive new uniforms, shoes, and blankets," I say. "And the food supply isn't as dire. They even have someone now to drill them on soldiering."

"We know all that and more," the Major says. "We've got informants everywhere. There's nothing they do that we don't know about first."

Jack's mouth is agape. "Real spies? Can anyone be one?"

The Major laughs. "We have friends all over. Some even fought for the patriots and became fed up with their nonsense. There isn't anything our people can't ferret out."

"I want to be a spy," Jack says.

"Jack, you know Quakers don't participate in war," Rachel says firmly. "Your father is risking his life right now for that very principle."

"But I want to be a soldier."

"I don't take kindly to that sort of talk, young man," she says.

The Major, evidently adept at smoothing over awkward social situations, turns to Rachel and asks if she's heard lately from her husband.

"Not a thing. It has to end soon."

The Major takes a long sip of his rum. He and his men have polished off an entire bottle.

"What I hear," he says, "is that the exiled Quakers have become a huge embarrassment for Washington and the Congress. Now the general and his cronies must find a way to end it and save face."

"I thought dinner would never end," Emma sighs as we climb the stairs. "I'm looking forward to a nap."

"Your major has given me an idea," I tell her as she plops down on my bed.

"He's not my major," she says.

"Have you told him that you know about his secret family?" I ask.

"Not yet," she says. "I'm struggling to find the right words."

"Good. Could you hold off a little longer?"

"Why?" She gives me a sharp look. "You're planning something, aren't you?"

"Well, yes. You heard him say the redcoats have spies everywhere who can find out anything."

"Yes, but so what?"

"Maybe they can find Rupert Pratt, the man Ethan and I believe could be behind Rip's murder."

"This is another one of your crazy schemes, and I want no part of it," Emma says pulling the quilt over her head.

CHAPTER 39

Emma is snoring in our room when I steal downstairs to the Major's parlor.

When I knock softly, he opens the door with a flourish—expecting Emma or even Rachel. Not me.

"Sarah? What do—"

"May I come in and talk with you privately?" I ask.

He's befuddled by my boldness. "Of course… come in."

I close the door behind me.

"Major Hammond, might I ask a favor of you?" I say, oozing politeness.

"You may certainly ask," he says a little hesitantly.

"I'm looking to find someone, a soldier with the rebels," I say. "You said your spies could find out anything."

"Nearly anything," he says. "Who are you looking for, a lover from the past or one for the future?" He laughs heartily and I manage a demure smile.

"Neither," I say, struggling to keep my composure.

"I need to find a Rupert Pratt. The most recent information I have is that he fought in New York at the Battle of Staten Island."

"Why do you wish to find this man? Rupert… Pratt, was it?"

I take a deep breath and proceed. "I believe he may be connected to the murder of Rip Ripley."

"Ripley! He's the poor sap from the coffeehouse who was killed by two of our men. The same drunken louts who attacked you, I believe."

"Yes."

"So you think this Pratt might have some valuable information for the case?"

"He could have had a hand in it." I tell him, hoping he doesn't press me for further information.

"Well, I certainly want to help you if it gets us closer to the truth," he says.

"Obviously, you're a redcoat and he's a rebel so I don't expect there's much you can do. But you said your spies can ferret out anything."

I expect he'll beg off politely. After all, there's a war going on and he has more serious business at hand than attending to an amateur sleuth stumbling into matters best left to the police.

"I may be able to help you," he says sunnily. "I'll do what I can. These are difficult times for everyone. We must help one another."

"Thank you," I say, practically dancing my way out the door.

Maybe I've misjudged this man. I'm beginning to understand what Emma saw in him. And Jack. The boy has come to idolize the officer who comforted him after the explosion, the fatherly figure who plays ball with him and the other boys once a week. Of course, a man like that would have a wife and children.

In the morning, I leave for work early to tell Ethan the news.

He's glad to see me, kissing my cheek in front of everyone. "Sarah, my dear, you lighten my heart so," he whispers. "Coffee? Would you like some bread pudding? It's fresh from the oven."

"Just coffee," I tell him, glad that he's not busy with customers. "I have news."

As usual every eye in the place is on me. You would think by now these successful merchants, these men accustomed to the rough-and-tumble of commerce, would be unflustered by the presence of a woman in their sacred refuge. I lower my voice.

"I asked Major Hammond to help us find Rupert Pratt," I say. "They have a network of spies who can find out what Washington had for breakfast. The Major said he'd—"

"Major Hammond? The damned redcoat quartering with you at the Porter house?" Ethan says in disbelief.

"Yes."

"You asked a redcoat for help?" he says, his eyes widening. "I can't believe you would do that."

I'm stunned by his reaction. "He's nice. He's not like the others. What's the harm?"

"We can't trust him, Sarah! Who knows what he'll do with whatever he digs up? Honestly, how could you be so—"

"Stupid? Is that what you were going to say?"

"No," he says, stopping to weigh his next word carefully. "Careless. How could you be so careless?"

"So what if he's British?" I say, my anger rising. "If it gets us what we want, I don't care if he's the man in the moon."

He's rubbing his hands together nervously. "Why do you think I fought against the redcoats? So we could all be friends again? I'll never trust them. Never!"

"Well, I don't see that the patriots did you any favors." I don't have to spell out the whole Spanktown debacle.

His face is bright red, and all eyes are on him now.

"I must get back to work," he says.

"I, as well," I say, leaving as fast as I can.

All day I stew over Ethan's reaction. Was I wrong to ask the Major for help? I corner Tess as she's washing a window and she gives me her customarily reasonable opinion.

"Perhaps he's angry that you took such a bold move without talking to him first," she says. "Or maybe he really does hate the redcoats that much. I don't know."

"Well, I can't un-ask the Major for help," I say. "What's done is done."

"I have some news of my own," Tess says, biting her lip to hold back a smile.

"What is it?"

"Amos has no plans to fire me, though I told him several times I'd leave if that was his wish."

"Bravo! The man has a heart after all," I say.

"We talked, really talked for the first time ever," she says. "He said, 'Tess, you are an enigma, and I suppose you know exactly what that is and how to spell it.'"

"What did you say?"

"Yes, I *do* know the definition of enigma, and I *do* know how to spell it—and I also know that you are a benevolent, gentle man. That's exactly what I told him," she says, smiling broadly.

"I'm so happy for you," I say, squeezing her arm.

"Oh, but there's more," she says, with the dramatic flair of a mother telling her child a story.

"He asked me to manage his library, to see that the books are organized and shelved in the right places. So, of course, I can read whatever I want."

"Wonderful! Does that mean you don't have to clean the privy anymore?"

"It does not. Sarah, be patient with the man. He's still adjusting to the fact that a former slave can read. And can also be his—well, his friend."

I could kiss Amos but restrain myself. I find him in his office, slumped in his chair, rubbing his temples.

"How can I help you, Amos?"

"Help me? Maybe you can help me make sense of this blasted war. Galloway was in here earlier crowing about the redcoats' latest victories, and I see only suffering and death."

"Victories? Where?"

"Near Newtown, not 30 miles from Philadelphia. Seems the British thought they needed to ramp up the patriots' suffering. What they did assaults even my sense of fairness."

"What did they do?" I can't imagine anything loathsome enough for such an admission from Amos.

"Everyone knows how desperate the patriots are for uniforms," he says. "They're out there freezing to death in the cold for want of a coat or even a shirt."

"Of course, I know. Uniforms are due any day."

"Not anymore. The redcoats attacked a woolen mill, stealing

2,000 yards of wool intended for patriot uniforms."

"Terrible! But maybe the mill can get wool elsewhere."

"Then they set fire to the mill," he said.

"I hate—"

"There's more," he says. "They raided a tavern where tailors had been holed up, feverishly sewing uniforms. They stole enough wool for 500 uniforms, then took 30 patriots prisoner, along with the poor tailors."

"I'll gladly help you write an article," I say, looking forward to denouncing the Brits.

Amos takes his time lighting his pipe. "Believe it or not, there's even more."

"More?"

"A week later the damn Brits commandeered a cattle drive—150 oxen bound for Valley Forge—and captured another eight patriots. Those oxen came right here to Philadelphia, where they were served up to redcoats whose bellies haven't missed a meal since the war began."

I gulp and wonder where the roast beef Major Hammond provided last Sunday really came from.

"The men at Valley Forge are desperate," I say.

"I don't know how they can go on," Amos says.

I wonder if Amos is again showing his true patriot colors. It gives me heart.

He rubs his temples again. "This puts us in a sticky situation. But I'm sure a woman with your considerable skills can write a comprehensive account that doesn't glorify or vilify either side."

I'm flattered but quickly return to my senses. It's a near impossible task, and we both know it.

CHAPTER 40

THE NEXT DAY I'M cleaning type with Tess and Joshua when Ethan bursts in.

"Sarah," he says breathlessly. "May I speak with you?"

I figure he's come to apologize for his abruptness yesterday.

"Yes, I'm glad to see you," I say, gesturing to Amos's office. "He's out wooing a would-be advertiser."

Ethan is still catching his breath. "The men were hanged this morning! Sam Hopkinson and Abe Jackson."

"What? That wasn't supposed to happen for another month." I'm stunned and confused.

"There was no big public hanging," he says. "The British did it quickly and quietly."

"How do you know?"

"Heard it at the coffeehouse. Couple of redcoats were boasting about putting away some damned outlaws. I asked them who, and they were delighted to tell me: 'The two swine who near killed that girl and then sliced your brother to death. If anyone ever deserved it, it's those two'."

I can hardly put my thoughts together but manage to croak out an objection. "Unless they had evidence we don't know about, they may have hanged the wrong men."

Ethan finally calms down. "I told my father, and he was glad it's over and done with."

"Well, maybe it was them," I say. "Maybe they were guilty."

Ethan is unimpressed by my willingness to get past it all.

"I don't believe it, and I don't think you do either," he says. "I don't trust the redcoats, any of them."

I tell him he's right. I don't trust them either—but it's wartime and if I can get vital information from Major Hammond or any other redcoat, I will. That's why I asked the Major for help finding Rupert Pratt.

"Do you still think me the fool for going to the Major?" I ask.

"No. As soon as I lashed out at you, I felt terrible. I'm the fool."

"No, I should have talked to you first," I say. "Tess says I have a habit of charging ahead without proper deliberation."

He takes my hand and gently squeezes it. "I think we can both do better."

I'm so relieved to see his warm smile. If we weren't in Amos's office, I'd give him a long, sweet kiss.

"To honesty," I say.

He still has my hand and pulls me closer. In one swift move, he gives me a kiss on the cheek. It happens so fast I barely feel it. I flush, and I fear my embarrassment—and pleasure—will show.

"What about Rip?" I say, trying to gather my wits. "Is that the end of our investigation? Is it a fool's errand now?"

"I'm sure that's what Galloway expects," he says. "Water under the bridge."

"That's probably what any sensible person would say."

"Probably so," he says.

"But that's not us," I say.

"No. It's not. I owe it to my brother to find his killer."

"I feel the same."

"Partners still?" He cocks his head and smiles. I think my heart will burst.

"Yes, partners. What's next?"

For a minute, he's at a loss but then comes up with an idea: "Since you're already on comfortable terms with the Major, maybe you can ask him why the hangings were rushed.

"I'll likely see him tonight," I say.

"Good. Maybe he also can help us retrieve Rip's pocket watch. I'd like to give it to Father. I think it would ease his grief."

Supper is not one of Molly's better efforts. It starts off pleasant enough when she presents a beautiful pie, the top crust a flaky golden brown. Even Jack, a picky eater, is impressed, as am I. Major Hammond is too busy trying to catch Emma's eye to notice. Emma is being coy.

"Molly, you've outdone yourself," Rachel announces. "A finer crust I've never seen."

"Is it an apple pie?" Abigail asks.

"Oh no," Molly says. "Eel pie."

There's a collective gasp. "Eel!" Jack screams. "That's disgusting!"

I'm on the verge of gagging.

"I'm not eating snake pie," Abigail says. "I'd sooner go hungry."

"And you will go hungry if you don't at least try it," Rachel says. "Eel is actually quite good. It's a delicacy in some cultures."

"The fishmonger told me it was caught fresh today," Molly says. "If you all are too refined for eel pie, I know families that would be plenty grateful for it."

Jack shrugs. "Let them have it."

"You, sir, will leave the table at once," Rachel tells him. "And without a scrap to eat. Now let's all be thankful for this blessing of food and eat heartily."

Emma gives me a look of desperation as she accepts a tiny sliver of pie.

I cut myself an even smaller piece, hoping it's mostly crust. The Major takes a piece that amounts to a quarter of the entire, vile pie.

"A fine dish, Molly," he says. "I love eel pie." Before the meal is finished, he's downed a second piece, pleasing Rachel no end.

Emma can't even choke down a forkful. Finally, out of desperation, she offers to put the twins and baby Mary to bed.

"Thank you, my dear," Rachel says. "I must get ready for a meeting with the other wives. We have much to do before our trip to Valley Forge."

"That's quite an undertaking for you ladies," the Major says. "Will your husbands approve?"

"We aim to surprise them," she says, smiling slyly.

"Bravo!" I say. "A bold move."

The Major, oddly, says nothing, focusing on his eel-filled plate. Even stranger, he's been silent about the execution of the men who assaulted me.

After supper, I knock on his door. He doesn't seem happy.

"Oh Sarah," he says. "I don't have any information on that Pratt character yet."

"That's not why I'm here. Weren't you going to tell me about the hangings?"

"Come in." He looks rattled.

"Yes. I just heard about it today. I was hoping to have more information before I came to you."

"I had to hear about it from the gossips at the coffeehouse."

"I'm sorry. Please, sit down."

"What happened? I'm worried the wrong men were hanged for Rip's murder."

"Oh, they're the right men," he says. "Here's everything I know, and I had to go to some lengths to find out."

I sit down, and he pulls his chair closer, so our knees are practically touching.

"Will you join me in some rum?" he asks.

"Of course," I say, hoping to sound as if I'm accustomed to men in their bedrooms offering me rum every night. He pours two glasses.

"What I heard—and this comes down from Howe—is that Hopkinson and Jackson were plotting their escape by paying off a guard. They told the guard they were going to defect and make their way to Washington's command at Valley Forge. Fortunately, the guard tipped off his superiors."

"Did they have to be hanged immediately for that?" I ask.

He takes a big swig of rum. "Yes, we take treason very seriously. And that's what this was. Those men were planning to defect, perhaps with valuable intelligence, and the penalty is hanging. We don't waste any time."

"It seems so hasty and secretive," I say. "And the very idea that those morons had any acquaintance with a thing called intelligence is ridiculous."

"This is war, Sarah," he says softly. "It's a messy business. I don't always agree with my commanders, but I trust them to do the right thing."

"I don't—"

"Look at it this way," he says, taking my hand. "Your attackers will never harm you or anyone else again. You can move on with your life. Forget all this, forget about Pratt. You deserve some happiness."

His kindness and a few sips of rum have made me feel comfortable. But my mind is clear. "I can't forget about Pratt. I still want to find him."

"Frankly, Sarah, it's a lost cause. Many men join up to get away from the messes they've made at home. Some even use false names and nobody in command wastes their time delving into the past."

"Please," I say. "Make just one more try to find Pratt."

He knows I won't drop it, so he grudgingly says yes. "But prepare to be disappointed."

His hand is gradually moving up my arm. "If I might ask one more favor before I leave," I say, quickly standing.

"Certainly, my dear," he says with limp enthusiasm.

"It would give Rip's father great solace to have his son's pocket watch returned to him. There's no further need to hold it as evidence, is there?" I say.

The Major opens the parlor door for me.

"We're at war, for God's sake!" he practically barks. "We have more important matters to attend to than some dead man's watch."

But he catches himself and suddenly softens his tone.

"But for you, Sarah, I'll see what I can do."

CHAPTER 41

Emma and I stay up past midnight huddled under our quilts. The fire has gone out and we're too exhausted to build it back up. There's a cold rain pounding the window, which I pray doesn't leak.

I tell Emma everything about the hanging and my talk with the Major. I even tell her about what I took as the start of his clumsy effort to seduce me.

"The rat!" She wants nothing to do with him.

"Nonetheless, I think he has a good heart," I say.

"You can think what you wish but he fancies himself quite the ladies' man," she says. "Your Ethan sounds much less troublesome."

"Yes! I do like him—oh, I might even love him," I say. "I know he loves me. I have a feeling he'll ask me to marry him."

"Marry? Would you...so soon after Tom...and losing Tom's baby?"

I detect a hint of disapproval, and I can't say I disagree.

"Oh, I don't know...honestly, Emma, I still think about your brother a lot. That's not fair to Ethan."

"Is Ethan still suffering from his time in battle?"

"Not nearly as much."

I fear he's harboring memories he has yet to tell me about, but I keep that to myself.

I pass Emma a ginger cookie that I liberated from Molly's secret stash in the kitchen. Biting into mine, I savor the tangy taste. Neither of us ate more than a few bites of Molly's eel pie, and now we're ravenous.

I go on to tell Emma about my perhaps insane quest to find Rupert Pratt, the patriot officer who forced Ethan to write the Spanktown Papers with a virtual gun pointed at his head.

"What a peculiar name," she muses. "Spanktown."

"It's a real place in New Jersey," I say, "but the Quakers never used it for their yearly meeting. The whole thing is a fraud, from start to finish."

"Why do you care so much about a place with a funny name?" Emma asks.

For a learned person, Emma sometimes astonishes me with her lack of curiosity.

"The patriots hate Quakers for not supporting the war," I explain slowly, as if she were a child. "Those papers were all they needed to grab Quaker elders off the street, insist they were helping the British, and imprison them hundreds of miles away."

"Maybe they *were* helping the British," Emma says.

"They weren't helping anyone," I say. "They're nonviolent to a fault. Won't favor either side."

We munch our cookies in companionable silence for a minute when Emma admits to a grudging admiration for Rachel and the other wives traipsing 20 miles to Valley Forge.

"Won't do any good," she says. "Washington's not going to listen to a bunch of women in drab dresses plead for their husbands, who've really had a pretty easy time of it in so-called captivity."

"You're being harsh, Emma," I say, though I've had similar thoughts myself. "I think the wives are plucky to make their way through a war zone when it's still winter. I wish I could go with them."

"You would," she scoffs. "You'll do any foolhardy, risky thing that makes you the heroine. I suppose you'd want to write about it too."

"Yes! People need to know about these determined women."

Emma snorts. "You mean foolish women."

"I know you don't want Rachel to go because you'll be left to care for five children. And you would hate it even more if the dreaded Gertrude steps in to take command."

"How would you feel," she pouts, "if you had to play mother to those untamed savages? It's hard enough teaching them all day."

"But they love you, Emma," I tease.

"They won't love me when I order them to bed in the middle of the afternoon."

The next day I can't wait to spring my proposal on Amos. I hold off until after he's had his mid-day dinner and a couple glasses of cider. That was Tess's idea.

"I've had practice," she tells me.

When he seems mellow, I make my move.

"Amos," I say sweetly. "May I have a word?"

"Of course. I also want to talk to you, about doing an article on the Smith Tavern's plan to hold cockfights in their courtyard. Maybe we can squeeze some advertising out of them."

"Of course, I'd be happy to do that. Cruel entertainment is all the rage, so why shouldn't we give the people what they want?"

Amos screws up his face. I immediately realize that once again I've blabbered myself into a losing position.

"Not that there's anything wrong with cockfighting," I quickly say. "It has great popular appeal."

He leans back in his chair. "What was it you wanted to talk about?"

I take a deep breath. "I have an idea for an article. As you might recall, Rachel Porter and some of the Quaker wives are planning to plead with Washington at Valley Forge for their husbands' release."

"It'll never work," he says flatly. "Washington has problems that go well beyond weeping Quaker wives wandering into a war zone."

"Maybe so," I say. "But these women are desperate, and they're doing something for their loved ones that few men would even attempt. I think it's courageous."

"So you want to write about this foolhardy mission."

"Well, yes," I say, ignoring his sarcasm. "I also want to go with them."

"Go with them?" He's raising his voice now. "On this fool's errand that could get all of you killed?"

"Yes." Amos is testing me but I'm trying to stay calm and logical.

"How long would this take you away from your duties here?" he asks, his voice precise and prickly.

"A few days, maybe four," I say. "I don't know."

He lights his pipe.

"What if you don't make it to Valley Forge, or if you do, the great General Washington decides he's too busy to see you? The man is fighting a war, after all."

I press on. "Even if they fail, the fact that these women tried to do this for their husbands is worthy of an article. And who knows? Maybe they'll succeed."

"And when are they embarking on this noble mission?"

"Probably not until the end of March, when the weather is better. That's my guess."

He's scowling, but I try appealing to his business side.

"We might be able to get some new subscribers out of it," I say.

"How?"

"Quakers will surely read about their own, especially if it concerns women doing something extraordinary. And with so many Quakers running successful businesses, they might come away with some special interest in supporting the *Sentinel*."

I see a spark of interest now.

"You might have something there," he says. "I'll consider it and let you know."

It feels like a victory, so I graciously accept it.

"I'll see to the cockfighting article right away."

Now all I have to do is convince Rachel to let me accompany them.

Before heading home for the day, I run into Tess hauling in logs for the fire.

"I think Amos will let me go with the Quaker wives," I tell her excitedly. "I appealed to his business sense."

"Smart," she says. "I have news of my own."

"What?" I fear Amos has changed his mind about promoting her.

"I told him all about my daughter, Dinah," she says, smiling. "We talk a lot now."

"That's nice." I say. "Sounds like you're becoming good friends."

"That's not my big news," she says. "It's this: Amos is going to help me find my girl."

I'm so surprised I wrap Tess in a big bear hug. "That's wonderful!"

She's flustered. "Now you can release me so I can go about my business—which does not include prattling on with the likes of you."

CHAPTER 42

Amos keeps me until 7 o'clock, yattering on about the latest snub from the loyalist Galloway, who failed to invite him to a lavish dinner and concert at his manor.

"After all I've done for the man and his gang of pompous redcoats," he pouts as he brushes a speck of pipe tobacco from his sleeve.

"That must be such a hardship for you," I say.

He's so steeped in self-misery that my sarcasm doesn't penetrate. Actually, I'm relieved that the chummy welcome he gave the redcoats last fall is wearing thin. He still pines for his horse Buttercup and is certain she's serving some damned redcoat.

Finally, I break away. "I'm late for supper with Ethan." I grab my cloak and leave before he can say anything about "that rebel boy of yours."

The cool air feels good on my face as I rush to the coffeehouse.

"Come in," Ethan says. "I've built a devilishly good fire upstairs, and I'm warming up some clam chowder."

"You're a devilishly good salesman," I say, heading for the stairs.

Between slurps of chowder, I fill him in on Major Hammond's explanation for the rushed hangings.

"Sounds as if there was nothing he could have done to stop it," I say. "He's still trying to locate Rupert Pratt."

"I don't trust him, and I haven't even met him—not that I want to," Ethan says. "Things don't add up."

"I think you're needlessly suspicious," I say, wondering if the trauma of battle is still clouding his mind.

"I'm just cautious," he says. "By the way, Rupert Pratt was declared a hero at Saratoga last October. The bastard won a commendation from Washington."

"How do you know this?"

"I have a friend who fought with me at Staten Island. He took a bullet at Saratoga, almost died. We've stayed in touch through letters, and I asked him about Pratt."

"Tell me about your friend," I say.

"Ezra. Ezra Cantwell from Connecticut," he says. "He went to Yale College, where he became friends with the brilliant David Bushnell."

"The one who built that tiny underwater vessel?"

"Yep. Ezra worked on that with Bushnell's crew. They nearly blew up that British warship in New York Harbor."

It's good to see Ethan getting so excited about his friend's accomplishments. He goes on to explain that Ezra worked with Bushnell again, helping to devise the underwater exploding barrels that raised such havoc here just last December.

I detect a hint of jealousy. "He sounds impressive."

"His father owns a shipyard in Connecticut, so he knows everything there is to know about ships."

"And bombs," I say.

"Yes. It's all very new and exciting. More exciting than brewing coffee every day and listening to peoples' petty complaints," he says.

"People depend on you. They couldn't get through the day without their coffee. I know I couldn't. That's important."

My earnestness makes him laugh.

"That is the most pathetic justification for what I do that I could even imagine," he says. "But I admire your valiant effort. Let me get you some more cider, and then we can toast the most extraordinary woman in Philadelphia."

I walk home in a daze on Ethan's arm. I think I'm falling in love with this gentle man. I didn't think I could love another after Tom. I used to think about him, his touch, night and day. But now those memories are just whispers.

"Would you like to come in and meet Rachel, the Major, and all the others?" I ask Ethan.

"No, thank you. Maybe next time," he says kissing my cheek. It's always "next time." I shrug it off, attributing it to a natural disposition that tends to lean inward.

Stepping inside, I'm glad I didn't push it. The twins are fighting over a toy soldier one of the Major's men carved. Emma is trying to comfort screaming Mary, who clearly wants only her mother. And Rachel is huddled in the dining room with eight other Quaker wives. I figure the women are engaged in Bible study, and I tiptoe toward the stairs.

"Sarah, come in my dear," Rachel says.

"Oh no, I don't want to interrupt."

"Please, we could use your counsel," she says. "We're planning our trip."

"I'm happy to help." It's too soon to ask if I might accompany them, but maybe they'll be open to it if they trust me enough.

"We're drafting a letter we can present to Washington," Agatha Nelson says. "Perhaps you can check our spelling."

I'm sure I can rewrite it more persuasively, but I hold back. "Of course," I say politely.

"Lawyers and men from our community have advised us to use these legal arguments," Rachel says, holding up a sheaf of papers.

"They know what's best," one of the women says.

"Do they?" Agatha says.

Rachel turns to me. "Read what we've written and see if our grammar and spelling pass muster, if you would please."

I read through four pages of tedium. "Spelling and grammar are fine. I couldn't have done better."

Rachel smiles broadly.

"What do you think of the message?" Agatha asks. I sense they're not all in agreement.

"It's not my place to—"

"Just tell us what you think," another woman says. "After all, you work with words every day."

"Go ahead, Sarah," Rachel says.

"Well, honestly, it sounds like something men wrote," I say. "And they failed."

Rachel looks crestfallen. I worry that I've overstepped my bounds.

"What would you suggest we do?" Agatha asks.

I take a deep breath. "What you're doing is bold—unheard of for women."

Another deep breath. "If I might suggest… the letter would have more of an impact if it's written from the heart. Mention how you and your children have suffered without the support and companionship of your husbands. How two of the men died, leaving grieving families. And how the rest are ailing from this and that."

"Yes, all that needs to be said," Agatha says. "What else?"

"I would keep it simple and humble," I say. "Mention charity and compassion, and how all families—Quaker or not—would suffer in the same circumstances."

"What about the war?" Rachel asks.

By this time, I couldn't stop if I wanted to. "I wouldn't even mention it. But do mention that your men are guilty of nothing and have endured all these troubles simply because of their religious beliefs."

The room is suddenly quiet.

"Would you like me to write it for you?" I ask.

"Thank you kindly, but I think we can take it from here," Agatha says. "This is our mission so the appeal should be written by us—not a lawyer, a man, or any other soul."

A chorus of approval rings out.

"We'll all sign the letter," Agatha says. "Then we must decide who among us will go."

"If there's more that I can do, please just ask," I say.

After a quick goodnight, I bound up the stairs, pleased with the entire evening. Emma is still up, writing a letter to her parents.

"I thought you'd never get home," she says. "It's late."

As I change into my shift, I tell her all about my evening with

Ethan and the Quaker wives. She tells me all about trying to teach French to Abigail, who has no ear for languages. Jack, she says, is finally adept at multiplication tables and even wrote to his father about it. And the twins: Even teaching them their letters is frustrating because they won't stop fighting.

I'm about to blow out the candle when someone slips an envelope under the door.

We look at each other. Nobody slips envelopes under our door.

"I feel like I'm in a novel," I say. "But I'd wager that it's for you."

With a heaving sigh, she gets out of bed to pick it up, but it's my name that's scrawled on the front. Inside there's a brief note.

Sarah,

I must talk with you in the morning.

Major John Hammond

CHAPTER 43

Emma is intrigued by the Major's note. I think she still harbors a spark of affection for him, though she claims to loathe him for hiding his marital status in all their cozy times together.

After a restless night, I'm dressing when she advises me: "Don't let him close the parlor door when you go in to see him."

"I have no interest in the Major nor he in me," I tell her. "I'm sure it's about Rip's murder."

As I knock on his door, I hope I'm right, and he's not just looking for another dalliance.

He's not smiling when he opens the door. "Come in, Sarah, I'm afraid I have some bad news."

That catches me off guard. "Bad news?"

"Please, sit down," he says. "That Rupert Pratt fellow you were looking for is dead."

"Oh, no." I'm not expecting that.

"Died at the Battle of Brandywine, not 30 miles from here," he says.

"How do you know?"

"Here's the official roster of dead from that battle," he says, reaching onto his desk for a printed list of names under the heading of *Battle of Brandywine, September 11, 1777*. "Says he died instantly from a bullet wound to the back of the head."

"That is terrible news!" Of course, I don't exactly mourn him. He was a rat and the world is better off without him. But now Ethan and I may never know for certain who killed Rip.

"I know that's not the news you were hoping for," the Major says. "I'm sorry you won't be able to pursue your investigation."

"That's very kind of you. Thank you for going to all the trouble you did to find this out for me."

An hour later, I deliver the bad news to Ethan when I stop in for coffee.

"Died on the battlefield," I say. "I don't think we'll ever solve Rip's murder. Maybe those two redcoats really did it. At least your father will be glad this is the end of it."

Ethan looks more forlorn than I've ever seen him. "Can't say I'm sorry he's dead, but this does set us back."

"I can scarcely believe he died at Brandywine, so close to us here in Philadelphia," I say.

"Brandywine?" Ethan looks puzzled. "When?"

"Last September 11. Why? What does it matter?"

"Something is wrong," he says.

"What are you talking about?"

"My friend Ezra saw Pratt at Saratoga last October."

Finally, it hits me. "How could he be in Saratoga," I ask, "if he died a month earlier in Pennsylvania?"

"He'd have to rise from the dead," Ethan laughs.

"What do we do now?"

"Could your Major Hammond have made a mistake?"

"I'll ask him. Tonight."

"Sarah, be careful. As I've told you before, I don't trust him."

At work, I plow through back issues in the storage room and confirm Ethan's suspicions about the battle dates. Either the Major made a mistake, or something is very wrong.

"What are you doing?" Amos is standing in the doorway, arms folded across his chest.

He doesn't look at all pleased.

"I'm just..." It's useless to lie and I'm sick of lying, so I tell him everything I know about Rip's murder. To my surprise, he's not miffed that I appear to have forgotten all about that article on cockfighting. And it's even more surprising—stunning, actually—that he offers to help.

"I could ask Galloway to make a discreet inquiry about this Pratt fellow and why the Brits were so anxious to hang the two brutes who attacked you. You're right: Something doesn't add up."

"Yes, that would be helpful," I say. "And maybe you could find out why it's taking so long to get Rip's pocket watch back. It would so please his father to have it back."

"Of course," he says, shocking me more. "And who knows? Maybe there's a good front-page account here for us."

But, more urgently, Amos asks me to help with an article about General William Howe, the British general now in command of Philadelphia.

"Howe's fed up," he says. "He thought he'd have this little rebellion snuffed out by now. But it's going on three years, and now he wants to retire back in England."

Clearly exhausted, Amos flops down in his leather chair. When Tess comes in with a plan to catalog his library using a numbering system she's invented, he brightens up and pours himself a generous shot of whiskey from the bottle he keeps in his desk.

"Let's get into the details tomorrow, Tess," he says, as he lifts the glass to his lips. "I've had quite enough for the day."

At home I can't wait to confront the Major. While Molly and Rachel prepare supper, I quietly knock on the parlor door.

He's clearly irritated. "What is it now, Sarah? What more could you possibly need?"

"Just a moment of your time. May I come in?" He gestures to a chair. "There's something I don't quite understand," I say.

"And what could you possibly not understand?" he says with a smirk.

"You told me Rupert Pratt died on September 11 at Brandywine—"

"Yes, yes."

"But he fought at Saratoga in October."

"And how do you know this?"

"I know it from someone who saw him there."

Instantly, the smirk is gone. His eyes dart about. I sense panic.

"What's going on?" I demand. "Are you hiding something? This time, please: Tell me the truth. All of it."

He lets out a deep breath, stands up, and closes the door.

"I can see I have no choice but to be completely honest with you," he says. "And that presents a great risk to me."

"To you?"

"Yes. What I'm about to tell you must be kept secret."

He looks at me and waits.

I nod, with some hesitation.

"I am not strictly a British officer. I'm a spy for General Washington."

"But..." I'm speechless.

"I guess I've been fairly convincing," he says with a smile. "I fooled even you, for a while. I hope that you're now relieved that we're both on the same side."

"Yes, I am," I say. "My... husband Tom died in battle for the patriots. I have no love for the redcoats."

"And now I hear you've taken up with Ethan Ripley," he says. "Emma tells me he fought for the patriots, and that the war caused him deep mental anguish."

"What difference does that make?" I ask.

"I've had my share of trauma," he says. "I fought at that miserable Battle of Long Island. Then in New Jersey. My luck ran out at Brandywine. The redcoats were thrilled to capture someone of my rank with inside information. They offered me a deal: I could go free if I pledged my allegiance to the bloody King. I said no—unless they offered me a position of rank."

"You took an oath to the British? How could you?" I ask. "All the patriots I know refused to switch sides."

"Sarah, my dear, you don't understand," he says. "I did it knowing I would use the opportunity to slip valuable information to Washington. That's exactly what I've been doing—and will continue doing if you promise to keep silent about this."

"Certainly," I say, wondering how I could have so misjudged

this courageous man.

"I know what I'm doing is extremely risky," he says. "I don't expect to make it out of the war alive, but if I don't, I will have at least done something honorable."

"Perhaps we can help each other."

"Perhaps," he says, walking over to open the door for me.

"Just one more thing," I say. "Everything you told me about the reason for the rush to hang the two men—"

"All true," he says. "I won't lie to you."

"That's good. But why did you tell me Rupert Pratt was dead?"

"I thought he was. War is chaos, Sarah. Mistakes happen all the time."

CHAPTER 44

I'M DYING TO TELL Emma about Major Hammond's secret, but I know she's incapable of keeping mum. She can't help it. It shows all over her face.

I can't tell Ethan either. He's in Reading at his uncle's funeral. Poor Mr. Ripley has had to brew the coffee himself, and it was undrinkable.

And for three days I've been tiptoeing around Amos while he recovers from a cold. He's so fastidious, he demands Tess fetch him a fresh handkerchief after every sneeze or two.

This morning, I find him in a good mood. I can tell because he's not bothered by the mess of papers on his desk.

"I have news from my dear friend Joseph Galloway," he says. "We had dinner at the Delaware Inn last night. Delightful place."

"And?"

"I asked him about Rip Ripley's pocket watch, the one found on the two men who were hanged. You'll never guess what he told me." He widens his eyes and tilts his head forward, as if awaiting a guess.

"Amos! Just say it."

"The pocket watch is gone."

"Gone?"

"It should have been in the trunk used to store evidence. That's what Galloway said. It was gone when his man looked for it yesterday to return it to the Ripley family," Amos says. "He asked around, and no one seemed to know what happened to it."

"It was a gold watch," I say. "Maybe someone stole it."

"Now I guess we'll never know," he says.

"I would still like to find Rupert Pratt."

"And ask him what? 'Did you kill Rip Ripley?'" Amos shrugs. "You may have reached the end of the road."

Amos's words echo in my head all day. I'm not ready to give up, but I feel hopeless.

I arrive home with a headache so bad my teeth hurt. Dinner only makes it worse when the twins fight over the last ginger cookie. The Major is off with his men at a tavern, and Rachel is short-tempered.

"The wives are gathering here tonight to make final plans for our trip," Rachel says. "I was hoping the Major would give us passes to leave the city."

"I'm sure he'll do it."

"Sarah, we'd be pleased if you'd sit in on our meeting," she says in a way that sounds more like an order. "We'd like you to look at our new letter to General Washington."

I grit my teeth, but I'm also flattered. "Of course. I'd be happy to, Rachel."

I wish Mother were here. She'd prepare a salve with feverfew leaves and willow bark to ease my throbbing head.

I ask Molly for the next best thing: Chamomile tea. Sipping it slowly relaxes me and soon I feel the pain ebbing to a bearable level. The wives start to arrive and gather around the dining room table.

"How nice of you to join us, Sarah," Agatha says. "Your suggestions have been most helpful." They nod in agreement.

"Here's our letter," Rachel says, "and you'll see that all 18 of us have signed it."

I take my time reading it. "Oh, good, you added the part about the mission being your own idea and not your husbands." After a second read, I tell them, "It's a fine job."

"Good," Rachel says. "Four of us are going: Agatha, myself, and two other younger wives, Sally Howard and Emily Grant. That's all we have room for. Even then it will be crowded."

Suddenly my hopes of accompanying them are dashed. Still, I'm awed by Rachel. This may be the bravest thing she's ever done.

"I've prevailed upon Gertrude to come and help Emma with the children," Rachel says.

I can't wait to hear what Emma has to say about that.

"I'm hoping my rheumatism doesn't trouble me too much," Agatha says.

Sally Howard reports that she has secured a carriage and four horses. "My two men will drive us and care for the horses," she adds.

Rachel tells the women that Josiah Morton, a Quaker merchant who wasn't among the abducted, insisted he come along to address Washington on their behalf.

"He said, 'It's not a job for women.'"

"I told him, 'It is for *these* women. Who better?'"

The whole table breaks into hearty applause.

"I have more good news," Rachel says. "As far as I can tell, no one knows about our mission except us and a few others. There's no way our husbands know, so no one can say they put us up to it."

Nor can their dear husbands stop them. If they knew, I doubt they'd approve.

I expect Emma to be in a foul mood tonight, and she is.

"Rachel just told me that she's going on this pilgrimage," Emma says. "She didn't even ask if I minded the extra work I'll be saddled with."

"What if she had asked? Would you say no?" I ask, as I slip out of my gown and collapse in bed.

"No. That's not the point," she snaps. "And don't get me all muddleheaded so I say something I don't really mean. That's what you do."

"No, I don't," I say, knowing that's exactly what I do.

"Enough!"

I fill her in on everything, except the secret that's burning a hole in my gut: Major John Hammond is funneling military intelligence to George Washington. Now that I know his true loyalties, I like him more.

"And another strange thing," I say. "They can't find Rip's pocket watch."

"The Major has a gold watch," Emma says, getting into bed. "He told me his grandfather gave it to him."

"Amos has one too," I say. "And so does Joseph Galloway. Anyone with some wealth is likely to have one."

"Why would Rip have one?" Emma asks. "He's not from money."

"I don't know why. It's baffling. But those were his initials engraved on it."

"And the watch was found in the belongings of the two redcoats who attacked you?"

"Yes, that's what Galloway told us," I say. "He must have heard it from General Howe's people. Emma? Emma…"

No answer. Then I hear the familiar sound of snoring. This time it's soft and almost ladylike. After a few minutes it lulls me to sleep.

Well before dawn I'm wide awake, thinking about Rip's murder. Emma is snoring louder than a stampede so there's no chance of nodding off.

At first light I go down to breakfast, surprising everyone. But I'm not really hungry and toy with my napkin while Abigail shows off her French.

"*Passez-moi le sucre, s'il vous plait*," she says, pointing to the sugar bowl.

The Major and two of his men shuffle in. "Good morning to you ladies," Hammond says as he sits down next to me. Molly dishes up fried hasty pudding and bacon.

"Molly, you've outdone yourself this morning," he says.

"You say that every day, Major Hammond, and every day I tell you that's what you said the previous day."

"And every day it's true," he responds, provoking laughs all around.

When Molly passes a slice of fried pudding to Abigail, the girl responds with a cheery "*merci!*"

"Abigail is practicing her French," Rachel tells the Major as she joins us. "She's made great strides with Emma's guidance."

"I can see. Emma's a fine teacher," he says in a way that suggests he's still enamored.

As he leaves the table, I motion to him. "May I have a word with you? I have news," I whisper.

He nods. Minutes later I'm in his room.

"I'm off to a meeting with Howe's men," he says. "I hope you'll pardon me for getting ready while we talk." His breeches are spotless, his wig is freshly powdered, and his coat pressed.

"It's all I can do to dress like a redcoat without puking," he whispers as he pulls on his polished boots.

"I can imagine," I say, helping him on with his white waistcoat, each one of the buttons polished to a shine.

"If you would be so kind as to hand me my pipe and tobacco from the mantle," he says, buttoning up the vest.

I grab the items and hand them over, but not before I spot his pocket watch on the dresser.

On it, I see all too clearly a set of engraved initials: R.R. Instantly, I freeze, working madly to make sense of it.

"What was the news you wanted to tell me?" he says.

For the first time in memory, I can't speak.

"Sarah?"

I say the first stupid thing that comes to my mind. "Emma has strong feelings for you."

"And I for her," he says. "What's wrong? You look shaken."

"Your pocket watch. The initials—"

He laughs. "My grandfather's initials, my mother's father. He was Rufus Reynolds, and he bought it in London just before he sailed to America. You didn't think I—"

"No, of course not," I stutter. "But you gave me a fright."

"Sarah, you need to put this murder case aside before you lose your mind," he says. "We're on the same side, you, and me, and your friend Ethan. In fact, there may be a place for you both in our special little group. And isn't it about time I met this Ethan?"

My racing heart finally settles down. "Yes, and I know it would please Ethan to meet a fellow patriot, especially one who fought in New

York under General Sullivan. You two will have much to talk about."

Only on my way to work did I realize the full import of my chat with the Major: Without saying anything that could come back to haunt him, he just asked me and Ethan to spy for the patriots!

CHAPTER 45

The next morning I stop at the coffeehouse and tell Ethan everything that happened while he was away. Predictably, he's suspicious of the major-turned-spy.

"Do you think it was just coincidence that Rip's initials are the same as this Major Hammond's grandfather?" he says pouring me a large bowl of steaming coffee. "Is he really a spy, or did he concoct a story to win you over?"

"I know what I feel in my bones," I say, adding nothing about our prospects of spying for Washington. "And I think I'm a fairly good judge of character."

He lowers his voice and takes my hand. "I just don't want anything to happen to you. That's all." He smiles at me in a way that makes my heart jump.

"I've received another letter from Ezra," he says. "His father will hire me on to learn shipbuilding, and perhaps I'll even have a chance to work with the great inventor David Bushnell."

My head is reeling. "Are you saying you're moving to Connecticut?" By now there are two impatient customers clearing their throats at other tables and pointing to their empty cups.

"I'm saying, I want you to come with me." His face reddens. The entire coffeehouse is leaning forward to eavesdrop. "I love you and want to marry you, Sarah."

I'm speechless. Dumbfounded.

"If you'll have me," he says. Now the three closest customers are hanging on every word, and they've hushed everyone else. "What say you?"

The place is silent. I feel all eyes on me, and I wish I could hide.

"I … I love you too," I whisper.

"Is that a yes?" He's grinning now.

"I think so. Yes, probably. This is sudden. I need a little time to think on it."

"Certainly. That's as good as a yes to me!" he says, exuberantly.

"Hear ye! Hear ye!" the man behind me yells. "She says yes!"

I'm excitedly telling Tess about Ethan's proposal when a note arrives for me from Major Hammond.

Dear Sarah,

I would very much like to meet Ethan tonight as I'll be off serving General Howe in the coming days. Because of my delicate position, neither the Porters' house nor a tavern is suitable. Might I suggest we meet at Lloyd's Coffeehouse after hours, if that is agreeable to you both. I'll meet you there at 7 o'clock unless I hear otherwise.

I'm looking forward to making a new acquaintance.

Later in the day, Ethan reluctantly agrees, though he tells me, "I was looking forward to an evening of quiet celebration with the lady I love."

I laugh. "There will be plenty of time for that after he leaves."

The only other person I tell about our little rendezvous is Amos. He's wary, in a protective sort of way that makes me feel good. On the other hand, his feelings about my future as a spy are decidedly mixed.

"You're getting in over your head," he says. He points to my habit of blurting things out and regretting them later—hardly the best trait for a master of concealment. And how would I feel about secretly gathering valuable information—and not being able to publicly report it?

"Of all the people I've ever known in newspapers, Sarah, you've got the temperament least fit for spying," he concludes. "Now, have you started going through that stack of Maryland papers for items our readers might actually enjoy?"

"Amos, maybe some news for the *Sentinel* will eventually come out of all this," I reason. "Think of the sales."

"Good point," he mumbles, but then he's back to being himself again. "Until you leave, I need you to help Joshua print today's issue."

I put on my heavy leather apron and hope, just this once, that I can keep the ink off my gown. I want to look my best for Ethan tonight when I tell him that I've thought about his proposal for half a minute, and my answer is a resounding YES!

Tess helps to make me presentable. Using a dozen hair pins, she wrangles my long, red curls into submission—a curvaceous mound perched precariously atop my head.

"There!" she says, as if putting the final dab on a portrait. "That should bedazzle him. If it doesn't, nothing will."

Ethan's eyes grow big when I walk in. "Do you have any idea how beautiful you are?" he laughs. "You don't, do you?"

I feel my heart will explode.

"I thought the last customers would never leave," Ethan says, readying a table for us. He brings out bottles of rum, whiskey, and Madeira. "Which do you think he'll prefer?"

"I've seen him down all three," I say. "Coffee for me, if you still have some. I want to keep my wits about me."

"Just brewed," he says, setting down a steaming silver pot next to me. "I thought you might want it."

"Thank you." It occurs to me that I may be the luckiest girl in all of Philadelphia.

Major John Hammond arrives precisely at 7 o'clock, immaculately dressed as a redcoat in full uniform with a sword swinging in a scabbard at his waist. His cocked hat sits jauntily over his powdered white wig.

He's so convincing that when I open the door and he strides inside, Ethan steps back, startled.

The Major extends his hand. "You must be Ethan. I'm Major John Hammond."

He looks around to see if we're alone. "I had to come in this vile uniform. I hope you understand."

"Of course," I say, glancing at Ethan, who still seems shaken. "I've confided to Ethan that you've done a little work as an agent for Washington. And, of course, I told him about your military service."

Ethan finally recovers his manners. "It's an honor to meet you," he says, extending his hand. "I served under Major General John Sullivan at the Battle of Long Island and later at the disastrous Battle of Staten Island."

"Disastrous? Yes, we did take more than our share of losses that day, unfortunately," he says accepting a glass of whiskey. "But I hope you don't mean Sullivan's leadership was disastrous."

"I do," Ethan says. "Staten Island was flawed from the beginning. I heard Sullivan was subjected to an inquiry for bungling it."

"He was exonerated and rightfully so," the Major says taking a swig. "He's a great commander. I swore my loyalty to him. I'd gladly serve with him again."

"Not I," Ethan says. "He was a powder keg. And totally wrong about so many things, like the Quakers."

"He was *not* wrong about the Quakers," the Major says. "They're America's most dangerous enemies, hiding behind the cloak of religion while they secretly help the British."

Ethan is suddenly quiet and looks uncomfortable.

"But you're accepting the hospitality of these 'dangerous enemies' every night," he finally says. "Will you be imprisoning Mrs. Porter?"

"Nonsense," the Major rumbles. "You do know about the Quartering Act? Mrs. Porter is safe but, no matter how badly your brain got rattled in battle, you surely remember that war has consequences."

This isn't happening the way I thought it would, and I'm worried.

"Ethan, Major Hammond says General Washington might want

our help in ferreting out valuable information that could be of use to the patriots."

"Spies?" Ethan looks bewildered. "He wants us to spy?"

"You two have shown you have the right skills—even you, Ethan, with your odd views of General Sullivan. Of course it would demand absolute loyalty to the patriots' cause, even when you don't always agree with your orders. Is that something you could do?"

"I believe I can," I say without a moment's thought.

"Ethan?"

"I'm not one to blindly follow orders," he says, sipping his whiskey.

I can feel a chill in his voice and worry that he'll spoil everything.

"A man who thinks for himself," the Major says. "Perfect in a coffeehouse but not cut out for the tougher side of war."

I can feel Ethan bristle, and I change the subject.

"Major, we just learned that Rip's pocket watch is missing from the evidence trunk," I say. "We'd hoped to give it back to Ethan's father to ease his grief."

"Missing? I had no idea. How odd."

"How odd, Major, that you happen to have a pocket watch engraved with the same initials as Rip's missing watch," Ethan says with a force I've never seen.

"How dare you imply I stole it," the Major bellows. He pulls out the watch and gently sets it on the table. "My grandfather, Rufus Reynolds, gave it to me just before he died. I have witnesses."

I turn the watch over and there are the initials R.R. I'm about to ask Ethan to apologize to the Major when I take a closer look at the initials. The two letters are not identical R's. The second R appears to have been tampered with.

"It looks like it was originally a P and someone with a sharp knife scratched in a leg to make it an R," I say.

The Major is flummoxed. "What? That's nonsense."

Ethan jumps up as if struck by lightning. "So the real initials are RP! That makes perfect sense."

"It does?" I wonder if Ethan has truly lost his mind.

"Yes, my dear. Let me introduce you to Captain Rupert Pratt, the rat who forced me to forge the Spanktown Papers!"

By now, the Major is standing. "You crazy fool. Sarah, don't listen to him. He's addled—couldn't take the rigors of combat."

"I wasn't sure until just now," Ethan says triumphantly. "The wig had me fooled. And you shaved off the beard that you had back then. But Sarah's sharp observation about the pocket watch sealed it for me."

"So what if I am Rupert Pratt," the Major says as logically as a lawyer mounting a case in court. "Men in service to the King often take different names. The French even have a term for it: *nom de guerre*. Using a preferred name in the bloody business of war is hardly a crime."

"No, but killing Ethan's brother is," I say finally making sense of it all. "You planted your own watch in the belongings of those two redcoats—"

"Knowing you could get it back after the hangings," Ethan says. "Rip would never own a watch like that."

The Major is backing toward the door as Ethan continues his barrage.

"I will never forget what you said to me that day. After forcing me to write the totally false Spanktown Papers, you told me I was a 'dead man' if I ever told anyone about it."

The Major is shaking his head no.

"When I told Rip about this travesty—and saw how the ridiculous Spanktown Papers were being used against our Quaker neighbors—he wanted to do the right thing: Get the truth out. And you killed him before he had a chance."

"You don't understand!" the Major shouts. "Either of you."

I take the opportunity to refill my coffee cup from the steaming vat.

Ethan's eyes are ablaze. "I understand that General Sullivan had to save face after the trouncing he got on Staten Island," Ethan says. "Turning over those papers would make him look like a hero to Washington, who never had much use for the Quakers anyway."

"Stop!" The Major whips out his sword. "Don't come any closer or you're both dead, just like Rip."

Ethan and I recoil at the sight of the sword. I'm frozen in place, terrified.

"I don't have to defend my actions," the Major says. "I was following orders—"

"To forge the papers, but not to kill Rip. You took that on yourself." Ethan can't stop himself.

"You don't know a thing about war and loyalty to your commander," the Major says, raising his sword to eye level. "General Sullivan is a great man, great leader, and I would do anything for him, even murder."

"So you admit killing Rip," I say, still transfixed by the sword.

"Yes, I'm proud of it. I'll probably get a medal for it someday."

"But you bungled it—I'm the man you wanted," Ethan says. "My brother had the bad fortune of looking much like me yet being more courageous."

At the very point of the Major's sword, Ethan is barely breathing. Ever in control, the Major—or shall I say that rat, Pratt—opts not to run us through then and there.

"Now I'm going to walk out this door and the two of you are never going to utter another word about it or you'll die. And not only will you die, but also Mrs. Porter and the Porter children. And as you know, I'm a man of my word."

I can't let him walk away. I won't. I pick up my cup and hurl the steaming coffee at his face.

He screams as the hot brew burns his eyes and cheeks.

Instantly, Ethan reaches for the sword and the two of them wrestle for it on the floor. I watch helplessly until I regain my wits and grab the big coffee pitcher. The Major seems to be gaining until I dump a river of scalding coffee on his handsome, traitorous face.

"My eyes! My eyes!"

Ethan grabs the sword and presses it against the Major's neck, nicking the skin.

"I've got you now, you bloody bastard," he says, as blood streams down the Major's white shirt.

I'm perched above him with the fancy silver pitcher. "You move a muscle, and I'll pour the whole damn pot onto your sorry manhood."

"Bitch!" he utters as he stops his writhing.

Then Amos strides through the door. "I heard yelling."

"It's under control, Amos," I say. "What are you doing here?"

"I was worried about you, Sarah, so I came by to keep an eye out," Amos says. He lowers his creaking knees onto Pratt's shoulders, placing the full weight of the *Sentinel* on his immobile body. As a final touch, he whips the white cravat from his neck and tosses it to Ethan.

"Use this to tie the bastard's feet.

The Major is still trying to issue orders. "You'll be sorry about this when Washington finds out."

Amos shrugs. "The first person we should notify is my dear friend Joseph Galloway. I'm sure the British will know what to do with this scum. What do you think, Ethan?"

"All right with me," he says. "As long as he pays for killing my brother."

"Oh, he'll pay," Amos says.

CHAPTER 46

AMOS IS WORKING ON an article about the so-called Major when I walk into the *Sentinel* the next morning. I'm already exhausted from telling the story of Ethan's bravery and the Major's capture to everyone at the Porter house.

Rachel was so shocked she slipped away to pray for his soul. Emma was less charitable.

"I knew he was evil, and I'm glad he'll probably hang," she told me as we undressed for bed.

I spent a sleepless night reliving every moment of terror and berating myself for being so trusting. Despite all that, I can't say I look forward to another hanging.

At the *Sentinel*, I walk into Amos's office, unsure of what to expect. He looks up and smiles broadly in a way that makes me uneasy.

"If it isn't the heroine of the day," he says. "Back from the precipice of death."

I moan. "Is that the way you're writing it?"

"It's the only way," he says nonchalantly.

"If I may intrude on your bliss, any more news on the Major this morning?"

He puts his quill pen down and takes up his pipe. "Yes. Quite a devious fellow. He took the name of John Hammond when he signed on with the redcoats. He told them his brother was a war hero, thinking it would buy him some special treatment from the

Brits, and it did. He rose in rank quickly."

It doesn't surprise me. The man could beguile his way into anything.

"What will happen to him now?" I ask.

"I'm no lawyer, but I suspect Howe will court martial him for treason or murder, maybe both," he says. "I can't think of a better outcome. Can you?"

"I hate him, but the thought of another hanging turns my stomach."

Since Amos is so forthcoming, I ask him the question Rachel so urgently asked me at breakfast this morning: "Will all this help the banished Quakers? Will they be set free now?"

Amos sucks on his pipe thoughtfully. "That should be the case. But the patriots and the Continental Congress and Pennsylvania's Council still despise the Quakers, and they'll not come around easily, even with proof that the Spanktown Papers were a fraud."

That will be hard for Rachel and the other wives to accept. But I resolve to tell them tonight when they meet again at the Porter house.

Meanwhile, I have to fill Tess in on Ethan's proposal. After the ruckus last night, Ethan and I had a quiet moment in the parlor. He presented me with his mother's wedding band and said that his heart's deepest desire is that we marry soon.

I find Tess on the floor in Amos's library, surrounded by books.

"What are you doing?"

"I'm numbering all the books," she says as if any fool could see exactly what she's doing. "That'll make it easier to catalog them."

"Why go to all that trouble? Amos certainly doesn't care."

"It's all part of my plan," she whispers.

"What plan? What are you talking about?"

"Can't tell you until I have it all figured out."

"Tess!

"No. That's final. Don't press me. Now tell me about the proposal!"

"I said yes!" I can't hold in my excitement. "He wants to wed soon."

"How well do you know this boy?" she asks.

"Aren't you happy for me? I know him well enough."

"Does this mean you're giving up all your dreams of becoming a famous writer?"

"No."

"Does he know that?" Tess asks as she lugs a pile of books to the shelves.

"No, but I love him. And this time, I'm sure."

Tess is throwing cold water on my happiness. "It sounds to me like you two have some things to discuss."

Supper is strange without the "Major's" commanding presence. The children are confused.

"He's not a redcoat?" Jack asks. "And Hammond isn't his real name?"

"And he killed someone?" Abigail says.

Jack is clearly upset. The man he knew as the Major couldn't possibly be a traitor.

Molly baked gingerbread—her way of making the bad news easier to take. It's an acknowledgement that we were all taken in.

Rachel appears especially sanguine about his arrest. "Even people who do unspeakable things can have some goodness in their heart."

I wonder if she's trying to convince herself that the so-called Major was at bottom a decent fellow. Like everyone else, she was blinded by his charm.

Except Emma. "I hope he burns in hell."

"You don't mean that, my dear," Rachel says, eyeing the children's reactions.

"Yes, I do," Emma says.

I catch her glance and raise my eyebrows in full support. Usually, I'm the one to instantly let loose whatever happens to be on my mind.

There's a knock on the door. "That would be the wives here for our meeting," Rachel says, apparently glad for the interruption. "Sarah, will you be joining us?"

"Of course." I put aside my plan to write Mother about Ethan's proposal.

The wives file into the parlor, now vacated not just by the purported major, but by the other officers as well.

"Where's Agatha?" Rachel asks.

"Her rheumatism," says Sally Howard, taking a seat. "Poor thing took to her bed. She won't be fit for the trip. It will just be the three of us: Rachel, Emily Grant, and me."

"How sad for Agatha. I will pray for her recovery," Rachel says.

I'm sorry for Agatha too. But now there will be an open seat in the carriage.

"I would like to go in her place." I can't believe I said it. I have no idea how it will go over or what I'd be taking on.

"What?" Sally says. "You're not a Quaker, much less a Quaker wife."

"No, I'm a writer," I say boldly. "I can document the whole trip. Maybe write about it for the *Sentinel*."

"Doesn't seem proper," Sally says. "This is about the wives."

"No, it's about the husbands," Rachel says. "Securing their freedom. And Sarah has already helped to prove that the Spanktown Papers are a fraud. She could help us make our case to General Washington."

"I'll help any way I can," I say. "Even carry the bags."

"This is a private matter," Sally insists. "Do we want to give that up for a newspaper article?"

"Sally, what you're doing is...revolutionary," I say. "Think of it: Quaker wives embarking on a mission to free their husbands. Risking great danger to travel behind battle lines and meet with General Washington. Even if he turns you away, you'll have made history."

I see a slight softening in Sally's face, maybe the barest hint of a smile.

"I doubt it's ever happened in Pennsylvania—or any of the colonies," I say. It sounds like I'm exaggerating, but I believe every word.

Emily finally speaks up. "I would be pleased to have Sarah accompany us. Yes, she's somewhat younger than we are and she's not of our faith, but she's already proven herself to be a capable advisor."

"It's unseemly," Sally says, "but I'll go along with it."

"Then we're agreed. Sarah will come!" Rachel is thrilled.

Emma is not thrilled when I tell her that night.

"You mean I'll have to manage the children by myself?" she says, as we climb into our beds. "You won't be there to help out, even in the evenings."

"Gertrude will come and stay," I say.

"The Empress Gertrude? I'd sooner do it all myself."

Amos is astounded that the women have agreed to let me come along.

"Well done!" He's even more excited about the newspaper's first story from Washington's headquarters.

I take the opportunity to ask for one more favor: "Perhaps this time you'll put my name on the article."

"That would go against all common sense," he mumbles. "What would people think?"

"They would think you're a very smart man," Tess pipes up from the doorway. "Someone not afraid to chart his own way."

Amos shrugs. "I'm also smart enough to know when I'm beat. Yes, Sarah, the world will be made aware that it's your writing."

Ethan is not nearly so compliant when I stop by the coffeehouse after work.

"You're doing *what*? It's not safe for them and certainly not safe for you."

"We have two men going along to drive the carriage and help with bags," I offer.

"Even so, I don't think you should go. So what if Amos doesn't get his big story?"

"It's not just Amos," I say as the last of the customers leaves. "This is what I want to do. And I'll want to do it again and again."

Ethan is silent for a while, and I fear the worst. Have I ruined everything?

Finally, he speaks. "I can see how much you want this. I'll not stand in the way. I love you too much."

My eyes grow wide and my jaw drops open. I've never been happier.

"This will take some getting accustomed to," he says, smiling. "You must be patient with me, my darling."

CHAPTER 47

"We're almost there!" Rachel alerts us.

God is merciful. After two days of being stuffed in this carriage with three pious Quaker women, we're finally on the outskirts of Valley Forge. There's not much to see so far, just a dreary plateau ringed by a couple of hills. That allows me to focus on my aching back and my aching head as the clip-clop of our four horses and the never-ending squeaks of our tiny carriage inch us closer with every bump and jolt.

I have no right to complain to these women who never complain. I'm lucky to be here, although last night tested my nerves. After leaving Philadelphia, amid a crowd of well-wishers, we spent the night with a sympathetic Quaker family. Just as we were bedding down, dozens of Washington's soldiers burst in, looking for the "Philadelphia ladies" who might be carrying military information to the redcoats. They ransacked the house and barn until they were satisfied we weren't spies.

"This is not a good omen," I remember telling Rachel, both of us cowering under blankets as a cold rain hammered the roof. Washington has made no secret of his disdain for Quakers, but I'd no idea it would come to this.

The 20 miles between Philadelphia and Valley Forge may as well have been a thousand. April's thaw has turned the roads into muddy trenches that test our drivers, the horses, the wheels, and our bottoms. More than once, we had to get out and walk through muck and high water.

Sally is still not convinced I belong here.

"Try to hold your tongue when we meet the general," she warns me yet again. "Unless we ask for your counsel."

"I'm here just to observe and record this momentous occasion," I say. That is, if we can get past the sentries and gain an audience with America's greatest general.

Just as I see the outline of the huge encampment, soldiers on horseback ride up to meet us.

"The ladies from Philadelphia, I presume," one of them says. Evidently the message we'd sent earlier had gotten through.

Rachel leans out. "Yes. We're here to see General Washington."

"He's expecting you. We'll guide you there."

Frankly, I'm amazed. I know that Rachel prevailed upon a prosperous Quaker woman who, with her husband, once dined with the general. I suppose her polite letter of introduction did the trick.

The soldiers lead us past the guard posts and into what amounts to a large, hastily constructed city. At least a thousand crude log huts, patched together with clay and straw, are laid out in neat rows connected by paths, all protected by trenches, cannons, and barricades in case of British attack. It's home to about 12,000 soldiers who arrived just in time for winter. There's mud everywhere, and a smoky haze can't disguise the overpowering stench. I can't imagine a more dismal place.

We rumble up to a stately stone house that George and Martha Washington have taken over, along with their entourage. We're ushered inside and I'm struck immediately by the flurry of aides, staff members and servants bustling about with everything from maps to squawking chickens.

"They must be severely pinched for space," I whisper, drawing a scowl from Sally.

We're led into the general's office on the first floor and take seats at a table covered with papers. The heat from the fireplace feels good on my damp, chilled, and weary body.

A short, plump, dark-haired Martha Washington glides in and warmly greets us.

"You must stay for dinner," she says. "You've come so far."

She listens sympathetically as Rachel describes the families' plight.

"How difficult for the wives and children," she says. "I know a little of what you speak—the separation of family, that is. Of course, your people have been through a much harsher time."

She asks each of the women about their own families and difficulties, until Washington himself strides in, ducking his head in the doorway.

He's in full uniform, and he's the tallest man I've ever seen—6 feet 2 inches, according to Ethan. I'm taken aback by his huge presence and hope I can remember every moment of this day.

"Welcome to Valley Forge," he says in a deep, calm voice. His eyes are gray-blue, and his red hair is powdered—not bewigged, as I'd imagined—making him look older than his 46 years. His face bears pockmarks from his bout of smallpox as a youth. He joins us at the table.

Rachel eloquently pleads for the release of the men, reading from the letter that I helped write. When she's finished, he asks a few questions, then politely concludes the meeting.

"I'm sorry you came all this way," he says, "but there's nothing I can do to secure the men's release. I will gladly give you this pass to travel to York, where you can plead your case to the Congress."

Then he's gone. "I thought we'd have more time with him," Sally grouses. "And that he'd be more sympathetic."

Rachel scans the general's note. "At least the pass seems sympathetic: *Humanity pleads strongly in their behalf*, it says." Rachel is the most optimistic person I know.

"And we're invited to stay for dinner," I add. I've been listening to my stomach growl the last hour.

At precisely 3 o'clock the grandfather clock chimes, and we're ushered into the front office. There, the staff have pushed together several desks to make a cramped dining table where we're seated with the Washingtons and his aides. As servants pile on dish after dish—venison, ham, cheeses, wine—I'm amazed. I thought the troops were starving, their feet bloodied for lack of shoes.

Martha, sitting across from me, must have noticed my surprise.

"It's been a hard winter, Mrs. Jordan," she tells me. "But Congress finally approved ample food, clothing, and supplies. We even have a master baker whose crews do nothing but bake bread all day."

I doubt the enlisted men are eating so heartily in their freezing, leaky huts.

I hear a horse and rider pull up outside. A moment later, a young soldier in uniform strides through the door.

"I have a message for you, sir," he says to Washington, who appears to be chewing an obstinate piece of ham.

"What is it, Captain?"

"It's Lafayette, sir. He's on his way here."

That voice! I know that voice.

I look up at the tall, handsome soldier. How can this be?

"Tom!"

As I stand, dizziness overtakes me, and I struggle to keep my balance.

Martha Washington rises to her feet and, in a voice of great concern, asks if I need privacy. I feel myself being led upstairs, where Rachel is hovering and Tom, suddenly pale, is standing before me in his best wooden-soldier pose.

"Tom, I thought you were dead. You're not dead?"

"Poor soul is still rattled," Rachel says. "The events of the day have been too much for her."

"Sarah, I'm very much alive," Tom says, his hand on my arm.

To steady myself, I sit on the edge of the Washingtons' curtained bedchamber. Am I dreaming? Have I arrived at heaven's gate—or is it, more likely, some ring of hell?

"You must be Tom Jordan, Sarah's husband," Rachel says.

"I am," he replies. "But I'm not Sarah's husband."

My head is starting to clear, and the awful truth of my deception looms over me.

Rachel, straining to make sense of it, asks me what on earth is happening.

"I can explain," I say weakly.

"I hope so," Tom says.

"Rachel, my real name is Sarah Barrett." Each word is painful to utter. "Tom and I were friends…lovers back in New York. I took his name, figuring life in Philadelphia would be easier for me as a married woman."

"So you weren't married to Tom?" Rachel says.

"No, she wasn't," Tom says curtly. "She took my name without even telling me."

"It was just a little fib at first," I say. "Then the baby made it a necessity."

"Baby!" Tom says. "I have a child?"

"No, I lost the baby." Suddenly I can't hold back the tears, and they come out as wrenching sobs.

"I'll leave you two alone," Rachel says, slipping away.

"What a time you've had," Tom says, pulling me into his arms. For a moment I'm back in New York, madly in love. But I pull back.

"Why didn't you write to me?" I say through the tears. "You said you would."

"I did write. I wrote to Miss Sarah Barrett at every newspaper in Philadelphia."

"*Barrett.* That's why I didn't receive anything. But why didn't you try harder to find me?"

Tom lets out a sigh of exasperation. "I was fighting a war. I still am."

"Why did you let me, Emma, and your whole family believe you were dead?"

"Since we're being honest here, I'll tell you," he says, all traces of kindness gone. "A bullet grazed my head at Brandywine and knocked me unconscious. I lost a lot of blood."

He pulls his hair back from his forehead, and I see a jagged scar.

"They took me for dead. At first, it was someone else's mistake. You know, in the chaos of war, mangled bodies and faces all look alike. So I was reported as killed in action."

"And then?"

"Well, I grew to enjoy life with all my previous ties cut," he says. "I was free."

I'm stunned. "Didn't you realize the hurt you were causing? I thought we would marry and have a family."

Heedlessly, he proceeds.

"I became part of Washington's inner circle," he says. "I'm a man of some importance now. The general trusts me with high-level military intelligence. It's easier to do my job without the entanglements of a woman or my family."

"Is that what we are, entanglements? Do you know what it's like to mourn someone you loved?"

He doesn't answer for a while. "Sarah, I care for you. You're smart, funny, daring..."

"But let me guess," I say. "The war comes first."

He nods, and I feel oddly free.

"It's a chance to make something of myself. Maybe gain a little fame, notoriety along the way."

"I see."

"You know, it was fate that you lost the baby," he says without even a glance in my direction. "If we'd been wed, I wouldn't be meeting with the Marquis de Lafayette. I wouldn't be sipping fine wine with the man who could win the war for us."

I'm on the verge of telling him it wasn't fate that took the baby. It was two drunk soldiers who beat me nearly to death. But I don't want his pity.

He has a faraway look in his eyes, as he gazes out the window. Being a father is the furthest thing from his mind. It pains me that he didn't even ask whether the baby was a boy or a girl.

"Now that I know you're in Philadelphia, perhaps I'll see you again soon," he says. "We had some fun in New York. Could do it again."

"Have some fun until you return to the business of war?" My head is fully clear now. I know I sound testy, and I don't care.

"Sarah, I never said we'd wed." Now *he* sounds testy. "It's not in my plans now, or maybe ever. There are things I want to do."

Suddenly, I can't remember what it was that drew me to Tom in the first place.

"Yes, there are things I want to do too," I say. "Goodbye, Tom."

CHAPTER 48

Dearest Mother,

I have so much to tell you.

First of all, Ethan and I are to be wed this day, May 25, 1777. I know you will love him as much as I do. The Porters have offered their home for the wedding. Emma is finishing my gown as I write this. She's a little miffed that it's not her own. I'm sure her day will come.

Charles Porter and the other banished Quakers are all back here. They got such a rousing homecoming! Molly baked two custard pies to fatten up Charles, who didn't appear to need any fattening up. Rachel is over the moon.

We may never know what led to their release. Some say it was Martha Washington's kind intervention. Their freedom was apparently already in the works when we journeyed to Valley Forge. The whole thing was a huge embarrassment for the patriots, who never apologized.

The man we knew as Major Hammond, the redcoat-turned-spy that I wrote to you about, is on the loose. Somehow he escaped! The British were holding him under heavy guard for treason and killing Rip. The whole thing sounds suspicious to me. He has many friends in high places. It makes me furious that he'll likely never be prosecuted for Rip's death.

Mother, I wish that you and little Benjamin could be here for my wedding. Hopefully, we'll see one another soon.

Your loving daughter,
Sarah

I'm addressing the envelope at my bedside desk when Emma, virtually weeping, lugs in my blue silk wedding gown.

"The wedding is in two hours, and I have yet to sew the lace around the bodice and cuffs," she wails.

"Emma," I say calmly. "I like it better without the lace."

"It will be too plain," she sniffs.

"Nonsense. I've never fancied lace and ruffles and those puffy sleeves that are so popular. They just get in the way."

"But—"

"It's all right, Emma," I say, pulling her in for a hug. "It's more than all right. It's the most elegant gown I've ever had. And I love that my best friend sewed it for me."

She tears up some more.

"I wish it was Tom you were marrying. Then we'd be sisters."

"I loved your brother once. But he's a soldier, and the war means everything to him. I love Ethan more for not being that person, and for being the kind, tolerant fellow he is. And he loves me totally."

"Well, I hate that you and Ethan are moving to Connecticut. When will I see you again?"

"It's not that far. We'll visit each other." Even as I say it, I wonder if our move will come to pass, with the war still raging.

There's a knock on the door, and Rachel sweeps in, followed by Charles.

"Sarah, is there anything I can help you with?" she asks.

"No, thank you. You and Charles have already done too much. Thank you a thousand times for letting us wed in your home."

"That's the least we can do after your fine account in the *Sentinel* about our banishment and the ladies' brave mission to Valley Forge," Charles says. "Thank you, Sarah, for giving the people the truth."

I think I shall burst with pride. "And I do so appreciate," I tell them, "that you've welcomed a clergyman from outside your faith to perform the ceremony."

"All are welcome here," Charles says.

At Ethan's suggestion, we're embracing one particular Quaker wedding custom to honor his mother's Quaker roots. Everyone attending the ceremony will sign our marriage certificate as witnesses to our bond. Maybe we'll even hang the certificate in the parlor, just as Charles and Rachel have done.

"Well, I must go check on Molly," Rachel says. "She's prepared quite a feast: clam chowder, stewed oysters, venison. And, of course, the cakes—one for the bride, one for the groom." Then she's out the door.

Not five minutes later, another knock. It's Tess, so stylishly dressed that I hardly recognize her. Gone is the bandana around her head, replaced by a bright yellow bonnet that matches her flowered gown.

"Tess, you look like a princess," I gush.

"Hardly," she scoffs. "The only princess today is you."

"I've never seen you in anything but…"

"Old tattered rags? Now that I'm in charge of Amos's library, I decided to fancy myself up a bit," she says. "Now let me get to work on your hair. See if I can bring some order to it, as I do to Amos's books."

I have no patience for fiddling with hair, but I gladly sit as Tess applies her combs, brushes, pins, ribbons, and such.

"What was the big secret you couldn't tell me about?" I ask. "Can you tell me now?"

"Yes, it's the most wonderful news! I convinced Amos to open his library to the public."

"You what!" I'm flabbergasted. "When?"

"Soon. He's going to make a grand announcement. You know Amos. He's got a collection to rival Ben Franklin's, and he won't let old Ben take all the glory."

"Does all this change anything between you and Amos?"

She pokes me with a pin. "Ouch!"

"Still sticking your nose in other people's business," she chides.

"I'm sorry, Tess. It's what I do. What I'll always do."

"Since we're baring our souls, I'll tell you. The law won't let us wed, so put that notion out of your head."

"That's not fair," I say, as I hand her pin after pin.

"You're right, but I'm as trusting of Amos's love as he is of mine."

I'm happy beyond words for her but, as usual, I ruin the spell by bringing up my concerns.

"What about your daughter?" I ask.

"He knows I won't rest until I find her. When that happens—and I'm certain it will—he'll find a small house for the two of us."

"Don't you mean the three of us?"

"Not at all. I'll continue to oversee the library, and Amos and I will go on as we have been. It's not perfect but it's the best we can do." She holds up a mirror. "Enough about me. Are you ready to marry this boy?"

"Yes!" I slip on the blue silk gown with the bosomy front and glance approvingly at my reflection.

Downstairs, guests are starting to arrive. "The pastor is here, and he stinks of garlic," Abigail, my spy, reports. "Emma is flirting with Mr. Tinkleton. He looks flustered."

Ethan, wearing green velvet breeches and a matching waistcoat, finally strides in with his father.

I start down the stairs just as Joseph Galloway arrives with his wife, whose cream satin gown would be more fitting at a royal ball.

At the bottom of the stairs, Amos is waiting to take my arm and do the honor of giving away the bride.

"It's a ridiculous custom," he whispers, "giving anyone away—and *you*, of all people."

"I know," I respond. "It's like I'm a wheel of fine cheese."

Amos chuckles and leads me over to Ethan, standing by the pastor in front of the fireplace. Ethan looks nervous until he sees me.

"I was afraid you'd had a change of heart," he jokes softly.

"My heart is bursting," I tell him.

The parlor is crammed. All the Porter children are lined up—even the twins, who smuggled the cat in for the ceremony. Mr. Porter grabs the yowling creature and tosses him out the front door.

The Reverend Silas Winthrop, a pastor from the nearby Methodist church, bids everyone be seated. Smiling broadly, he ventures a mild joke about ordinarily being up in the pulpit rather than down in the parlor. Then he begins.

Dearly beloved, we are gathered together here in the sight of God to join together this man and this woman in holy matrimony.

Ethan tries to look somber until one of the twins announces an urgent need for the privy. The pastor, who has no doubt seen a lot in his time, chuckles with everyone else but gamely keeps the proceedings to the point.

Suddenly he asks me a question I didn't anticipate:

Wilt thou obey him, and serve him, love, honor, and keep him, in sickness and in health?

Obey him? The words chafe. I'm silent. Ethan looks at me and seems to know what's holding me back. Then he winks, and I let out the breath I've been holding.

I do.

The next thing I realize, Ethan is struggling to slip his mother's ring on my sweaty finger.

Soon after, we're all sitting down to the first of Molly's five sumptuous courses.

All the talk is about France finally agreeing to back the patriots.

"I predict the British will leave Philadelphia within a month, and the patriots will soon win this miserable war," Amos announces. "But enough of war. Today we're celebrating the union of this fine couple."

He rises, holding up his glass. I have no idea what's coming next. Ethan squeezes my hand for support.

"I would like to propose a toast to the bride," Amos says slowly. "Here's to a fine writer whose name will eventually be known well beyond Philadelphia and the colonies."

He smiles at me. "Sarah taught me something about women: I will never underestimate them again. Gentlemen, you would be wise to heed my words."

"A point well taken," Ethan says, raising his glass. "To my wife, Sarah."

I think I shall die from happiness. I draw Ethan's face closer and kiss him soundly on the lips, taking my sweet time.

AUTHOR'S NOTE

WHEN I FIRST SAW the name Spanktown I laughed, wondering if it was something out of Dr. Seuss. But it was a real place in New Jersey during the American Revolution. How it got that name is a mystery, though one legend holds that it was so named after an early settler humiliated his wife with a public spanking.

Today it's part of Rahway, a bedroom community of 30,000 near New York City. During the American Revolution, it was the site of a brief battle. More intriguingly, it lent its name to a document that unjustly doomed a group of peace-loving Quakers to imprisonment for nearly eight months.

My novel, *Spanktown Papers*, draws from this little-known niche of American history. In September 1777, patriot forces rousted 20 Philadelphia men—almost all of them prominent Quakers—from their homes and banished them to western Virginia. Their crime? They refused to support the patriots and their revolution, even in such mundane matters as donating blankets to the troops. Their religion forbade them from taking a side in war—any war.

They were never given a hearing or charged with a crime, no less convicted. Two of them died during their imprisonment. The Spanktown Papers, however, accuse them of something far worse than not supporting the revolution. According to these documents—none of which are known to exist today—the Quakers were allegedly funneling military secrets to the British.

Most scholars agree that the Spanktown Papers were fraudulent. No one knows for certain who was responsible. In my novel, I suggest it was Major General John Sullivan. While that's literary speculation, it's not so farfetched. Sullivan claimed to have found them in the baggage of a deserter before turning them over to the Continental Congress. The unpopular general despised Quakers for their pacifism and was in dire need of some positive press after leading his men into a disastrous raid on Staten Island.

Revolutionary War scholars cite obvious blunders in the papers themselves that seem to absolve the Quakers: The document purportedly came out of an annual Quaker meeting in Spanktown, which was never held; the papers named the days of the week, against Quaker custom; and the supposed military intelligence they conveyed was simply wrong.

A non-fiction account of the injustice against the Quakers is vividly brought to life in *Prisoners of Congress, Philadelphia's Quakers in Exile 1777-1778,* by Norman E. Donoghue II. Published in 2023 by The Pennsylvania State University Press, this meticulously researched book was invaluable to me in crafting my novel.

I was drawn to writing *Spanktown Papers* by one of Donoghue's many cogent observations. What happened to the exiled Quakers, he wrote, is "both a cautionary tale and an unfortunate precedent for future generations." One has only to look at the internment of Japanese-Americans during World War II, the arrests of women suffragists in 1917, and the Red Scare during the McCarthy era, he noted.

In our current era, I would add the mass roundup and deportation of residents who are undocumented or simply thought to be undocumented.

Other fine books aided my research: *World of Trouble, A Philadelphia Quaker Family's Journey through the American Revolution,* by Richard Godbeer; *The Diary of Elizabeth Drinker*; *The Diary of Christopher Marshall*; and Rick Atkinson's *The Fate of the Day*.

Writing historical fiction is a delicate dance—weaving fact with fiction to make a compelling read. In reality, Major General John Sullivan never had a top aide named Rupert Pratt. He is my creation, as is the British Major John Hammond. Rip Ripley, the murdered coffeehouse proprietor, is also fictitious.

The wives of the exiled Quakers did indeed make a risky pilgrimage to Valley Forge in early April 1778, which was highly unusual for women of that time. But, as I learned from writing this book, Quaker women often have been ahead of their time when it comes to speaking up for themselves and others. They were early opponents of slavery and supporters of women's suffrage.

In *Spanktown Papers*, I have not used the actual names of the exiled Quakers and their wives to give myself more literary freedom to tell an engaging story. The Porter family is fictitious, though I relied heavily on the published diary of Elizabeth Drinker, whose husband Henry was one of the exiled Quakers.

I took other liberties with regard to the Quakers. In colonial times they used so-called Plain Speech: "thee" and "thou". I opted not to do that to make it easier for present-day readers.

As a former newspaper journalist, I've always been amazed by newspapers from the colonial period, partly because of the monumental effort it took to produce one page of type, painstakingly setting each letter of each word backwards and upside down so the page could be properly transferred to paper on the press. In 1776, Philadelphia had no fewer than six newspapers.

A global shipping hub with at least 30,000 residents, Philadelphia was ground zero for the American Revolution. On July 6, 1776, Benjamin Towne's Pennsylvania Evening Post became the first newspaper to publish the Declaration of Independence. The Post had an advantage because it published three times a week when most newspapers in the colonies were weeklies. Among the other Philadelphia newspapers were the Pennsylvania Gazette, founded by Ben Franklin, and the German-language paper Pennsylvanischer Staatsbote, printed by Henrich Miller.

I could not have written this book without the encouragement and guidance of my husband, Steve Chawkins, a former writer and editor for the Los Angeles Times. He edited *Spanktown Papers*, as well as my two previous novels in the series, *Outcasts of Essex* and *Prisoner of Wallabout Bay.* His judgment is spot-on, and his humor carried me through the trials of putting this book together.

Also, he appreciates my love of diving down the rabbit holes of American history.

I want to thank friends and colleagues who encouraged and aided me along the road to publication. Author Kathleen Sharp read a draft and provided valuable suggestions. Marty Foley, former teacher and Philadelphia tour guide extraordinaire, was a fountain of local history and kept an eye out for errors in my manuscript.

My publisher, Open Books, has always been enthusiastic about my novels, for which I'm grateful. I so appreciate the wise counsel of David Ross and Kelly Huddleston and their efforts to put out the best book possible. I want to thank them for believing in Sarah's stories and in my ability to tell them.

www.ingramcontent.com/pod-product-compliance
Lightning Source LLC
LaVergne TN
LVHW030918080826
845145LV00013B/2953
9781948598927